# DREAM STEALERS

## Suzanne O'Neil

WESTBOW
PRESS*
A DIVISION OF THOMAS NELSON
& ZONDERVAN

WestBow Press books may be ordered through booksellers or by contacting:

WestBow Press
A Division of Thomas Nelson & Zondervan
1663 Liberty Drive
Bloomington, IN 47403
www.westbowpress.com
1 (866) 928-1240

ISBN: 978-1-5127-2622-0 (sc)
ISBN: 978-1-5127-2621-3 (e)

Library of Congress Control Number: 2016900242

Print information available on the last page.

WestBow Press rev. date: 01/20/2016

To my children

Levi

Jesse

&

Shara

# Chapter 1

The beautiful white city glowed in the soft morning light. Pale sunlight fell on the curves and lines of the Greek-like architecture that stretched without break as far as the eye could see. Overhead the dome of the sky was a light blue that was almost white. There were no roads or fences in this city; no street lights, signs or shops, not a blade of grass or even a persistent weed could be seen from one end to the other.

It was peaceful and silent as it always was at this time of morning just before the City awoke for the day. A balmy breeze wafted lazily around the buildings. The weather was calm and mild as usual. There were never any storms here and it never rained. No sound or raised voice could be heard through the wide, arched windows of one of these palatial homes. The pale light softly illuminated the spacious rooms with their cool white marble walls. The furnishings were clean, creamy whites tastefully interspersed with glowing ornaments and colourful wall hangings of vividly contrasting reds, blues and greens. It was very beautiful and encouraged feelings of tranquillity.

Four people woke simultaneously and began to go about their usual morning routines. It seemed to these four as though this day would be a normal day similar to the many, many days they had had before. Each day they would carefully follow their schedule; waking, eating, enjoying some family time together, then departing from the house for their various locations around the City. Their schedule was never boring as each day contained a perfectly balanced variety of rest, recreation and productivity.

Outings and holidays were scheduled regularly making their lives exciting enough to prevent their days from becoming mundane but predictable enough to feel safe and secure. Why should today be any different? But something subtle had changed that morning, just a slight deviation from the ordinary but it was a beginning of things to come.

The luxurious carpet muffled the footfalls of the family; Mum, Dad, a teenage boy and a younger girl, as they assembled together for breakfast. The man sat back in his large, comfortable, squashy-looking chair watching as his family gathered. He was taller than average, solidly built and athletic looking. He had a shock of dark hair, carefully clipped in the square hairstyle that was in vogue just then. It gave his face the appearance of strength, which matched his name, Petra, meaning rock, but his brown eyes were soft as he regarded his family. He gazed fondly at his partner who was white-blonde and petite with her long, carefully styled hair rolling down her shoulders in perfect waves. She was beautiful in a Barbie-doll fashion; wide blue eyes and full lips skilfully made up, straight nose and perfectly shaped eyebrows. Any alterations that had been made to her face were tastefully and artfully done. Her name was Amiria.

Petra did sometimes wonder secretly how she might look naturally without the enhancements. On occasions he had strange visions of her with her long hair blowing crazily in the wind, a wind that never blew here inside this peaceful city. Here there was only ever a gentle fluctuation of circulating air. In his imagination he saw her hair flowing around her face instead of in the immaculately neat and tidy style with not-a-single-hair out of place that was usual for her. However he was really very satisfied with his current partner and knew he had nothing to complain about; they were a perfect match of course.

Amiria had her hands clasped in her lap, sitting a little rigidly as she observed the children. Dayzie was a little blonde version of her mother with her hair in long plaits. Their teenage son, Az, smirked at his mother as he munched on a chocolate bar. Az generally took after his father in looks but where his father's eyes were a deep brown, his were hazel and sparkling with an inquisitive light. He was the picture of good health as they all were, his teenage body toned and lean. Chocolate bars were a rare commodity in the City and only available very occasionally. Amiria was profoundly puzzled as to where he had got it from. Az was fully aware of his mother's alarm that he was breaking rules and crossing boundary lines by eating that chocolate bar. For some reason just lately he often felt an almost uncontrollable urge to break out of the schedules carefully laid down for him. Even this very minor transgression gave him a small thrill.

Amiria could not contain her concern at his behaviour. "You know that will cost you later don't you? You haven't done enough exercise to warrant that treat. Your lunchtime diet will have to be adjusted to compensate, why don't you just stick to the diet schedule?" Her anxiety caused her speech to flow a little more rapidly than usual as she protested with a slightly plaintive note in her voice, pouting her perfect lips. Az shrugged and licked his fingers as he dropped the wrapper onto the floor. The eyes of his family watched unbelievingly as that rebellious wrapper fluttered downwards.

"I just felt like it" Az muttered and got up, disappearing through the door to his room.

"Where is he going?" Amiria questioned Petra petulantly, "We haven't had all of our morning family time together yet."

"Let him go Amiria," Petra suggested calmly touching her arm gently with just the tips of his fingers, "he'll learn. There are always consequences and sometimes they have to learn the hard way."

He smiled at her and by way of distraction changed the subject. "So, what shall we view this morning?"

Amiria leaned back frowning at the space where her son had been sitting. The wrapper had disappeared from the floor. She breathed in deeply letting out a controlled breath. Turning to her partner she forced herself to relax and speak calmly. "How about we watch a short history piece?"

"History again? I prefer the future, at least I would if it wasn't so predictable," Petra laughed.

"What about you Dayzie?" he turned to his young daughter who was sitting dutifully eating her morning nutritional commixture, "what would you like to view?"

Dayzie looked up at her father with her big blue eyes, kicking her feet up and down which were still too short to reach the floor. She seemed to have an excess of energy and was swinging her head from side to side enjoying the feeling of her shiny plaits flapping backwards and forwards across her face. At the end of each of her plaits was attached a silky-looking blue butterfly. This hairstyle was popular among the girls in her class right now. The butterflies were tiny mechanical creatures, their wings whirling with an almost imperceptible sound. Whenever her head was still enough to allow them flight, they raised her plaits in the air around her head like a couple of playful snakes.

"The old day's daddy, the ooold days," she chanted in a sing song voice.

Her father sighed, "Just like your Mum ae? Okay the old days it is. Are you sure you won't find it too scary?"

"No Daddy it's not like that now, things are much better, it's safe, I'm glad I didn't live in the old days but I like watching it. Let's watch it now."

Dayzie laid her spoon down on the table eagerly waiting for the viewing to begin.

# Chapter 2

The table descended smoothly into the floor, along with the dishes and cutlery from their breakfast. The big soft chairs moved closer together so that she was situated between her parents facing a large concave screen that stretched from floor to ceiling. The butterflies were causing her plaits to hover gently beside her face.

Her father looked over at the screen and gave a voice command to select the right piece. "We can start from where we left off yesterday" he said.

On the screen a beach scene came into view and pulled itself around them three dimensionally so the family really felt as though they were sitting on that beach. Amiria kicked off her shoes to enjoy the simulated feeling of sand under her toes. Dayzie reached down and picked up a handful of it. She let it run through her fingers towards her lap but the sand seemed to disappear as it fell.

They looked out at the sea which was washing soothingly backwards and forwards on the seashore with just a little wind ruffling the tops of the waves. Dayzie's hair fluttered slightly in the gentle breeze.

A family was playing in the sand with buckets and spades. They were digging holes and building a sandcastle. A very young child was sitting there eating a melting ice-cream. Ice-cream was dripping down his hand and onto his protruding brown stomach. As he ate he smeared ice-cream all around his mouth. His Mum looked around at him and grimaced at the sticky mess. Noticing her looking the little boy chuckled gleefully at her. With his other hand he wiped ice cream off his tummy and licked it. His Mum pulled a face, then laughed and went back to digging and patting the sand making a sandcastle.

"I can smell the sea Daddy," sang Dayzie as she watched delightedly. Then she scrunched up her face with disgust as she saw what the little boy was doing.

"Eewh! He's getting sand in that white stuff he's eating." She looked away from the little boy, her eyes scanning the beach. "I can see shells on the sand Dad, do they have dead things in them?" She looked up at him wrinkling her little nose.

"Yes probably, dead and rotting things." he answered with a distasteful look on his face.

"I can feel the wind from the sea Dad, it feels nice." Whenever Dayzie said the word, Dad or Daddy she gave the word an odd emphasis as though unused to using it.

"That's just the simulator darling," Petra said smiling down at her, "same as with the smells."

He looked over at Amiria. She was sitting with her chin in her hands enjoying the scene and the feel of the sand on her toes and the breeze on her face.

"What are you thinking about love?" He asked her.

"Mmmm, that I would like to go there just once and feel the sand and the wind and swim through those waves like some of those people are doing," she answered dreamily.

"You know it wasn't safe; people drowned in the sea or were eaten by ferocious water creatures." He was looking at her curiously and with a little bit of amusement.

"I know, I know I just have this longing."

"You can feel the sand and what it's like to swim in a simulator anytime you want to."

He knew he was giving her the standard answers but he was also enjoying her apparent fascination and wanting to probe her thoughts a little.

"But is it the same as the real thing? We'll never know will we?" she sighed wistfully.

"May be we shouldn't watch it if it makes you feel that way," he replied teasingly.

"Maybe, but I like it. Let's watch the one in the bush next."

"Teacher says people could get diseases from dirty and rotten things. They made them sick and then their life cycle came to Completion while they're still young," chimed in Dayzie still thinking about the shells.

Dayzie was seven years old and thought her teacher at school was just perfect. She was always quoting the things she said.

"Yes Dayzie that's exactly right," said the Amiria vaguely, her mind still far away, "you should always listen to your teacher."

Dayzie smiled in agreement and carefully leaned, very slightly, onto her Mother's shoulder.

On the screen a bush scene appeared and then surrounded them, encircling them with dim, forest greenness. Curling ferns were growing profusely around the massive trunks of ancient Kauri and Beech trees. A rustling sound could be heard amongst the bushes and the musical tones of Bell-birds and Tui's came from high up in the branches accompanied by the melodious chattering of dozens of other birds. The family was silent for a few minutes as they drank in the awe-inspiring other-worldliness of this place.

"When is this one?" Amiria asked dreamily. She reached up to lightly stroke a curling fern frond.

"Mid twenty first century sometime. There were still forests then that people could walk around in. Look there's someone now," Petra said excitedly pointing.

A brown face appeared from behind a tree with big green eyes that gleamed with fun accompanied by a cheeky grin. As he came out from behind the tree they could see his muscular, young body, dressed in a pair of black shorts. The young man looked to be about seventeen, very tan and fit looking with a big mop of frizzy black hair that stuck straight up all around his head.

"He looks funny," chortled Dayzie, "look at his hair!"

"That was the fashion then honey," said Amiria, "and look at how brown he is, the sun has baked him darker than anyone you see now. I wonder if he got skin cancer and had a shortened life cycle?" she mused, "the sun was very fierce in those days and people didn't seem to bother about covering up very much."

The young man on the screen suddenly smiled a bright, toothy grin and his eyes widened in glee as he grabbed a rope that hung down from the sturdy branch of a tree and swung himself forwards. The scene swung round in time to see him land with an almighty splash in a clear, green river. He came up gasping and shouting, "Woo-ah! It's cold! Come on in you fellas, you chickens, get in here!!"

Two others, a girl and a boy appeared running through the trees and jumped into the river with him laughing and splashing. The girl, who looked to be in her early teens, had long, dark, very curly hair that was thick and tangled. The boy had shorter hair in the same sticking up style as the other but he looked to be a few years younger than him. Both of the children were as brown as the older boy. After they had swum and splashed for a quite a while they crawled out of the river and lay on the grass of the riverbank talking and laughing. The girl grabbed a string bag she had left under a tree, pulled out an apple and began to munch.

"What's that? What's she eating?" demanded Dayzie excitedly, bouncing up and down on her seat.

"You know what it is," said Petra encouragingly, "you learnt that at school. What is it?"

"Um, um, um, it's, fruit that grows on a tree!" she said eagerly.

"Yes, very good but what kind?" he encouraged.

"I don't know Daddy, it's too hard there's soooo many," she said looking perplexed, frowning in concentration.

"It's an apple dum-dum" said a surly voice from the door way. Her brother stood there frowning, leaning against the doorway with his arms folded, watching the scene.

"'Calling names is detrimental to a humans overall confidence and ability to produce,' Az, you know that. No more name calling," said Amiria with slight distress in her voice.

Az gave a dismissive huff and disappeared from the doorway. His parents looked at each other with some concern.

"That will be noted you know," said Amiria worriedly in a low voice to her partner across the top of Dayzie's head.

"Yes darling, he will have to learn, but try not to worry too much, anxiety is unproductive; and remember the Information Giver will answer all our difficult questions and solve our problems for us." He leaned sideways to tap her nose playfully, smiling down into her eyes. She smiled back at him, her anxiety seeming to evaporate for a moment as she responded to his warm tone. She leaned back in her comfortable chair with a contented look on her face.

"You have learnt very well how to facilitate a relationship Petra," she said softly, giving him what she knew was an appropriate, standardised complement, "I will recommend you when it's time for a new cycle."

"Thanks," he said lightly but with a sudden tinge of pain on his face that she didn't appear to observe.

"And now," he said in a more definite voice turning to look at his little daughter, "it's time for the next phase in our schedule. You need to go to class young lady, and you're Mother and I to Production."

"Mummy can we follow them? I mean keep following them? They look nice and happy even if their lives will probably be short?" Dayzie's eyes were still on the scene, where the young man and the two children were leaving the riverside and getting into an old time vehicle. The vehicle suddenly roared to life and took off throwing up smoke and dust as it rattled away along a dirt road through the bush.

"Yes why not." Amiria said to her with a smile. "I would like that too."

"Mum," said Dayzie a little hesitatingly, using the same curious emphasis when she said Mum as she had used when addressing her father, "they can't see us can they?"

"No of course not my dear. Why do you ask?"

"It's just that the girl who was eating the apple, she looked at me. She looked right at me Mum." Dayzie looked up at her mother, her eyes wide and questioning.

"Well," began Amiria uncertainly, "they do say that sometimes people seem to look directly into the viewer and it appears as though they can see us or sense us somehow, but the Information Giver says of course that's impossible. Sometimes we hear them talking amongst themselves saying they felt a presence or feel that someone or something they couldn't see is there with them. The Information Giver says it is just their imagination and of course he is right."

She said the last part with a firmness in her voice she didn't fully feel. She was a little troubled by these things as it did all seem a bit strange but she forced herself to speak confidently. It was her responsibility to re-enforce confidence in her little daughter for the Information Giver as this would make her life happier and trouble free. She knew this for a fact after watching some disturbing scenes from the past. Watching these was restricted of course as viewing too many of these kinds of scenes could cause emotional distress of the mind, which was not conducive to Production. Production was the most important thing in the world, and no-one questioned that.

"Off you go now, 'go and learn and grow wise and be at peace with the world.'" She gave her daughter a kiss on the forehead in the prescribed way, quickly wiping the spot with a hygienic wipe. Mixing of body fluids was strictly forbidden and a horror of this had been impressed on every human being in the City. Her daughter jumped up and bounced rather than walked to the door, her plaits jumping along with her, butterflies still fluttering.

As her mother watched her leave she thought, she seems so happy and carefree but oh so curious.

"I think *she* will be fine" she said to her partner. She emphasised the *she*, indicating that she had some concerns about their son.

"I wouldn't worry about Az too much, every boy goes through that difficult stage; it's what makes them maximum producers later on. And if not, well you know there is still time left in our life cycles where we can nurture and enjoy more children." He said this easily and flippantly giving no hint of the turmoil of emotions that lay under this statement. He was well aware of his role to soothe and calm the more tremulous emotions of the female sex reassuring her of the realities of life. His partner seemed unware of the sadness in his eyes that belied his tone.

"Yes I know but it's different for mothers somehow we don't let go so easily, I so want him to be okay." She leaned slightly into her partner for body comfort which was allowed to a degree within certain strict guidelines.

"We can get a consultation from the Information Giver about him, so we know how to handle him best," he said evenly. "I'll check to see if he's gone to class, then we need to be off too."

He got up and went through the doorway, coming back a few minutes later. "Yes he's gone and the locater says he is on his way to class so that's okay."

His partner was still sitting staring at the now blank screen.

"Are you all right? You look as though you are thinking hard about something. Penny for your thoughts?"

"What's a penny?" she looked up at him in enquiry, distracted for a moment.

"Old-time money. Funny thing, like a round disk, made of brown metal. It wasn't worth much. They used it to buy things. Carried it around in their pockets. Probably Lost it most of the time; *and* it was a great way to spread diseases, Yuk!"

"Buying things? That's so weird; our system is so perfect, no problems, and no worries, everything we want or need is given to us."

"Yes but what were you thinking about with your fascinating female mind?" he prompted her in a playful tone.

"That brown boy. His life is so different from ours but he seemed happy, and something else I can't quite understand. He didn't have a schedule or routine or a diet or an information Giver but he looked healthy and happy and, I don't know, different from us anyway," she trailed off uncertainly.

"You only saw a tiny part of his life; you don't know what other horrible things were going on or what his life would be like in the future. He probably doesn't even know when his life cycle is going to end. It could end in so many horrible and painful ways in those days."

"I know, I know, everything is so much better now but, but…" she trailed off lamely.

"But what my dear? I will have to get some advice from the Information Giver about *you* soon if this carries on," but he spoke kindly, so that she knew he wasn't being serious. He had been taught well about how females responded to tone and facial expression and physical closeness. Her way of thinking was intriguing to him but he also knew that too much wondering and longing could be detrimental to a person's mental health. Thinking that there may always be something better took away happiness from a person and reducing happiness always diminished Productivity.

"You have a great life, a perfect life" he told her gently. Glancing up at the schedule lights on the wall he announced, "It's time to go now, are you ready?"

"Yes it is and I *am* ready." She stood up purposefully and followed him to the door. At the doorway she looked back briefly at the screen still puzzling a little but as she left their home and joined the rest of the day travellers she pushed these thoughts aside. She revelled in the morning meeting and greeting and in the contented chatter around her. She was eager to speak to her particular friends about what a great man she had this cycle.

# Chapter 3

The day Amiria had met Petra was a cherished memory. It was always such fun when it came time to acquire a new partner. The Pairing Ceremonies were public events and were an important part of life in the City. Even when she wasn't personally involved she loved to attend just because she enjoyed the excitement and entertainment of watching the new couples coming together. It was always enjoyable to receive an invitation for one of these occasions.

The ceremonies were held in the great Oval House. It was a massive oval-shaped stadium with a high curving, sculptured roof. Inside there was a raised stage with majestic marble steps surrounding it and row after row of seating flowing outwards. The audience always dressed in evening wear when attending these occasions; the women in long beautiful, flowing gowns, the men in exquisite shimmering suits. These outfits were specially designed for these celebrations and in response to loud clapping they would light up all over, flashing brilliant colours and animations of realistic explosions and bursting fireworks. This added to the atmosphere of excitement that always surrounded these ceremonies.

Watching the pairings from the audience was one thing, but being personally involved was a whole new level of enjoyment. Such was the extent of the preparations and the build-up that Amiria would be in a heightened state all day. Her favourite part was the full makeover that she would get as a participant including full body glitter, makeup, hairstyle, a purpose-designed dress, accessories, shoes, exquisite perfume and just about anything else she might request to enhance her appearance on the occasion. After these extensive personal preparations which took many hours, those starting a new cycle would assemble with their current partners in the foyer of the Stadium. Linking arms to parade up the aisles together in long lines, past the applauding audience in their brightly flashing clothes and up onto the stage. As they reached centre stage, one by one, they would give each other a fond farewell hug and separate to the left and to the right. They were then positioned behind screens where they would wait in excited anticipation for the moment when they would be lifted. One by one the screens were removed and their new partners revealed to tremendous applause and screams of delight from the audience as they came together as a new couple. Projections of gold streamers and shimmering glitter explosions would float down onto the stage. Dazzling lights flashed and dramatic music played during these revelations.

Pairings initially began at age fourteen. The audience especially loved watching these young ones being paired for the very first time. Most of them appeared quite shy and nervous about coming before such a crowd. At that age of course, they didn't stay with one partner for an entire cycle and partners were changed on a regular basis, at least once a year. They were little more than friendships and were merely a rehearsal for the real thing.

The Pairing Ceremonies also marked the time when teenage children left home to begin their career training. However in the intensified state that was reached during these ceremonies, the separation of parents and children wasn't given much thought. Upon leaving the stadium with their first partners these fourteen year olds would merely embark on a traveller to be taken to a career house according to which career had been chosen for them, and a new Cycle was begun.

It was in the cycle that followed this one, when you turned twenty one that you began a proper seven year-long relationship and moved into your own house. It was believed that seven years was the optimum duration time for a relationship to provide feelings of security and consistency without becoming tediousness. The subsequent cycle beginning at age twenty eight was the time when you were allocated children and began the parenting phase.

Children were assigned to families when they were seven years old. Before seven they were brought up in the children's homes where they were trained and prepared for life in the City. Sometimes they would stay with the same parents for a full seven years till they turned fourteen, and at other times they would be reallocated to different parents part-way through the seven years depending on how far through their relationship cycle the parents were.

The seventh cycle leading up to your funeral was often considered to be the best phase of a person's life. You were honoured during this time for your contribution to Production and commended for successfully parenting a new generation. This was the final cycle of life where you were given positions of respect and your advice was sought for the benefit of the new generations. Often these Seventh Cyclers would visit the career classes to help prepare the future producers for their roles in various areas of Production. Seventh Cyclers were given extended recreation activities and were no longer expected to spend five days of the week at Production. Any modifications they wanted to make to their faces or bodies during this time was seldom denied so they were able to maintain a perfectly youthful appearance right up till Completion. Their final year, leading up to their funeral when they turned forty was entirely given over to pleasure seeking with non-stop pleasure and entertainment.

The Seven Cycles of Life would usually follow one after the other in smooth succession without interruption, unless of course something went wrong. In that case you might be put back into the relationship pool to be allocated a new partner by the CCS or to be allocated new children to parent depending on what had happened. If something did go wrong this was never discussed either openly or even covertly.

New beginnings was a strong theme that was promoted in the City. When you were allocated a partner you were happy and you accepted them without question. You were always perfectly well-matched and any little problems were quickly resolved using specific relationship instructions that were laid out by the Information Giver. 'Understanding brings solutions,' was a standard wisdom for life message. Understanding how to conduct a relationship successfully was also comprehensively covered as part of their education.

Life was smooth and harmonious, then before your body began to experience the debilitating effects of old age, your life was brought to a close. You celebrated your happy perfect life at your own funeral along with your close friends. Funerals were occasions that it was a privilege to be invited to. At funerals all the guests gave speeches of thanks for the perfect contentment of their lives and especially for the person who had arrived at 'Completion of the Life Cycles.' The Information Giver was spoken of with respect and honour. The forty year old would then say their final goodbyes and step backwards into an open chamber that had been prepared for them. It was a beautifully prepared room with soft lighting, calm music tinkling in the background and fragrant scents in the air. A special drink would be waiting for them which they would raise in salute to their guests, speaking the traditional toast; "To the new generation," and then swallowing it with a flourish. As they raised the empty glass, the gathering of people would cheer. The final phase would be enacted as they lay down on satin covered slabs, closing their eyes as they drifted peacefully towards Completion.

# Chapter 4

Amiria's mind at this moment, however was more concerned with her own memories rather than with contemplating the Life Cycles. She wanted to recall all the details of her meeting with Petra. She remembered vividly the dress she had worn at her last Pairing Ceremony. A beautiful silky white dress that floated around her, her hair swept up stylishly with soft tendrils hanging down around her face and brilliant diamond clasps in her hair. These exquisite jewelled accessories were kept exclusively for these important occasions, adding to the glamour and excitement.

She had been very aware of her own beauty as she waited expectantly behind her screen. She had felt special and important, waiting for her moment in the spotlight. She hadn't given much thought to her previous partner, although she had been perfectly content with him. It was expected that the cycle would come to an end, it had been fun but now it was time to move on to the next new beginning. This time around she would not only have the excitement of being in a new relationship, she would become a parent and she was happily looking forward to that. She would have a boy and a girl and the boy would be like his father and the girl would be like her. It would be such fun to be a family.

She remembered from her own childhood the first time she had been introduced to her parents. She had been carefully prepared for this phase, learning how families functioned and how she would be expected to behave. If you followed all the instructions you were given you would have no problems and you would be perfectly happy, that was how it worked. It was simple and straight forward and the same thing applied to relationships; or so she had always thought.

When the screen had suddenly gone up and she had caught sight of Petra for the first time she had been so caught up in the moment that she had barely registered him. She swept across the stage as she had been taught, smiling and acknowledging the crowd. The next thing she knew she was being lifted up in the strong arms of a tall, dark-haired man and whirled around in the air to the delight and amusement of the audience. Her perfectly coiffured hair had slipped half-way out of its gleaming clasps to fall about her face. He had lowered her gently to the stage then and gazed at her with open admiration.

At the moment when they had looked into each other's eyes something strange had happened to Amiria. Normally she was very aware of herself and the audience and how they were responding to her, but for that single moment of time she had forgotten everything except him. It was as though the noise of the crowd, the music, the bright lights and cascading glitter had all been shut off. Something about Petra made her lose her self-consciousness if only for several heartbeats of time.

Then the roar of the audience reached her ears once more and the scene around her swirled back into focus. She smiled and flirted as was expected, blowing the audience kisses, twirling her beautiful dress. The audience was delighted with her loveliness and her effervescent personality. All too soon she was leaving the stage arm in arm with her new partner to begin another seven year cycle.

Later they would find out each other's names and occupations. Other than that there was usually not much more to know. Relationships were conducted in a standard way and there were standard expectations and solutions to any concerns that may arise. As each person was taught thoroughly at school how to facilitate a relationship with the opposite sex, there were usually very few problems. Advice was always readily available, life was generally stable, tranquil and calm. It never got boring as emotional levels were constantly read by the personal robots, reported to the CCS and activities scheduled to compensate for fluctuations.

The memory of that unprecedented moment she had experienced on the stage often came back to Amiria's mind especially as now, when she was relaxed and unoccupied on the traveller on her way to Production. That moment was something she didn't understand but she had always kept the memory close to her heart wondering what it might mean. She had no name for it, she couldn't explain it and she had never spoken about it. All she did know was that was anticipating the next seven years of her relationship cycle as she had never done before. There was also another indescribable feeling, dimly perceived, pushed back into the far recesses of her mind. Yes, she was looking forward to the next seven years, but what after that? She brought her mind back to the present chatting animatedly with her friends for the rest of the journey, purposefully ignoring the strange undertone of her thoughts.

Later that day on her way home Amiria had felt the need to sit quietly as she travelled, thinking more about what her partner had said to her that morning. It was true, she thought to herself, as she gazed out of the window of the traveller, she did have a great life. What more could she possibly want? She thought for a moment but couldn't come up with anything that she wanted but didn't have. Everything was worked out for her. She got up at a specified time, stood on the machine that took a reading of her health levels and nutritional needs. She ate the food that appeared before her that always tasted pleasant and was just right for her body. She would go to Production when it appeared on her schedule. She went to the Exercise Arena and did the prescribed amount of exercises along with her contemporaries and felt wonderful afterwards. She took part in family interactions each day for a specified amount of time; not so long that it tried her patience but long enough to satisfy her emotionally. The family took holidays when it was deemed appropriate. She knew she could request a holiday or a weekend of recreational activities for herself whenever she wanted and if this was turned down it was because it was the right decision for her well-being and she accepted it. She had faith in the system. It worked perfectly well.

What more could she possibly want? There was that question again, there was no answer to that question. It was strange that it seemed to go around and around in her mind. She decided to just ignore it. There were some things it was better not to think about.

She frowned as she recalled that day she had visited her friend Lila. She had been shocked when she had entered her friend's house to find her curled up on the sofa sobbing. She had never seen someone cry like this before; sobbing as though her heart would break. She sat beside her and greeted her as usual with a smile. Unsure what to do she had begun cheerfully chatting about her day and her family, things that Lila would normally be interested in. But Lila had just raised her wet, tear-streaked face to stare at her for a moment, then continued to sob. Amiria had stopped talking then and sat in silence wondering what to do.

Finally Lila had wiped her face with a tissue. "I can't stand it anymore," she said tragically.

"Can't stand what? Everything is so good, so perfect…"

"Is it?" Lila asked abruptly cutting her off.

"Of course it is," she had replied bewildered. What a strange question, she had thought to herself.

Lila looked as though she were about to say a whole lot more but instead she said, "you'd better leave, they'll be here soon, to take me away."

Amiria had jumped up then and after hesitating for a brief moment at the door had quickly left. She knew this was the kind of situation it was best to stay well away from. Later, after Lila had disappeared, she had wondered what she had meant. Why hadn't she been happy with this beautiful, perfect life? That was the moment when she had started asking herself that question, but there was no answer to it. She knew that she would have a perfect life and when she turned forty she would attend her own funeral along with all of her friends, celebrating their lives together and that would be it; Completion.

It was curious that she felt a little flat at this thought. She would never see Lila again and she knew it was best not to think too much about it. Psychology of a healthy mind was one of the subjects she had been taught thoroughly at school from a young age.

After seeing Lila that day she had been granted an unexpected holiday with two of her friends. She had enjoyed a full week of socialising and fun at the Bubble-spa where she had been appointed a new friend. This new friend was a very lively, hilarious young woman who had them in fits of laughter every night. If it had occurred to her that this friend was a replacement for Lila she didn't let herself dwell on it. What did it matter anyway? She knew the computer always did a fantastic job of matching people together and it was best to just relax and trust the system. She had been so flat out busy with activities during this time that she had been left exhausted but happy. She knew the best thing now for her to do was to concentrate on the happy times and on her family and Production.

She pulled herself out of her musings and consciously settled her mind. Just then her personal robot flashed indicating it had a message for her.

"A night of musical enjoyment for you and your current partner has just been added to your schedule," it announced in an up-beat voice. "You are now being detoured to the beauty salon to prepare for your evening out."

Amiria clapped her hands delightedly, the surge of excitement and anticipation that welled up inside her completely erased any residual feelings of concern she had about Lila and she forgot entirely about her. When she eventually arrived home after her visit to the beauty salon she was happy, relaxed and excited about the coming night out. She had a new high, spiralled hairstyle, dramatic make-up perfectly applied by the Beauty Salon robot to highlight her natural beauty and new accessories to dress up her outfit. Petra's eyes nearly popped out of his head when he saw her. It made her glow inside to know she could affect him like that and she gave him a flirty smile.

"So what did you do while I was at the Salon?" she asked, curling up in a chair near him that moulded itself to fit her.

"I was awarded a game of hyper-golf with my closest friends," he said twinkling at her. "I guess the CCS must have thought I would be feeling lonely with my lovely partner out later than usual.

He continued to smile at her and she wondered what he was thinking about, although, she had a fairly good idea what it might be.

"Looking forward to the concert?" she asked sweetly.

"That's one of the things I'm looking forward to tonight," he replied meaningfully.

She giggled. This was definitely her best cycle yet; one to remember.

# Chapter 5

Zak roared around the corner in his Mark IV Zephyr. Dust flying, all the windows wide open, the cooling air rushing over his damp body and over his two young cousins in the backseat. Gypsy's tangled mop of hair was flying around her head wildly in the swirling wind. Rangi was hanging his head out of the window as they sped along.

It was a stinking hot day in the small farming community in Aeotearoa, New Zealand. They had just been down to the river for a dip out the back of the farm. They weren't in a hurry, but Zak felt good having his foot hard to the floor causing the solid old car to judder and veer on the dusty gravel road. All around them were rolling, green hills, dotted here and there with white, woolly sheep.

There's no chance I'll meet any other cars on this road through the back paddocks so no worries there, Zak thought confidently, at least not much chance, at least...!

He slammed on the brakes and slid sideways past a startled looking man on a tractor. He just managed to swerve around him and stay on the road, leaving the man behind him coughing under a cloud of dust.

"Sorry Uncle!!!" he yelled out of the window. He whooped and slammed his foot back down on the accelerator as he tore up the last stretch, skidding to a halt outside an old farm house. Leaping out he shouted to his cousins, Rangi and Gypsy.

"Common, I'm starving, time for some kai." He ran into the house with Gypsy and Rangi following closely behind. He slowed down immediately as he spotted his Grandmother standing in the kitchen with her hands on her hips glaring at him. She was shorter than average, with rough grey hair pulled back tightly from her face. Her body was of motherly proportions and her wide-spread feet were planted firmly on the floor.

"What's your hurry?" she growled her lips pinched together in displeasure, "come back just in time to eat but not in time to help around the house ae? Leave all the work up to your old Grandmother will you?" She shook her dishcloth at him menacingly.

"Aww Gran it was hot so I went down to the river for a dip. Took the two youngies with me," Zak said pleadingly as if hoping this would get him off the hook.

"You took them so they could open the gates for you, I know you, young scallywag" and she aimed a whack at his ear with the dishcloth but he was too quick and leapt aside. He wasn't really worried by this grumpy reception, he knew she wouldn't stay mad for long. He dropped into one of the old kitchen chairs at the table grinning up at her as she stalked past him to the bench. Rangi and Gypsy plunked themselves down as well, grinning sideways at Zak in trouble with Gran again. Gran started dishing up the food, still looking stern. She looked up as she heard the tractor putting past with their Uncle, her eldest son, driving it. Uncle looked in at them for a moment but didn't wave as he usually did. His face was covered in a mantle of dust and his normally springy, black hair looked ash-grey.

"Hey what's up with your Uncle, he looks grumpy about something?" she looked suspiciously at Zak who shrugged nonchalantly as though it had nothing to do with him, then changed the subject.

"Something smells great Gran, what have ya made for us? I'm starving, bring on the kai woman!"

"Put on your shirt and act like a gentleman at the table and I might decide to feed you," she replied shortly. Her tone was strict but it was obvious she had a lot of pride in her handsome young grandson.

If only he would find a nice girl and settle down a bit, she thought. She shook her head resignedly.

Not many families of our race in this area might have to send him up North to find a nice Maori girl, she mused, someone who would fit into the family. God forbid not a Pakeha girl coming in with her finicky ways, turning her nose up at good kai and not understanding our culture. Still, it wouldn't pay to say anything to him, she thought as she dished up the meal. He would probably do the opposite just to annoy me, "young rat bag," she muttered to herself.

She carried the plates of steaming hot foot over to the old red Formica kitchen table. Her two other grandchildren were seated waiting patiently to be fed as well. Rangi was eyeing his older cousin whom he copied to the last detail and followed everywhere.

He would copy whatever Zak did even if it was jumping off a cliff, Gran thought with a chuckle. They were prodding and punching each other right now and chattering nonsense she noticed. Plunking down another two plates, one for herself and one for Gypsy she dropped herself into a chair with a big breath out as though thankful to sit down. Her eyes fell upon Gypsy who was sitting quietly waiting patiently to start eating her meal. She was rubbing her nose with the back of her hand and blowing stray strands of her unruly, damp hair off of her face.

Ridiculous name her daughter had given her, Gran thought as she often did, tucking into her meal and nodding at the children to start as well. It should have been Aroha or

Miriama or something pretty like that but no, she had to have her way. Rangi, now that was a decent name. She gazed upon Rangi fondly. Just then Rangi gave a great snorting laugh at something Zak had said and a lump of snot flew out of his nose and landed amongst the green peas nestled on his plate. Gran's fond smile fell off of her face and was replaced by a look of outrage.

"Why you disgusting little, little.....NGNGNGNG!!!!" Gran went red in the face and became incoherent from the effort not swear in front of her grandchildren and so set a bad example. She was very particular about things like swearing and table manners. She had been brought up in a household where every second word was a curse so it was an effort for her not to fall back into the bad old habits.

"What's the matter Gran your face is going red are you having a stroke, shall we call for an ambulance? Ha, ha," Rangi teased her.

"Don't you NNNGNGNG...!!!" Gran shook her finger at him eyes bulging with the strain.

"What was that Gran" asked Zak teasingly? "Ngngng *what?* Hey Gran how do you *spell* that?"

"Never you mind!" she blustered, "You just go and scrape off those peas into the pig bucket Rangi."

Rangi went and did what he was told, waggling his tongue at Gran behind her back.

"You should act more respectable," Gran continued with a little more coherence, "like me, you wouldn't see me snorting out snot balls into my food like that." She lifted her head proudly.

"Oh. Respectable? Like you? You mean respectable like when you get all dressed up in your nice big hat and coat Gran?" Zak spoke with wide-eyed innocence.

"Yes that's right, I know how to dress nice," Gran was looking slightly mollified.

"And then go down to the pub and get drunk Gran? Ha, ha."

"Oh you, you mind your own beeswax."

"Yeh," chimed in Rangi, "or when you stop on the side of the road and pick up other people's old clothes to bring home for us to wear, ha, ha, ha."

Gran glared at him. "Nothing wrong with that," she snapped, "waste not want not…"

"…as Grandad used to say," the two boys chorused together completing her sentence with a laugh.

They had heard her quote Grandad so often, it was like an old record being played over and over. They didn't really mind, they just liked pulling her leg. Gran fired up easily but she had her pride and refused to let them annoy her for long. Gran drew a deep breath and exhaled it in a huff as though breathing out all of her frustration. She started munching on her kai muttering under her breath, "Those boys, I'm getting too old for their carry on." She looked over at Gypsy who was sitting quietly and pensively looking down at her plate, holding her fork poised but not eating very much. Something about her face made Gran ask. "What's up sunshine, cat got your tongue?"

"I was just thinking Gran," she murmured, still looking at her plate.

"About what?" Gran prodded, looking at her with interest.

"Aww nothing really." Gypsy fiddled with her fork and didn't look up.

The boys stopped their high jinks to look around at her too.

Something about her face made Zak ask, "Did it happen again Gyps?"

Gypsy said nothing but looked uncomfortable.

# Chapter 6

"Common my girl, you'd better tell us" Gran prompted Gypsy, "you might have the gift, you might be seeing the spirits of our ancestors. Wouldn't *that* be something?" She said it with pride in her voice.

"Or she could just be plum crazy," laughed Rangi.

"Enough of that, I'm not too old to take the wooden spoon to your hide," Gran admonished Rangi.

Rangi looked scared enough and shut up quick. Gran only let the teasing behaviour go on so long, once she was really mad she didn't mind dishing out punishment in the old style.

"Well Gypsy?" Gran encouraged.

"I saw them again today," she whispered. She looked at Gran uncertainly, slightly fearful of what she had seen, then back down to her plate, shifting some peas around absently.

What were they like? Gran asked curiously.

"A man with dark hair and brown eyes," Gypsy said slowly, staring into the distance as she remembered the strange apparition in the bush, "a woman with light-coloured hair flowing down her shoulders in waves," she continued, "and a little girl, younger than me with long, blonde plaits and big round blue eyes. The little girl kept bouncing around but her eyes stayed staring straight ahead, fixed on one spot, like she was watching us, and her plaits were floating in the air around her head," she added. "It was funny," she giggled. Then she stopped abruptly, as her fear and uncertainty about what she had seen came back to her.

"Their clothes were different too," Gypsy said remembering their strange appearance.

"How different?" Gran demanded.

"Beautiful silky, pale colours and they looked soft and clingy like they were part of their skin."

"Can't have been spirits of your ancestors then, because they wouldn't have worn much clothes at all." Gran seemed to think this was hilariously funny, her plump figure heaving as she chuckled, slapping Zak who was nearest to her on the arm.

"Cut it out Gran" Zak said to her with an offended look. Then he turned back to his cousin.

"What else Gyps?" he prompted.

"Well they had pale skin."

"Humph Pakehas," snorted Gran little bits of mashed potato flying out of her mouth as she emphasised the letter P. Rangi stared with feigned astonishment at the little wet pieces of potato on the table cloth. He opened his mouth to say something but catching Gran's eye shut it again quickly and turned back to listen to Gypsy.

"Yeh, really white like huhu grubs that you find in rotten wood," continued Gypsy, "you know all pale and soft looking."

"Sounds like Pakehas alright," Gran said in a low voice then burst out laughing again. Zak leant away from her so she couldn't give him another slap.

"Far out Gran," he mocked, "you been drinking?"

"No I haven't you disrespectful young scamp." Gran had suddenly gone back to being grouchy again. She never discussed her regular visits to the pub and it was a very touchy subject. She never meant to drink too much but, well, one thing led to another and when did you stop? When you fall down, she thought giggling to herself. Then seeing her granddaughter's serious face she said, "Well I don't know what to make of these visions of yours young Gypsy, best not think about them too much ae. Eat up and shut up that was what your Granddad always used to say. Good advice I reckon. Who's doing the dishes tonight?" She stared meaningfully at the two boys who suddenly went into motion, stuffing the last of their meal into their mouths hurriedly.

"Um sorry Gran gotta run just gotta do this thing you know out there, you know," and Zak was gone with Rangi in hot pursuit.

Gran sighed as she watched them disappear out of the door. The only time she saw Zak and Rangi moving that fast was whenever she mentioned chores or when they were tearing madly around the rugby field. They would come home from their rugby games so exhausted they could barely walk, covered from head to toe in muck, handing her their stinking filthy clothes to be washed. Funny then that they never ever seemed to have enough energy to even dry a dish unless she threatened their lives.

"Just you and me again ae Gypsy," she sighed, "never mind boys will be boys. I'll get them on the weekend. They're having a hangi at the Marae. Old Joe Awarangi is putting a whole pig down to cook. They want workers to help clear the bush and fix up the gardens around the Marae. It's a big job. I'll tell the boys about the hangi but not about the work till after they get there."

She threw back her head and laughed again, her big brown face crinkling and revealing yellowing teeth with several missing.

"Hah, hah, ha, that's how you handle boys, through their stomachs ha, ha."

"Well let's get these dishes done my girl." Grans good humour was restored and she heaved her ample body up from the table. Brushing back the straggling pieces of her grey, bushy hair, collecting the dirty plates she headed for the sink.

Gypsy followed still deep in thought and got out the tea towel without complaint to dry the dishes.

As they worked Gran chattered away about this and that while she listened vaguely her mind still busy with her strange experience. She tried to shake off the funny feeling she had when looking directly into the eyes of the little girl in her vision. It was a weird feeling, as if, if she could just remember where, that she had met her before or knew her from somewhere else. How could that possibly be? They were strangers, wearing strange clothes and in a strange place. Yet the feeling persisted. It was almost as though she had known them once and forgotten or would know them at a future date. As if their paths hadn't yet crossed but inevitably would. She shook her head to clear it and tried to concentrate on Grans cheerful remarks about meaningless things.

Listening to Gran didn't really require much attention though and she soon found her mind wandering back to her peculiar abilities. She remembered how worried her Mum had been when she had first started telling her about the strange people she sometimes saw fleetingly. For a start, when she was very small, she had seen them only out of the corner of her eye, a flash of colour or a shape. Sometimes she would seem to glimpse someone disappearing as though through a door she couldn't see. Later on she had seen them more clearly, usually far away, sometimes, startlingly, looking back at her for an infinitesimal moment from a mirror or a pool of water. Those were the first times she had seen them really clearly if only for a brief moment.

She had prattled all about it to her Mum saying they were her friends and describing in such detail what they had looked like that her Mum had marched her off to the doctor to figure out what her problem was. This had resulted in a referral to a psychiatrist.

The psychiatrist was an elderly man who had listened to her seriously for a time, leaning forward with his hands clasped together as though concentrating on every word. After a while he had relaxed, laughed and then congratulated her on the originality of her thoughts. He had refused to give her the medication her Mum had demanded and sent them both away, saying she was a perfectly normal little girl with a great big imagination.

Her mother had next taken her to a psychic. Gypsy remembered the bead curtain they had to walk through to get to the inner room and the strong scent of incense that had billowed around her. The psychic had hummed and haa-ed over her, closing her eyes as she invoked unseen spirits. Even at that age Gypsy had thought it was all a bit silly and had been more fascinated by the big gold earrings the woman had worn and the colourful scarf wound around her head. The psychic had waved her hands over a crystal ball impressively, then triumphantly announced that Gypsy had the sight and was seeing the ghosts of the long ago dead. Her Mum had been quite excited about this until Gypsy had pointed out innocently that all the people she saw were dressed in unusual, silky clothing not at all like something their ancestors would have worn. The psychic had been pretty grumpy about this and declared Gypsy was just an ordinary, prosaic little girl after all with nothing very interesting about her.

Soon after that Mum had met another one of her boyfriends and lost interest in the whole thing. That was the usual pattern with their Mum. She loved them, Gypsy knew that, but drinking and relationships always got in the way.

She didn't really mind, she was used to it, and it meant she got to spend time on the farm with Gran. Gran's place felt more like home than anywhere else anyway. She had learnt not to mention her visions to her mother anymore which became clearer and more frequent over time.

One memory stood out. She had been brushing her teeth one morning and had glanced up at the mirror. Instead of seeing her own face reflected there she had found herself staring confusedly into what appeared to be a long dim tunnel. There were colourful lights here and there shining in the semi darkness and somewhere, a child was crying heartbreakingly. She had felt a powerful urge to go to that child to give comfort, so much so that she had found herself pressing hard up against the glass of the mirror as though trying to push her way through. Then the vision abruptly disappeared and she had found herself staring only at her own distressed face with toothpaste bubbles dripping from her lips. She had been ten years old then. Even now, at thirteen she still recalled that particular vision vividly and the strong feelings she had experienced along with it.

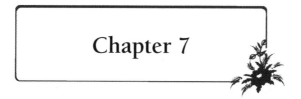

# Chapter 7

Dayzie was sitting in the child traveller kicking up her feet as usual. She was keeping her head still and not flapping her plaits around just for a moment but only because she was asking questions. Sometimes she asked them so fast they overlapped one another.

"Why, she said out loud, "do we go to class every day except two?"

"To learn to maximise your productivity and because ..." began the tiny robot floating in front of her face. But it didn't get a chance to finish before the next question was fired at him.

"What does my name mean?" Dayzie loved to know things and she squeezed information out of the little robot like squeezing juice from a lemon.

"You are named after an ancient plant called a daisy that grew in extremely unhygienic circumstances and ..."

"Why are you shaped that funny way?" she giggled, interrupting again as she looked up at the tiny black and white shape hovering in front of her.

"I am shaped this way," said the robot in an even voice, "because in the past humans kept animals as pets. Mainly small furry creatures called dogs and cats, that brought them comfort and enjoyment, but of course they were very unhygienic, covered in tiny creatures called fleas and carrying a multitude of diseases. So robots are formed in the shape of....."

"What is an elephant like? What does it look like? What does it smell like? What does it *taste like*?" She covered her mouth and giggled at the last question.

The robot, unfortunately, for all its vast suppository of information, did not understand humour in any form and so had no choice but to answer the question seriously.

"An elephant was a large animal, grey in colour that had big, flapping ears, a small tail and round feet with toenails but no toes. I really don't know what they smelt like and I have no data at all as to what they might have tasted like. It is possible that humans may have consumed them as food. It was common for those in the far past to consume the flesh of animals. You may experience what an elephant is like in a simulator during your leisure times; but not the taste of course," he added meticulously.

"How funny," said Dayzie, stopping her kicking and bouncing for a moment to stare at the robot.

"Which bit is funny?" the robot enquired in his patient voice.

The tiny robot always spoke in a patient voice, it had been programmed that way. No human could endure the kind of questions that were fired at it all day long from this gregarious human. If it could have sighed and rolled its eyes it would have frequently done so.

Dayzie seemed to have lost interest in questions for the moment and was craning her neck to stare out of the window. The tiny robot's name was Acne. A most unsuitable name he knew. Dayzie had named him and also told him he was a 'him.' He knew she had got the name through her viewing of ancient people on the history viewer. He also knew by his own recall of historical knowledge that acne was a skin disorder that used to appear on a human face in the form of oozing, red spots. Not a flattering name, no, not flattering at all. One day she had even painted little red spots all over him. They had never been fully removed to his satisfaction. Strange really, most people were naturally very fond of their personal robots since they had been with them from the time when they were first fully developed humans. Each child was constantly looked after, watched over, comforted and guided by them. It was unusual that she had given him that peculiar, unflattering name. Often the little personal robots, named affectionately by young children, were called things like teddy, brainy, puppy or honey, so why she would choose that name for him was unfathomable. Acne had stored this anomaly away in his data banks to be presented to the Information Giver as he had been programmed to do. It may not be something that would ultimately affect Dayzie's future Productivity as far as he could calculate, but you never knew and anyway that was something for the almighty computers in the Central Information System to work out.

"Dayzie I sense you need to urinate," he informed her. "It is a little before time so it is possible we may need to adjust your liquid intake in the mornings."

"I can hold it" said Dayzie bouncing harder.

"That may well be true, but to ensure your bladder performs its function well throughout your Life Cycles you need to urinate regularly when I say so."

"Oh all right then," she capitulated with good humour.

The seat she was sitting on disappeared so quickly it seemed to have vaporised and was instantly replaced with a spongy substance instead. After a few minutes the spongy substance vanished leaving no trace of fluid and the soft, rubbery seat similar to all the other seats on the traveller reappeared. The girl who sat the prescribed distance away to her right, far enough away to allow for comfort but close enough to converse if desired, glanced at her, then looked away again without interest.

Dayzie stared at her with her usual overactive curiosity. The girl looked a little bit older than her and she was sitting with her ankles crossed neatly and her hands clasped on her lap. She was looking out of the window with her head leaning slightly to one side.

"I'm seven, how old are you?" Dayzie asked the girl engagingly.

The girl looked around slowly, glanced over her once and then said, "I'm ten," as if to say ten was much better than being only seven.

Dayzie crossed her ankles and clasped her hands in her lap too, mimicking the older girl. She tilted her head on just the same angle and looked out of the window, glancing back at the other girl briefly, checking to make sure she had it just right. She straightened her head and tilted it again, straight, tilted, straight, tilted. It didn't look any different to her whichever way she held her head, so she went back to bouncing. They would be there soon anyway. Outside looked pretty much the same as they sped past, though very nice to look at. White buildings, artfully designed and perfectly spaced spread across the landscape. Colourful wall paintings blazed in contrast with the clean, pristine white. They were abstracts and the dynamic blends of colours and dramatic sweeping lines were pleasing to the eye. The scenery was very pretty but she loved the sky the best. The sky could be many different shades and was changeable depending on the time of day or the weather. She had questioned Acne endlessly about why this was so, so she knew what caused the fluctuations in colour and the different types of clouds. She really wasn't as interested in why as much as just enjoying it. It was so beautiful and seemed so alive compared with everything else. There weren't any plants or trees of any kind here in the City not real ones anyway. Of course you could go into a simulated forest anytime you wanted to. Apparently there was a massive, real forest somewhere, far away across the sea that produced just the right kind of air for people to breathe. It was controlled though, so it never got too big or too small but was just the right size for producing air for the number of people who lived in the world. It was a pity that it was so distant you couldn't get to it. The numbers of people in the City were also carefully controlled but she wasn't sure just how. She did know that she was produced from a sperm and an egg, that she had been grown in a perfectly safe environment until she was fully developed. She was then nurtured by the Caretakers and Nanny Robots until it was time to be assigned to a family. The stories were all the same for everyone so no-one really talked about it and what did it matter anyway? She was far more interested in the sky that was never the same with its constantly changing colours, cloud patterns and pictures. She had to lie almost sideways on the traveller to see it above the buildings.

"Time to get off and go to class," said Acne in that no-nonsense voice that is hard to disobey. Everybody waited their turn and got off in orderly fashion, taking turns row by row. Dayzie jumped up when it was her turn, bouncing along in her usual energetic style. She was blissfully unaware that she stood out from the others who were all patiently standing in line waiting to take their turn. She was also unaware of her personal robot scanning and recording her every move, sound and emotional fluctuation. She was looking forward to going to class to learn all kinds of interesting things. Today she remembered they would be learning about the Seven Cycles of Life. She knew the first two already. From zero to seven years old was Development and Preparation for living in the City, next was Allocation to a Family. That was her current cycle and that one would go on until she turned fourteen. At fourteen she would leave home and her Careers Training would begin. Being allocated to parents was the most momentous thing that had ever happened to her so far in her young life. Moving from the Preparation Centre where she had lived amongst all the other children her age to go into a home with her own parents and a big brother had filled a longing inside herself that she couldn't understand or explain. The cycles that came next after this one were a little hazy in her mind but she did know they were Relationship Cycles and the beginning of Production duties. Then came the Parenting cycles and then one more cycle before your funeral that was extra special. She couldn't quite remember why it was so special, but her teacher would explain everything to her and make it simple and easy to understand. Happily she jumped off the traveller and entered her classroom along with her classmates.

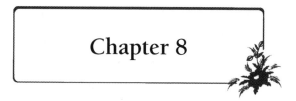

# Chapter 8

Az sat in class listening intently to his teacher. He was an intelligent boy and had always enjoyed learning. Up till now he had maintained an impeccable record both in and out of school. He absorbed information like a sponge and could memorise and spout quotes and Wisdom for Life messages 'till the cows came home.' He smiled to himself at that phrase 'till the cows came home.' It was one he had heard while watching a history view of a family from long ago. He knew what cows were and he even knew how people used to extract milk from them. He had been revolted by the piles of steaming manure and the dirty looking animals trudging through the bacteria filled dirt and mud in the view. Farming they had called it. They were so dumb back then. They actually waited for rain to make the grass and crops grow and if it didn't rain then hard luck and the plants shrivelled up and the animals died. Funny way to live life, so uncertain and scary.

He had heard of but had never seen the great Sky Gardens where all the food for the people of the City was grown. He knew it was grown on platforms high in the sky where the sunshine, temperatures and rainfall were rigidly controlled. Clouds were siphoned from the atmosphere, condensed and the water released at just the right times. This was so much better than old time farming. Everything was certain and predictable, safe and secure.

It was strange then that just lately he had begun to feel differently about things. He had felt a little restless, moody and even a little bit dissatisfied. Hormones probably, he told himself. He had studied hormones in great detail in class so he knew how they affected his body, mind and emotions.

He tuned back in to what the teacher was saying and as he did so he noticed something that had been bothering him unconsciously for a while. Every time the teacher said anything about anything he always added a 'Wisdom for Life message.' He liked his teacher who was of course very good at teaching. Everyone was good at what they did. One day he would be an engineer when he had completed the correct amount of education and he was proud of this. The Information Giver had been recording his every move and word since he was a baby so that he would be given the perfect career suited to his abilities, resulting in the ultimate degree of happiness, satisfaction and of course, Productivity. It was a simple and effective formula. He listened to his teacher and made careful, orderly notes on his auto-pad as he always did but with another part of his mind he mused on what it was that was annoying him.

The teacher was finishing his lesson on technology and logic with another message: "... and of course all this leads to 'maximum results for the yielding of greater Productivity.'

There it was, that was it! He had been hearing it all his life. That last sentence said in a certain tone which made it sound as though it couldn't ever be challenged and it was the same old thing he had been hearing over and over again.

I wonder why they feel they have to say it over and over again, he thought irritably, if it's true we'll know it's true without having to be told over and over, won't we?

The teacher was asking them to recall images on their auto pads to reinforce what he had just taught them. Lessons always involved all the senses; listening, viewing images, simulated touch, shapes and patterns, recitation, smells and practical application were all important for maximum learning potential and recall. With lunch break approaching Az was regretting eating that extra chocolate bar this morning. It hadn't been on his diet list and it would mean a reduced meal or more time exercising so that he stayed in perfect health. Only students who were involved in highly physical activities such as dancing were usually given these small sweet bars of chocolate to bring their sugar levels back to an optimum level. They contained a blend of natural, healthy plant extracts, oils and sugars. He had taken the chocolate bar from a girl in his class who was training to be a gymnast while she was distracted talking to her friends. She hadn't noticed him take it. No one expected anyone to take something that didn't belong to them. Why would they when everything they needed was provided for them? It was also impossible to fool the health and nutrition monitor. You stood on it before each meal and it measured exactly what you had eaten previously through the ratios of sugars, fats and nutritional elements in your blood. It recorded your weight, calculated your muscle and fat mass for your age and height and within mille-seconds and spat out a list of items on a disc it was permissible to eat. This disc was then presented to the cafeteria machine which processed your lunch. The machine would record his higher levels of sugars and fats in his bloodstream and adjust his lunch accordingly. When the girl's levels were measured it would show she was short of these things and would most likely spit her out another chocolate bar. She might think she had misplaced it somewhere and quickly forget about it, but the CCS would know exactly where it had gone.

Still it had been good, he thought, as he remembered the taste and there was something else about it too. He remembered the thrill of breaking out of the careful boundaries that had been laid down for him. It was almost as though he were daring the authorities to do something about it. Nothing had happened so far. Maybe he would get a light lunch and that would be it.

He questioned himself why he felt this urge to test the limits. Was he normal? He looked around surreptitiously at the other students. They all seemed to be studiously focusing on their work and appeared perfectly content. For just a second he caught the intense gaze of a girl with green eyes. It was only for a moment but in that tiny space of time he suddenly felt as though he were not alone with these thoughts. The girl had red hair which contrasted sharply with her pale skin and bright eyes. He had seen something there, behind her eyes, seemingly familiar. He decided he would try and talk to her when he got the chance. She wasn't one of his designated friends but something about her intrigued him. Not just her looks but something different, something deeper.

He thought too about the history view that they had watched with that brown young man in the funny, rattley vehicle, speeding along the dusty road. Now that looked really exhilarating. That boy had been driving very fast along a rough road with the real possibility he could get hurt if something went wrong. Az closed his eyes and tried to imagine what that would be like, knowing that you could get hurt but doing it anyway.

"Az. This is class time not dreaming time. Please recall your mind to the task." His teacher was speaking directly to him, not unkindly, but firmly.

Az came abruptly out of his imaginings and refocused on the images on his auto-pad, quickly becoming absorbed in the fascinating information. He put his inner thoughts aside to be considered during rest time in his schedule.

# Chapter 9

Gran had her big, old-fashioned hat and coat on.

"I'm just popping down to the shops dears" she called in a fake, cheery voice, fooling no-one.

Zak had already gone out for the night and no one was expecting him back anytime soon.

Hanging around with his good-for-nothing friends I'll bet, thought Gran. Wonder if he's drinking tonight? I guess it's inevitable, she thought with resignation.

She remembered her own childhood when her parents used to drink themselves stupid most nights. She recalled them yelling and screaming abuse at each other. When things got too bad she would hide, crawling into the recess under the stairs along with her little brothers and sisters, peeking out to watch fearfully as they bashed each other. Oh yes her mother was just as bad as her father, sneaking up on him and bopping him around the head with the fry-pan. Knocked him out cold once too. She had taken her fair share of beatings though. It had been a crazy household. All of her six brothers and sisters had grown up to be big drinkers, and then her own children too. Alcoholics and drug addicts and couldn't even look after their own kids properly, she thought with sorrow. Well it would be more of a surprise if her grandkids didn't drink, she supposed.

'The sins of the fathers...,' she quoted, to herself sighing and shaking her head sadly, seemingly oblivious of her own hypocrisy.

Her own daughter Anahera, mother to Rangi and Gypsy, had it hard always seeming to pick the wrong man. If only she had the courage to go it alone, for the kids' sake, she had often thought. That was her weakness, she had to be in a relationship even if it was a bad one and the father of the kids was nowhere to be seen. At least her eldest son was doing pretty well these days. He had taken over the farm when the old fella had no longer been able to keep it up properly. He still drank heavily she knew, but at least he kept it mainly for the weekends or when the All Blacks were playing a game of rugby.

She'd really done her best to bring her kids up right. The years when they were young had been hard years, trying to scrape a living off the land. The old man had worked hard morning, noon and night clearing the scrubby hills by hand, up before dawn and not home till after dark. When the kids were little he had almost been a stranger to them, leaving before they woke up and coming home long after they were sound asleep in bed. She had practically raised their four kids alone. They had earned barely enough from the farm to pay the mortgage and the bills living only on what she could grow in the garden, meat from the farm or whatever they could catch. There were plenty of eels in the river and they had often feasted on them. There were pigs in the bush too and when he had brought one home slung across his back she would invite the whole Whanau around and they would have a hungi.

The kids all had to wear homemade or hand-me-down clothes. The girls used to complain about how embarrassing it was to have to wear undies made out of flour bags which everyone could see when they did handstands at school. She'd given them a piece of her mind about that, showing off your knickers to everyone indeed! They had both worked so hard and they had done it all for the kids, so they would have something in this world after they had gone and not nothing.

Thinking about the old days Gran's mind flicked back to when she was a young thing and had first met the old man. He had been referred to as the 'old man' for so many years now that people barely remembered his real name was Henry. Henry had been quite the looker in those early days. A charming, good-looking young scallywag he had been and a bit of a heart-stopper. He was well known around town for his drunken carousing and his string of lady-friends. Oh yes she hadn't been the first girl to catch his eye, she well knew that, but he had settled down with her and she had discovered he was a family man at heart. There had been a few disappointed young ladies in the town when they had tied the knot. There had been that Pakeha girl, peroxide-blonde hair, long red fingernails, just dying to get her claws into her man. Henry had enjoyed the attention, had flirted with her, teased her a bit and then told her he was getting married so she may as well get lost. She remembered the triumphant feeling she had experienced to be the one to catch him.

On her wedding day she had walked up the aisle as if in a dream. He had been unbelievably handsome in his new black suit, really quite respectable looking. He was grinning at her with his twinkling brown eyes, black curls slicked back under a heavy layer of grease. She had asked him once why he had chosen her when he had all those other girls chasing him. His reply had surprised her. 'Because I knew you would be a good mum,' he had said, revealing his true nature underneath it all, "and you're not afraid of hard work', he had added, 'not like that young miss with her painted talons, sitting around powdering her nose.' That had been good enough for her and she hadn't questioned him again.

It hadn't all been sunflowers and sunsets though, more like get on with life and don't complain. Still, she had some good memories from those days in spite of the struggles. It was a good life on the whole, living out in the country, swimming in the river, plenty of bush and surrounded by the rolling green hills, but there had been some bad times too. They were both drinkers and, especially when all the Whanau was around, there would be parties. The kids would be left to fend for themselves while the adults partied it up. When the extended family wasn't around it was straight down to the pub on a Friday night. If she'd had a few twinges of guilt about leaving the kids home by themselves during these excursions, they had disappeared after the alcohol started flowing. She had taken a few beatings from Henry too, when he had drunk way more than he should have, especially in the early days, but somehow they had stuck together to provide some sort of stability for the kids.

The old man had been blessed with his own peculiar sense of humour and now after he had been gone so many years it was one of the things she remembered best about him. That and his constant 'sayings.'

Every single morning it was, 'time to put both feet on the floor,' that was his way of telling his aching old body to get up out of bed and get to work. After a cuppa when it was time to get back to the job it was always, 'time to put the boot under the ball,' an obvious rugby reference. He had always been a great believer in mind over matter.

If he saw someone speeding he would always say, 'that fellas late for his own funeral,' then he would chuckle appreciatively at his own joke. She had thought him funny the first few times she had heard it, but it had worn a bit thin over time. Strange though, now that he was gone those repetitive sayings that had so irritated her so much stayed in her mind and they helped her to carry on. She sighed. He had always said he would die with his boots on and that was exactly what he had done. Pushing seventy but still working a full day on the land when he had collapsed from heart failure. The doctor had warned him over and over again to cut down on the smoking and drinking but he had never listened. He had always thought he knew what was best for himself.

She still missed the old man every day. He could be hard but she had admired him for his sheer determination. There were also plenty of times when she had wanted to whack him around his stubborn old head with the frying pan like her mother used to do to her father. He'd been stuck in his ways no doubts about it but there wasn't a lazy bone in his body, and it had all been for his family. She respected him for that. She shook herself. No good thinking too much about the past and what she had lost. What she needed right now was a bit of company and a maybe a little drink or two.

She peeked into the lounge. Rangi was playing x-box furiously and didn't look up. She popped her head round the door into Gypsy's room and saw her lying on the bed with her feet up against the wall, reading.

"Just going out, won't be long dear" she said with that false gaiety in her voice that everyone including herself hated.

"Okay Gran" said Gypsy, "see ya later, take care of ya-self."

Gran nodded and smiled at her briefly before moving quickly towards the door. She had worked hard all day and surely she deserved a night out at the pub with some friendly company. She wouldn't stay long this time, just a few drinks then home. She marched down the road as quickly as possible before she could argue with herself that she knew very well she wouldn't be back before the early hours of the morning.

# Chapter 10

The house went quiet after Gran had left with only the sounds of the x-box in the lounge and a gentle rustling as Gypsy turned the pages of her book. Gypsy enjoyed the peacefulness and silence of the country-side. The only sounds that broke the silence of the night-times were the possums cackling in the trees or the thumping sounds as they ran across the old tin roof. Sometimes you heard the *'mooor pooor'* of a little Morepork owl calling eerily from the shadows. They were small shy little creatures that only came out at night so it was hard to catch a glimpse of them. Once while Gypsy and Gran were sitting yakking on the couch in the evening there had been a loud bang on the window behind them. They had pulled back the curtains to find one of the little owls with its face pressed up against the pane, clearly stunned from hitting the window mid-flight. It must have seen the light through a chink in the curtains and tried to fly right through. Maybe it was after the moths that fluttered around the light bulb in their lounge. It sat there on the window sill for about five minutes, large round eyes staring sightlessly into their lounge, clinging to the thick ivy vines that surrounded the window frame before it finally fluttered off into the night.

Another night Gypsy had been sound asleep in bed when an unholy commotion had shattered her dreams and brought her into startled wakefulness. Gran was pounding around the house like a mad thing, broom raised above her head while a possum skittered around and around the house with terrified round staring eyes. It zipped into a bedroom in its panic faster than you would believe, under the bed of a deeply unconscious Rangi, out of the bedroom up the hall into the next room and round and around again with Gran panting after it ineffectually trying to catch it. Gypsy had watched the comedy act for a few minutes before calmly opening the back door wide so the possum could flee out into the night with Gran in hot pursuit. It turned out that the possum had come in through the cat door and had wandered into the kitchen drawn by the smell of food. Gran had discovered it sitting up on the bench helping itself to apples from the fruit bowl. Gypsy wished she had seen the moment when they had caught sight of each other. She could imagine the possums bulging eyes with its tiny pinpoint pupils staring into Gran's astonished face for a few shocked seconds before the chase had begun.

Often at night after lights were out, Gypsy would hear galloping sounds around the house. In the morning the only sign that there had been anything there was the small sharp hoof imprints in the lawn. Deer coming down from the forest behind the house would leap the fences and come out into the open during the safety of the night to eat the grass in the paddocks. It all added to the interest of being in the countryside for Gypsy but the farmers considered them to be a nuisance.

There were some kinds of wildlife she wasn't so fond of though. There had been those mysterious trails of food scraps running from the pig bucket along the floor and disappearing through a crack in the fireplace that appeared during the night and were discovered in the mornings when they came into the kitchen for their breakfast. This had been when Grandad was alive and eventually after trying to stop up the cracks in the fireplace he had got to work ripping the old tin firebox out of the wall. Behind it he discovered a family of tiny pink rat babies. Gran had been entirely disgusted that the big fat cats that slept on the beds at night had let a family of rats move in right under their snoring, be-whiskered noses.

Tonight all was quiet and peaceful as Gypsy allowed herself to become deeply absorbed in her book. If she had listened very carefully she would have been able to hear the sounds of the whistling tree frogs faintly in the distance. Eventually Gypsy lay back with the book lying on her chest knowing that she would probably fall asleep soon and should really get under the covers. It was school holidays so she didn't have to get up for anything in particular in the morning. She lay there with the cool evening breeze blowing through the window, fresh smelling and promising rain.

As she lay staring at the ceiling she started to get that prickly feeling again that always came along with her visions. Oh no, she thought, not now, not while I'm alone. Unlike the brief glimpses and distant visions she had experienced as a young girl, these visions lately had been clear and lasting several minutes at a time. She saw them long enough to remember the details of each person and their surroundings. She lay frozen to the spot, not knowing what would happen next, unable to move a muscle. It was bad enough seeing them when she was in the bush with her brother and cousin close by but here, now, alone in an old house as evening approached... She shivered and waited for whatever was going to happen next.

The face shimmered on the white of the ceiling. She saw the dancing plaits and the big, round luminous eyes. It was like looking into a pool of water with a slight breeze disturbing the surface. They stared at one another as the seconds passed. Finally Gypsy realised the face looked just as scared as she felt and that it was a much younger child than she was. She decided to try something. She looked towards the door but the house was still quiet other than the x-box sounds. She turned back to the face and spoke loudly and clearly.

"Who-are-you?"

The face looked so surprised that she was sure the girl had heard her speak. She saw her mouth opening and shutting as if she were trying to say something to her but she could hear no sound. She saw another face appear behind the young girl, peering down at her in her room, saying something to the girl and pulling her rapidly away. It was the man that she had seen sitting beside the girl in the vision in the bush. She thought he must be her father and he looked worried.

As they disappeared from her view she caught sight of the room behind them. It was beautiful and spacious, clean whites with splashes of lively colour. She thought they must be very rich to afford a flash house like that. Then suddenly the vision was gone and she was staring at the yellowing ceiling of the old, cobwebby house again. She lay quite still on her bed as it got darker and darker trying to process what had happened. This wasn't just a vision, the girl had heard her, she was sure she had. She had even tried to reply, but for some reason, wherever she was she couldn't make herself heard. She found herself desperately hoping she would see the little girl again. She felt a strange affinity for her. It was almost as though she were looking at herself in another body or like a little sister that she had once had and was very fond of but had forgotten all about. That was a bizarre thought. She mentally shook herself, but could not eliminate the feeling that the little girl was connected to her somehow. Finally, stiff and chilled she crawled under the covers. It wasn't really scary after all, she thought as she snuggled in, not like seeing ghosts, more like looking at someone on TV, except they could see her too. Eventually she fell asleep wondering, was this something from the spirit realm or was it a flesh and blood little girl that was alive somewhere in the world? She had a strong sense that the girl needed her in some way.

# Chapter 11

Amiria was in bed sound asleep as usual that night. Nothing ever disturbed her sleep and she always woke fully refreshed and ready for a new day of Productivity. She loved her job of course as everyone loved their jobs. Each day she worked producing the things that she found most enjoyable and which gave her a deep sense of satisfaction. Amiria's occupation was an Interior Designer. Her job was to match colours and furnishings to please the eye and create an atmosphere of peace and tranquillity in homes, classrooms and areas of Productivity. She was naturally very good at her job. Thanks to her no two dwellings in her designated area were ever the same and stepping into each home was an absolute delight to the senses. Everyday presented a new challenge to her and sometimes she even undid something that looked perfectly good just to have the pleasure of doing it all over again in a slightly different style.

On the weekends she enjoyed the balance of social and family times that were allotted to her. It was always pleasant to meet up with the particular friends who had been skilfully selected for her, to relax, chat, and to discuss hair styles, Production and of course relationships. This was a very feminine thing to do, she knew, and was as important to her and other women as actually being in the relationship. Each cycle the computer expertly matched couples together who were highly compatible and who would extract maximum enjoyment from each other's company. Men studied at school how to interact with females and women were taught the best ways to interact with men. In this way all a person's needs were fully met. The fifth Life Cycle was deemed to be the right time for children to be introduced into a relationship. Parenting was also carefully studied and taught and the Information Giver was always on hand for any problems.

Life was so peaceful and certain and, what was it Petra had said? *'Predictable,'* that was it. But he had said it almost as though he thought it was a bad thing. She had lain on her bed before falling asleep contemplating this. She had thought back over her life and then forward to the future, right to the day of Completion of the Life Cycles which she knew would be on her fortieth birthday. In class she had been taught, of course, that after this age the human body began to fail and become sick and painful. She shuddered, who would want to live like that? But, she thought, he is right our lives are predictable. She felt strange at the thought, sort-of empty. It was as though her happy state was a shiny, fragile bubble that could burst at any moment. She had fallen asleep not long after this with the comforting thought that whatever she was feeling the Information Giver would find a solution for her. Something exciting; some change in her schedule that would cause her emotional levels to return back to their normal peaceful state.

The next morning she poked her head into Petra's room on her way to get breakfast. She saw him lying in bed with a perfect image of herself enfolded in his arms. She smiled down at him.

"Enjoying yourself?" she asked teasingly. The image disappeared and Petra stretched and sat up in the bed.

"Morning darling, and yes I was, perfectly. No morning-breath with simulations thank goodness."

"I know what you mean," she rolled her eyes at him and laughingly continued towards the dining area.

He jumped out of bed with energy and followed her just in time for their morning weigh in and to eat the breakfast prescribed for them. The breakfast, as usual, perfectly satisfied their appetites and nutritional needs giving them energy for the day.

Amiria checked the flashing light on her personal robot as the children came in and exclaimed with delight, "Oh Petra, I've been invited to share in a funeral celebration. Darlia has invited me, it's her funeral. I've never been to one before, how exciting. I've heard they are so much fun." Amiria noticed the light on Petra's personal robot was flashing as well. "Oh look you have a message too."

"I've been invited as well, it's for Saturday afternoon. That should be interesting darling." Petra seemed less excited than Amiria at this prospect.

"What is a funeral?" enquired Dayzie with a hundred questions shining out of her eyes.

"No, no, no sweetheart," smiled her mother, "you need to ask your teacher those questions, it's an important subject and you need to hear it just right. It's not one of the things parents are supposed to talk about to their children."

"Ok Mum I'll ask my teacher at school today," Dayzie answered contentedly.

Amiria smiled at her daughter and then looking out of the window she noticed that the usual soft light was even dimmer than usual. Then she heard a distant rumble. The children looked up from their breakfast with surprise and interest.

"Did you hear that thunder?" said Az.

Just then their four personal robots lined up as they did when they were about to make a joint announcement. A calm voice spoke from them in unison.

"Today you may see some flashes of light in the sky. This is called lightening. It is a natural phenomenon but it is advisable that you stay indoors until it is over. School and Production will begin at a slightly later time than usual today. Please enjoy the extra time resting and relaxing with your family. Thank you."

The children looked at each other. This kind of thing did not happen very often. The weather was usually the same day after day after day; the same dim sunlight with clear, pale skies.

"Mum what's a phe-nomin-omin-nom?" Dayzie asked quizzically.

"It's, just something that happens," answered Amiria vaguely.

"Something they can't control," added Az.

"That's a strange thing to say," said Amiria with a worried look on her face and then she began speaking hurriedly as her anxiety for her son broke through. "What do you mean something they can't control? It's good that things are controlled, so they can't hurt us. What would the world be like otherwise?"

Az shrugged, refusing to elaborate on his comment. Then changing the subject he asked, "What are we going to do with our extra time?"

"What would you children like to do?" Petra enquired.

"Let's watch that family again, the ones in the bush," said Dayzie excitedly, not noticing that she was holding her spoon in the air with commixture dripping off it and onto the table.

Petra looked at Amiria. "What do you think darling?"

Amiria exhaled to release the anxiety that had built up following Az's comment. Closing her eyes she consciously restored herself to calmness. Learning the art of mentally controlling your emotional state was included in the education of everyone in the City.

"Yes, I'd like that," she looked up at him smilingly. She wilfully relaxed her body as their seats moved together to form a comforting proximity. The viewer switched on and they became immersed in the scene of the farm in the bush. The scene they saw this time was quite different from the last time they had viewed it. Then the hot sun had been streaming through the branches of the trees and bouncing off the sparkling water. It was a dim day there too.

"How strange," murmured Amiria, "their weather is the same as here."

The girl with the long tangly hair was in the garden near the old farm house alongside a grey-haired, old women. They were both bending over pulling at the plants, throwing some away and piling others up. Every now and then the old women rubbed her back.

"You see that," Petra pointed out, "she's in pain. That's what happens when you keep living after forty."

"Mmmm" said Amiria musingly. She was fascinated by the old women. Her grey hair, her outsized body, her amazingly crinkled face. No-one like that existed in their world now.

The old women looked up at the sky and they heard her say, "rain coming soon my girl, good for the garden."

"Let's get these inside quick Gran before it buckets down," the girl urged.

The City family watched in fascination as drops of water began to fall from the sky. The girl in the viewer squealed, laughing as the drops came down thicker, and faster. She gathered up the vegetables, working as quickly as she could but they could see her hair was beginning to drip.

They disappeared indoors leaving the City family to watch the rain fall more and more heavily; gathering in puddles on the dirt driveway, hammering on the old tin roof of the house, water streaming down the gutters. Amiria glanced away from the scene to look out of the window. The day still looked dim and dark but no rain of course. The only way she would ever see rain was through a viewer. Why was that, she wondered. She was a little mystified by this momentarily before becoming reabsorbed in the scene.

They could hear a rushing sound and the view switched to the river which looked browner and fuller than before. The rain continued to pound down, torrents of water now flowing down the driveway. Bits of tree branches began to appear rushing past on the surface of the river. Eventually the rain softened and stopped. For a time all they could hear was the soft plopping of large drops of water dripping from the trees as the sky lightened and the clouds dispersed.

Then quite unexpectedly the sun burst through, shining so brightly on all that wetness that the family gasped in unison.

"It's so bright" said Dayzie, "it's brighter than our sun isn't it?"

"Yes I think your right" said Petra thoughtfully. "What do you think Az?"

"It's the same sun" Az said frowning, "why would it be brighter? I wonder what happened to it to make it so much dimmer now."

"Well it's nothing to worry about any way," said Petra heartily. He was interested too but he knew better than to encourage his children to wonder too much. Their natural curiosity needed no assistance and it was better that their questions were answered in the proper fashion at school.

Just then the calm, pleasant voice spoke once again. "The lightening is now over, please proceed to School and Production."

The four of them jumped with surprise. How long had they been watching the rain, transfixed?

"Why don't we ever get rain here?" Az grumbled.

"Would you really want to live in a world where water fell out of the sky any old time and wet everything and turned rivers into dangerous floods like that one?" Petra asked him.

"People's life cycle's sometimes ended in floods." Dayzie interjected automatically. She had a dim, far-a-way look in her eyes. She knew this fact was true but the rain did look so lovely. What would it be like to be out in it and to jump in those puddles and watch the river rise and wonder what was going to happen next? She felt a tickly feeling in her stomach at the thought. The next time she was in the simulator she would programme a rainy day and pretend for a while that she didn't know what might happen next. That sounded exciting.

"Time for school Dayzie," said the friendly voice of her personal robot in her ear.

She jumped up. She did so love her classes, her teacher was so sweet and learning new things was always fun. The day was much lighter now as they went outside to get into the traveller a little later than usual. She looked up at the sky. She saw the clouds moving very quickly away to her right, in the same direction they always disappeared to, and the pale, far-away sky re-appearing. There were no sunbursts though.

Why?! Why?! Why?! She thought to herself, stamping her feet as she walked each time she thought it. She imagined splashing through water as she stamped, but the ground was perfectly dry.

"What are you doing?" Wondered Acne.

"Stamping" she said. She didn't tell him about the imaginary puddles or the questions that were bouncing through her brain. She knew there would be some perfectly good answer all about safety and stuff and she didn't want to hear about it just now, she just wanted to think and imagine.

# Chapter 12

Petra gazed out of the window for a few appreciative moments, contemplating the superb view from his area of Productivity. Being an architect his productivity space was in one of the few buildings that were built higher than ground level. It had been constructed as a square tower, three stories high with a flat roof that was useful as a launching pad for small one-person hovercrafts. Although it was built for practical purposes, the design and layout was also a thing of beauty as was every building in the City. Petra enjoyed observing the products of his creativity. The simple, beautiful lines pleased him, and he was constantly searching for possible improvements.

He turned and walked purposefully over to the large table that held a perfect scale model of his sector of the City. He ran his hands over the smooth marble surfaces marvelling that it felt so completely real to his touch. Placing his hands together over one of the domes and then moving them apart using the hand gestures he had been taught, he easily pulled open the seemingly solid structure. In this way he could break down the entire building to study every portion of it right down to the most trivial detail. Complementary to his love of beautiful architecture Petra was also skilled at ensuring a building was functional and practical.

He studied the inner workings of the building for a time performing several minor changes, then when he was satisfied he moved the outer walls back into place. Whatever enhancements he made on this model, whether minute or extensive, those changes would be effected overnight. He might come to work the day after completely remodelling a building, look out the window and there it would be, exactly as he had designed it. It was almost as though it had grown up from under the surface of the city. He didn't know how this happened but in his imagination he saw an army of robots working feverishly and silently through the night as he slept to achieve such rapid changes on such an immense scale. Once again Petra laid a finger on the cold marble of the model. He stood motionless thinking and wondering. A troublesome thought fell into his mind like a stone shaking the surface of a tranquil pool, sending quivering thoughts to the outer edges of his consciousness.

"Petra," his personal robot interrupted his contemplations, "are you considering a new design?" Petra withdrew his finger hurriedly blinking to return himself from the strangeness of his thoughts. "No, I was just thinking..." He stopped unsure if he should reveal his inner imaginings to his robot helper or not.

"Yes, you were thinking...?" the robot prompted persistently.

Petra turned to the tiny floating machine. His thoughtful expression cleared as he made his decision. Revealing his thoughts would just trigger a detailed response that would explain everything and explain nothing. Instead he chose to allow the robot to believe he needed inspiration.

"I think it's time I went to the creative room to search for new ideas," he answered as though he merely was in need of new stimulus.

"A splendid idea Petra," the robot agreed enthusiastically, "it will be a good opportunity for you to see things from an entirely different perspective."

The creative room was a fully simulated interactive experience allowing Petra to see his work from any size, perspective or angle and to try out different ideas on varying scales. Petra was soon deeply engrossed. First he enlarged himself to a size big enough to look down on the simulated buildings as a whole gaining an overall perspective. He then reduced himself to the size of the mythical mouse, enabling him to examine more intricate details. He liked the idea of creeping around like the bright-eyed little creatures that featured in ancient stories. The creative room simulation also allowed him to move massive buildings around by simply waving his arms and, in an instant, to completely change their structures. He spent an enjoyable afternoon occupied in this way, developing new, exciting and inventive ideas. He became so distracted he forgot all about those troubling thoughts that had been forming in his mind while staring at the small scale model of the City. Although gone for now, lost in the experience of the moment, these thoughts would return later, triggered by an unexpected train of events soon to unfold before his unsuspecting mind. If his mind was a tranquil pool, then something dark was disturbing its depths.

The small inoffensive-looking robot watched Petra as it had been programmed to do and as it had done for the whole of his life. Its view of the world was quite different to Petra's, stripped of any simulation. He watched as Petra stood in the bare room twitching and jerking his arms and body as a dog twitches in its sleep while dreaming. The little robot knew all about dogs and all the other creatures from the past. It had full access to information about the world as it previously was but it had strict encoding guiding what to present as fact and what to withhold. As it monitored Petra throughout the day it recorded, stored and assessed what information should be reported and what should not. Right now it was replaying over and over the moment when Petra had been staring down at the model of the city. Something about it and about Petra's response when questioned caused it to analyse and re-analyse the moment. Its meticulous appraisal brought nothing further to light however, so it stored the information away as unworthy of being reported; at least for the moment.

# Chapter 13

Meanwhile in another part of the city Amiria was finishing up her day of production duties. She stood back and gazed around the room she had just been arranging with satisfaction. Anything she could imagine she might need to complete the layout of a room she could request and it would be supplied for her. These items were manufactured almost instantaneously so that her imagination was allowed to flow unchecked. When she was working on a project she would become deeply immersed in what she was doing, focusing with intense concentration. Colours, fabrics, contrasting shades and thoughtfully arranged furnishings designed to enhance feelings of harmony, peace and calm leapt from her imagination into reality. Soothing, assuasive shades flowed throughout the living spaces with vividly contrasting splashes of colour here and there. Her designs strongly reflected life in the city: an even flow of harmonious events with some exciting highlights thrown in for interest. Transforming a room from top to bottom was something Amiria never tired of, rather it gave her energy and immense gratification. With one final satisfied look she turned to clock herself out, swiping the panel on the attending robot which assisted her in her work. Her personal robot was hovering nearby as always.

"A very nice achievement Amiria," it observed conversationally before pointing out the next phase of her schedule. "Following production today you have been allocated some social time with your friends. I believe this evening you will be having your nails done together." Her robot was like a tiny, polite and fastidious butler, advising her of her routine and providing the constant reassurance that humans seemed to require.

For Amiria this was a perfect end to another perfect day. She headed out towards the travellers eagerly anticipating spending some time with her friends. Sometimes after production she would go to the exercise arena to keep her fitness levels optimal, sometimes, like today, she would be allocated social time. At other times she and Petra would be given special couple time together where they would be engaged in enjoyable, relationship-enhancing activities.

One evening they had been taken to the space restaurant where they had been given a fabulous meal while watching the earth revolve slowly beneath them. All simulated of course, even the food and drink, but very romantic in Amiria's opinion. She remembered Petra had been a little distracted that night studying the giant globe beneath them. He had pointed out how most of the earth was now ocean except for the large piece of land covered entirely by buildings where the City was situated and the gigantic forest lands far away. He had wondered what it must be like to live in the sector of the City where you could see the edges of the land and the sea. Amiria had never heard of anyone who had been to that place. This thought had set off some wondering questions in her mind until Petra's personal robot had interrupted. It had reminded Petra firmly that this was supposed to be a romantic evening out not a science exposition. Petra had quickly apologised and immediately focused his attention back onto her. He enquired politely about her day and complemented her looks and outfit as suggested in the 'recommended conversations with your partner' instructions. Amiria had enjoyed the rest of her evening very much and forgotten all about pondering what it might be like to be able to see the edge of the sea.

Happily Amiria disembarked from the traveller to join her friends at the nail salon. They had a very enjoyable hour together choosing colours and patterns for their nails, chattering animatedly about their day and their lives. Amiria chose gold for her nails with minute silver swirls. The salon robots soaked their hands in soothing lotions then shaped their nails skilfully. Her friends, Alexis, Tamara and Janeece chatted enthusiastically with her about fashion and who was paired with who and any other items of interest in the City.

"How are you enjoying being a parent again," Alexis questioned Amiria smilingly.

Dayzie was only a recent addition to Amiria's family. Having just turned seven she had been brought from the preparation centre for family allocation.

"Oh she is just adorable," Amiria gushed, "she has long golden hair and big blue eyes. It's so lovely having a daughter. She looks so pretty in her cute little outfits and she is always asking questions." "Really?" Janeece enquired. "Always asking questions?" Janeece looked up from her nails, which were being painted a bright metallic blue with wave patterns, to stare at Amiria with a slightly startled face.

"Oh, you know," Amiria dismissed her concern easily, "just the usual little girl's chatter. I always refer her back to her PR or to her teacher of course. Didn't your daughter ask a lot of questions when she was only seven," she enquired. Janeece's daughter had recently turned twelve and was now seriously thinking about her career.

"Well no, she didn't. She knew all she needed to know would be taught at school. She is a peaceful child. She is going to be a teacher," Janeece added proudly. After a short pause she commented, "how nice that Dayzie has golden hair just like yours," but the observation sounded slightly forced to Amiria's ears. She agreed pleasantly, but felt a little uncomfortable.

Dayzie did ask a lot of questions she realised, was that bad? Maybe in her concern about Az's behaviour she hadn't noticed Dayzie as much as she should have. She reminded herself to be more firm with her, encouraging her to ask her questions at school or to her personal robot. She was so sweet though, it was hard to deny her. Amiria suddenly realised there was an unusual quiet in the salon. Alexis and Janeece seemed to be very focused on their nails, but their usual animated prattle was absent. Amiria wondered uneasily what was going on.

"What do you think girls?" Tamara suddenly burst out, breaking the awkward silence. She flashed her now completed nails which were a livid florescent pink. Tiny strobe lights had been inserted into each nail, and they were flashing garishly as she fluttered her fingers in the air.

The four woman burst out laughing at the sight and the momentary tension dispersed.

"I hope Jade likes them," Alexis giggled referring to Tamara's current partner.

Their hour was up so the four friends left the salon together still talking and laughing.

Arriving home Amiria greeted her children and her partner, enthusiastically recounting her achievements of the day and showing them her nails. She sat with Dayzie for a while, chatting companionably while Dayzie gazed adoringly up at her. At first Amiria did notice the frequency of Dayzie's questions but soon forgot as they babbled away to each other much more like sisters than mother and daughter.

Petra and Az also chatted easily, then after the prescribed amount of time they changed conversation partners so that everyone had equal interactions with each other and equal and opportunities to speak. The little robots silently monitored them as they completed each phase of their evening routine. After their meals, which were produced specifically for each person's nutritional needs, they wished each other peaceful dreams and retired to their rooms. Their healthy bodies and unfettered minds drifted easily and serenely to sleep, not stirring till they were all awoken at the usual time the next day.

This was how life in the City went on. No need to think or worry or fear, certainly no cause to question or to be curious. It was only necessary to live peacefully and allow the cycles of life one after the other to follow their course. Who could complain about a life like that? And yet, strangely enough, there were those in the city who were not content with this seemingly idyllic lifestyle. These ones were like tiny illuminating sparks of light, wildfire that sprang up unexpectedly, and that the eyes that carefully watched over the City felt necessary to systematically douse.

# Chapter 14

It was a terrible shock to Amiria when her partner woke her in the night.

"Petra why are you waking me?! My sleep cycle isn't finished! I don't understand why you have woken me?"

Her partner's normally calm face looked disturbed and worried.

"I'm sorry honey but I heard a noise and got up to see what it was. I know we are supposed to allow the house robots to deal with it but I guess I just got curious."

"Curious? How strange. Everything you need to know is taught as part of our education and every problem is dealt with by our robot helpers, you know that. There is no need for curiosity."

"Yes but listen, when I went into the lounge I saw Dayzie. She was up, in the night watching a history view."

"What? In the night? What's wrong with her Petra?"

"I don't know darling, maybe she's just curious too, but it's what I saw that's concerning me."

"What was it?" Amiria was puzzled but a part of her was intrigued to know what these strange, unusual happenings were all about.

"You know that family that we've started following?" Petra spoke quietly and earnestly, "Dayzie was viewing that girl, the one with the long black hair."

"Yes?" Amiria waited, wondering what he might be going to say next. This situation was unprecedented and she didn't like the sensation that whatever was coming next was unpredictable.

"Well," he said falteringly knowing how strange this was going to sound, "the girl spoke to us." He stopped, waiting for the reaction he knew would come.

"Did you wake me up for this? There must be something wrong with you. Petra your crazy, that girl wasn't talking to you, she was just talking." Amiria had a slightly hysterical note in her voice as she struggled to comprehend her partner's unusual behaviour.

"Listen," Petra spoke pleadingly, willing her to understand, "the girl was in her room staring up at the ceiling. She was looking right at Dayzie and speaking to her and I know she saw us."

Amiria was shaking now. "Oh no, oh no, I just know this will end with you leaving, and you were the best one, now I will have to start over with new children and a new partner," she looked up at him with a distressed face, "I don't want you to disappear," she breathed frantically.

"Please don't talk like that, you need to trust me," he implored her softly, "there are some things we need to find out, things they've been hiding from us. There's something about the history views they are not telling us and if they can lie about those, then what else could they be lying about?"

"I don't care, I don't care I don't want to lose you or my children."

"Amiria, I found out something else strange today when I was at work." Looking down at her innocent, troubled face he wondered what impact this next revelation was going to have. "I was working on the simulated model of the City as usual, I was touching the surface and noticing how cold it was, like real marble. I was thinking you wouldn't know the difference if you didn't know it wasn't real. That really got me thinking. So when I got home that evening I tested the walls of our home. Amiria, they-are-simulated," he emphasised each word to ensure she really understood. "There seems to be something solid behind the simulations but all of the outer layers are not real. I didn't have a chance to investigate any further because I didn't want my PR to notice anything."

"No, no," Amiria moaned, "it can't be, it just can't be true." Amiria covered her face with her hands as if to shut out the new and disturbing information she was receiving. Lila's face suddenly popped into Amiria's mind. She remembered the distressing sound of her sobs. Was the same thing going to happen to her, she questioned herself with a sickening feeling? Was this how Lila had felt? It frightened her to think that the carefully controlled world she lived in could so easily and unexpectedly break apart at any moment. Her breathing was coming in short gasps now, she could feel her heart rate increasing.

"You know if you don't calm down *they* will be on their way here," Petra whispered gently with concern.

"I know, I need to take some deep breaths." She slowly calmed herself down, controlling her breathing, stilling her racing mind.

"That's better, now look at me. We need to talk and we don't have much time. If we stay awake too long there will be an alert. We need to talk quickly and calmly. Where do people go when there's something wrong with them? I've lost a partner and children. Why? Because they became curious and started looking into things, questioning them. Those kinds of people always disappear. Where do they go?"

"I don't know, that's a question that has no answer to it and what do you mean you've lost a partner and children? Is this your fault? Is that why there's something wrong with Dayzie and Az? Have *you* made this happen?" she stared at him fearfully.

"Amiria, think about it. What's so bad about being curious? Why do people who can't keep to the schedule disappear? Why?" He was holding on to her arms now, his face too close to hers. She could feel his warm breath on her skin, something that was forbidden due to the dangers of moisture in the breath. She pulled herself away from him abruptly.

"I DON'T KNOW!! I'm sorry I need to calm myself again." She closed her eyes and focused on her breathing again for a few moments. When she felt composed again she turned to Petra. "Alright, tell me why?"

"Because, Amiria, there is something to hide!" he whispered intensely. "Someone is afraid people will find out what it is, so they disappear. I don't know where they go to but maybe, I guess, maybe they die young." He had hesitated to say this last part to her but he wanted to be honest and let her know everything that was in his mind.

"Before their Life Cycles are completed? Like in the old days? That's horrible." Amiria opened her eyes wide disbelievingly.

"Yes it is. I'm sorry Amiria, I have to find out what's going on, and I'm not going to let them take my children away again. We need to leave here. Will you come with me?" He knew he had no right to ask that question of her, to pull her away from everything that gave her a sense of security.

"Where? Where would we go?"

"I don't know but it will be different, not part of the schedule, maybe outside of the City."

"There is no outside of the City. There is nowhere else. There's just the City and the Sea and the forest far away across the sea where we can't go. Even if there was another place what would it be like? How would we know what to do or know that we are healthy? How will we stay happy?" Her words tumbled quickly out of her mouth as her mind struggled to imagine a life other than the one they had right now. If she started questioning, disbelieving what she had been taught, where would that leave her? What was truth and what were lies? This was all so strange and yet, she had to ask herself why she had never thought of these things before?

"I'm sorry I don't have any answers only questions. Do you want to stay, lose your children and me and have another family chosen for you, or will you come with me?"

"Petra." Amiria looked up at him with something new in her eyes as though she had just understood something.

"Yes Amiria?" He waited with trepidation for her reply. This was the moment when he would know if he was going to lose her or if she wanted to be with him more than she wanted a seemingly safe and secure, although highly regimented life.

"I know what it is now, what that family in old times had that we don't have. I think I'm beginning to understand. I don't know what to call it but I'm coming with you, I want that with every part of myself, I want to, to, make my own schedule," she said the last part with more energy in her voice. Then she covered her mouth fearfully as she realised the enormity of what she had just said.

"Yes love," he said quietly, "but we need to choose our time right. Go back to sleep and stay as calm as you can. Do everything according to the schedule. I'll tell you when its time. He leaned over and kissed her gently on the lips.

"Why did you do that?" Amiria said with shock in her voice, "you know that's unhygienic."

"I, I, don't know. I just wanted to so I did." Petra sounded apologetic. "I'm sorry would you like to disinfect?"

"No, no it's okay, good night darling." Amiria watched him begin to leave her room, then pause for a moment by the door to look back at her. He had an unfathomable light in his eyes as he regarded her briefly, before quickly sliding the door shut behind him.

Amiria lay wonderingly on her bed till eventually she fell asleep, her lips still tingling, from her first ever, real, un-simulated, kiss.

# Chapter 15

Az was heading towards the traveller as usual at the end of the school day. He was pleasantly tired from a full-on day of intense study and exercise and was looking forward to his rest hour. As he lined up with the other students, for a reason he couldn't explain, he flicked his head to the right as something subconsciously caught his attention. To his astonishment he saw a flash of bright red disappearing amongst the buildings. It was her, he was sure of it, the girl with the red hair who had shot him that intense, knowing look in class. Where on earth was she going when she should have been getting on the traveller along with everyone else? He glanced around him. No one else seemed to have noticed anything unusual and were looking directly ahead, patiently waiting to file onto the traveller one by one in the prescribed and orderly manner that was expected of them. Az's mind was in a turmoil. How could she be breaking out of routine like that, and why? He wondered too about her PR. Surely it would report her to the CCS? He struggled with an urge to run after her to find out what she was up to, but he didn't want to attract attention to himself or to her. There was nothing he could do, he was being constantly monitored. He felt trapped as he stood in line not daring to do anything out of the ordinary. He experienced a strong pang of jealousy for the girl who had the courage to break out of boundaries like that. He puzzled about her as he waited his turn to board the traveller. When finally everyone was inside and they were ready to go, he saw her slip on board just as though she was running late from her class. Some of the students glanced at her briefly, then away. No one seemed particularly interested. Her robot was bobbing beside her as usual. The whole thing was extremely perplexing. Az looked around again at the other students who appeared oblivious that something extraordinary had happened. Why was he noticing what had happened when no one else was? He felt isolated in his difference from the others and he didn't enjoy the feeling.

The next day after school he made sure he was right behind the girl as she left the classroom. He watched her as she casually moved towards the door along with everyone else. As she stepped outside she seemed to accidently drop her recall ball. All of the students carried these small metallic balls which were used for recording everything that was taught during class so they could be reviewed later. Many students used them to review the highlights of the days teaching points during the ride home. The ball rolled away to her right and after pausing for a moment she followed it. As she bent to pick it up, she turned suddenly and glanced at him. A mischievous gleam issued from her eyes for a second, then she disappeared around a corner. Az was shocked at how quickly she vanished. Her personal robot was still bobbing in the space where she had been standing a moment ago. It seemed to waver for an instant then disappeared also in the direction she had gone.

He stood dithering for a moment or two as his curiosity battled with his inner conditioning to follow along with the schedules set out for him. Impulsively he made up his mind. He had to know what she was doing. He pulled his recall ball out of his bag and as stealthily as he could, let it go. The ball rolled away in the direction where the girl had vanished. He chased it and mimicking her, whisked around the corner. He just caught sight of her as she disappeared amongst the buildings. That bright red hair was a dead giveaway. He gave chase and after turning several corners came to a halt, unsure what to do next.

"Are you lost Az?" his robot was bobbing patiently in the air right beside his ear.

Az tried to think up an excuse for what he had done. "I, ah, I dropped my recall ball, it rolled in this direction and…and…" He got no further. The tiny robot was there one minute and the next, gone.

"Come here quickly before someone sees you, hissed an angry voice from the shadows. The red-headed girl appeared in front of him momentarily then disappeared again. Az stepped cautiously into the shadows, nearly bumping into her as he did so.

"What, what happened?" Az stuttered, "where did it go?" He had never been without his personal robot for a single moment of a single day of his life for as long as he could remember. It was almost as though a piece of himself was missing.

"Oh don't worry its ok, I just stuffed it in a bag," she responded to his question impatiently. "They get confused when you do that, they think it's night time and switch themselves off. I'll let him out later. I couldn't stand listening to you trying to lie like that," she ended with a funny mixture of amusement and irritation on her face.

"Where are you going?!" Az's question burst forth with the intensity of his need to know.

The girl dropped her exasperated tone and winked at him conspiratorially, "come with me." She crept further into the shadows with Az following closely behind. They moved silently between the marble walls of the buildings and the massive marble columns.

The girl pointed upwards. "There," she said softly, "and there."

Az strained his eyes to see in the gloom cast by the shadow of the buildings. High up, on the sides of some of the columns where it was lighter he could see large black circular objects.

Staring up he could just make out that the appearance of their immediate surroundings was slightly distorted, the way heat distorts images.

"What are they," he whispered.

She didn't answer but gestured to him to keep following her. In a couple of minutes she slowed down cautiously, then stopped. "Ah here it is," she said.

All Az could see were the usual marble buildings, grey in the semi-darkness. He noticed nothing unusual.

"Close your eyes," the girl commanded.

Az was doubtful, but shut them as she requested. The seconds passed but there was only silence.

"What now?" he asked. When there was no reply he opened his eyes to discover he was alone. He turned his head this way and that, then turned right around in a circle but all he could see were walls and columns. What is the girl up to, he wondered with annoyance. Had she really brought him here just to run away and hide, leaving him alone without even his robot? He felt oddly empty at the thought. Then he heard a giggle.

"Do you believe in ghosts," the whisper came from strangely close by. He stared around, up and down but couldn't see her.

"Nooo," Az quavered, uncertainly, "like the old-timers? Of course not, that's just superstition…," he trailed off uncertainly. Where was she?! He was feeling frustrated and a little nervous. Then to his horror, right through the wall in front of him he saw pales fingers reaching, slowly towards him. He froze as the ghostly hand came closer and closer. Then with another giggle the girl's whole head appeared through the wall as well.

"Boo!" she said, right in his face. Pulling her whole body through the wall to stand in front of him she stood shaking with silent giggles holding her stomach as she pointed at his white, scared-looking face.

"Try it for yourself," she suggested when she had recovered. She stretched out her hand which went right through the wall.

Az looked at the wall. It appeared solid enough just like any other wall. Cautiously he stretched out his hand. As expected his fingers touched the cold stone of solid marble. He lay his palm against it. It didn't go through. He looked at the girl questioningly.

She had that impatient look on her face again. "Try again," she urged. "Your mind believes the wall is there. Your fingers touch a solid wall because that is what you expect to feel. Push through. Mentally see yourself pushing your hand through the wall."

Az closed his eyes in concentration. He stretched out his hand and felt nothing. He opened his eyes and saw his hand halfway through the wall. Az gasped as he comprehended. "its not real, its simulated!" He had spoken aloud and the girl shushed him furiously. Az stood stock-still staring at the seemingly solid wall, with his hand still stuck halfway through it, contemplating what this meant.

He turned to stare at the girl with a bemused expression. He took in her bright hair, her shining eyes, her vivacious personality. She was so different so unique but the thought that was pounding through his mind was not how fascinating this girl was. It was one word which lit up, glaring like the sun from the long-ago past; Dangerous! Unexpected fear hit him like a punch in the stomach. She was someone who could do anything, absolutely anything, someone unpredictable. She was exactly the kind of person you didn't have anything to do with, because she was the kind of person that usually disappeared. He desperately wanted to run as far from that place as possible. He wanted to be back on that safe traveller with all the others heading for home as he was supposed to be. She would disappear and maybe he would too. This wasn't something small like taking a cholate bar. This was big. They had discovered a secret that someone may not want uncovered. He wanted to escape but he couldn't seem to get his legs moving.

"We need to get back or we will be missed," the girl whispered urgently to him. When he still didn't move she put her hands on his shoulders and shook him a little.

Her unexpected proximity snapped Az out of his immobile state and he began to run with her beside him back towards the travellers. Slowing down before the last corner where they would become visible to the other students they arrived just in time, jumping on last of all. As they were about to part and sit on separate seats, Az tugged at the girl's arm for a moment. She didn't flinch at the contact but instead switched on her mocking grin.

"What's your name?" he whispered feeling a twinge of guilt as he said it. Usually you didn't need to ask someone's name. When you were designated a new friend your personal robot introduced you. Having to ask someone's name was a peculiar and unnatural thing.

She was nodding approvingly at him as though commending this breach of protocol. "It's Marama," she breathed barely moving her lips, then she moved quickly away from him to find herself a seat.

Somehow Az's personal robot was hovering beside him again. The girl must have released him while they were running he guessed.

"Well that was strange," his robot was muttering, "I seem to have had a black out. Is it morning?" It swivelled its small head looking around as though trying to get its bearings. "I must need to get my circuits rewired. Very strange indeed." Then he turned his attention to Az as information reached his sensors. "Az I notice your breathing and heart-rate are accelerated, are you in a healthy and stable physical and mental state?"

"I'm fine, fine," Az stuttered, "just dropped something and had to run after it."

He noticed the girl, who had taken a seat a few rows ahead, throw him a patronising glance, as if to say, "couldn't you lie better than that?"

Az gazed silently at the back of the girls red head. His personal robot was blathering on about something to do with punctuality and keeping calm but he tuned himself out, thoughts racing frantically through his head. Marama steadily ignored him throughout the rest of the journey, acting as though nothing unusual had happened. She seemed entirely relaxed and unconcerned he noticed enviously. The event was both frightening and confusing to Az. Previously he had grumbled inwardly about the schedule but breaking out of it was harder than he could have imagined. As he worked to lower his adrenaline levels he began to try and understand what this discovery meant. As usual he had far more questions than answers. What was the meaning of the simulated wall? Just how much of the City was simulated was the next astonishing question that pushed itself determinedly into his mind. Why would they simulate parts of the City? The next thought that naturally popped into his head sent his mind into a frenzy; what were they trying to hide?! Questions became tangled up in one another as they triggered thoughts and ideas and possibilities that he had never dared contemplate before. Several times he had to pull himself up to purposefully calm his mind in order to prevent his robot noticing his mental disturbance. He felt a little bit resentful that the girl, Marama, had somehow dragged him into this. In honesty he had to admit he couldn't really blame her as it was him that had followed her. He had followed her because she was different. Did that mean he was different too? He stared out of the window at the beautiful but monotonous scenery of pale, white city structures. Wilfully he turned his thoughts to calmer things. He had to stay calm, had keep his heart rate steady and think this through logically. It was hard to be rational and calm while his whole conception of reality was crumbling into confusing pieces about him.

## Chapter 16

"Wakey, wakey!"

"Wha..! What? Whadduya want?" Gypsy groggily came to consciousness from a deep sleep.

"Time to wake up sis." Rangi was hanging over Gypsy, grinning and rocking her bed violently.

"Stop it Rangi! Why what for?"

She tried to prise her eyes fully open, looking at him through slits.

"Gran's got religion again." He said grinning and plunking himself down on the bed beside her. "Often happens after a few nights out on the town. She wants to take us to church."

Gypsy groaned and rolled over.

"Which one this time? I hope not that one where they say the same thing every week, over and over and over, like chanting."

"I don't think Gran will ever show her face there again," said Rangi with a giggle.

"Oh yeh, that was the one where you fell asleep and started snoring."

"Yeh, Gran wanted so much to hit me but was scared to with all those Pakehas watching. She was worried someone would call Social Services. Didn't stop her from chasing me round with the wooden spoon when we got home though. Good thing she couldn't catch me. Ha! She says she's had enough of Pakeha preachers anyway, she's found one that's got a Maori preacher, wants us to go there."

"Do we have to?" Gypsy groaned, sitting up and rubbing her eyes.

"You know what she gets like. She's got the guilts, worried we're gonna turn out like the rest of the family; drinking and smoking and swearing, wasting our lives, beating people up, ending up in prison like Uncle Jacko. He's gone down for a long time."

"What did he go down for?" Gypsy was interested.

"Dunno but must have been bad, she won't talk about it, just rambles on about the demon alcohol.

She goes on and on about a generational curse or something. You should see her ranting and raving out there. It's pretty entertaining. She thinks it's too late for Zak but maybe not for us. She doesn't know I sit outside the pub sometimes and Zak hands me booze out the window."

"Do you want to end up like that? Like Mum and Dad? Drinking and drugs and we hardly ever see them?"

"Aww it's just a bit of fun, what else is there to do for fun? It's boring without the drink. Scary getting in the car with Zak after he's had a few though, had a few near misses." He shook his head at the memory. "Need to drink quite a few to stomach that, fear goes away after I've had a few more."

"Then your kids will be the same and it will carry on."

"Not me I'm not having any, hah!"

"Sure but everyone does ae."

"Anyway get yourself out of bed ya lazy thing, leaving in twenty minutes, got to wear good clothes not your stinky, old, smelly ones."

Gypsy didn't enjoy going to church much. She always felt uncomfortable and out of place. She didn't know what to do and felt stupid trying to keep up with what was happening. This new church looked okay though. Plenty of Maori faces anyway that made a nice change. Once the music started she sat up a bit and took some notice. The singing was good she thought with pleasant surprise, and the music was very good! Maybe they hire the band, she thought, but then who pays for it? Bunch of Maori? Not likely. Gran looks happy anyway, repenting away like usual, she noticed, glancing sideways at her with a grin. Gran marched them home after the service with a big smile on her face, her outsized floppy hat flapping up and down as she stomped along. Gypsy and Rangi trailed along behind. Zak hadn't come home the night before and was, who knows where, but most likely sleeping off a headache.

"I like that church," announced Gran, "we're going to go every week from now on," she said with decision in her voice."

"Sure Gran" chorused Gypsy and Rangi tonelessly. They'd heard this lots before.

Seeing is believing, Gypsy thought with an inward laugh. Yet I've seen some things lately that I could only call miracles, she mused, things that couldn't be explained. Could she talk to that preacher about it? She felt unsure. What had he said today? Something about curses attaching themselves to bloodlines and they needed to be flushed clean. How though? Maybe I'd better listen to the whole thing next time, she thought. Something she did know for sure this morning was that she wanted to get to know the little girl in the vision better. She wanted to communicate with her somehow and find out who and where in the world she was. Could she be an alien, an angel, or from another time, she wondered? Didn't look like the past with those clothes. The future maybe? She believed now that the girl could hear her, and she just needed to find a way to make the communication go both ways. In the meantime I guess I will just have to wait till she re-appears again, she thought with resignation.

———◆———

Later Gypsy lay on her bed willing the vision to appear but nothing happened and after a while she fell asleep. She awoke with a start very early in the morning. Everything was still and quiet but she had that feeling. The little girl was here somewhere. She looked up at the ceiling and there she was looking back down at her. She didn't look so frightened or confused this time. Maybe she was just as inquisitive as herself.

"Hello," she said aloud. The girl nodded, smiled and mouthed something. Gypsy put her hand up to her ear and frowned, shook her head to show she couldn't hear. The face disappeared. It was so sudden that Gypsy thought the vision had ended but in a moment she was back. She was holding up a square flat object with a word printed on it in large letters. It said 'Hello' backwards. Just like looking in a mirror, thought Gypsy.

"I can read the word but I see it backwards," she said to the girl. "My name is Gypsy, what's your name?"

She could see further into the room now, and she saw that the girl was leaning over a table writing on some kind of electronic pad. She soon came back and held it up. 'Dayzie' was spelt backwards on it.

"Hi Dayzie, I want to learn about you. Where are you from and why can I see you?"

Dayzie frowned and shook her head, frustrated that she couldn't speak to her and explain.

"Okay," said Gypsy "I'll ask you questions and you nod or shake your head okay? Just like a game of charades?" The girl nodded happily.

"Okay first how old are you? Are you six?" Shake. "Seven?" Nod.

"Where do you live? In New Zealand?" Shake. "America?" Shake. "Australia?" Shake. "Britain?" Shake. "Europe?" Shake. "I give up, do you know the name of the country you live in?"

Dayzie shook her head again obviously puzzled at her questions. She wrote quickly on the pad and held it up. It said 'The City' in back to front letters.

The City? Thought Gypsy, but where?" Maybe I'll try something else.

"Are you from earth?" Nod.

"Good. Are you from the future?" Shake. Nod.

Dayzie looked uncertain then started pointing at Gypsy saying something rapidly and excitedly. At that moment she turned to look behind her as though she had heard a noise and then abruptly disappeared from view. Gypsy was disappointed.

We were getting on so well too, she thought. She doesn't seem to know which country she lives in, that's strange. At least I know she's from earth and she understands English. She was a bit confused about the future question. I guess I couldn't expect a seven year old to know stuff like that. Oh well, this is pretty exciting. What was that? She suddenly realised someone was standing in the doorway. She leapt up to see Rangi standing there as pale faced as it was possible for any Maori boy to be. They stared at each other for a minute.

"You saw it too didn't you?" exclaimed Gypsy excitedly.

"Shhh don't wake Gran, and Zak's just come in, he's got a roaring headache, better stay away from him today." Then as though snapping out of shock he exclaimed, "What was that thing on the ceiling!? You were talking to it!"

"I don't know but it's not a ghost I'm sure of it. It's just a little girl from another place, maybe even another time. I'm gonna keep talking to her find out more about her. Did you see that room? Wild! Beautiful, like Greek architecture on a small scale, all white marble, columns and arches and the artwork, wow, and that carpet looked like you could swim in it," Gypsy gushed excitedly. "It was perfect, absolutely perfect. Wish I could get there. Wonder if we can get there somehow."

"Your raving sis, going crazy. Maybe I didn't see nothing after all. Just you talking to the ceiling."

"Aren't you curious?" she demanded, "This is a pretty big mystery and we need to find out more before we gotta go home after the holidays." She looked a little deflated at his lack of enthusiasm and the thought of home seemed to further depress her mood. Back to that old flat with Mum and the latest step-Dad, she thought miserably. "Wish we could live here all the time," she said aloud. "Hey, she said, brightening up, let's set the alarm for this time every morning and see if we can see the girl again."

"Okay I guess it is pretty interesting. Spooky though, hope it's not something evil, like the things Preacher was talking about. Think we should ask him about it?"

"Dunno let's get to know him better first, find out if we can trust him," suggested Gypsy non-committedly.

"Anyway, we have to help Uncle with the shearing today," Rangi informed her without enthusiasm, "that's what I came to tell you."

"Oh great, all day in that stinking hot shearing shed." Gypsy rolled her eyes towards the ceiling.

"Yep, my favourite part is picking up the daggs" said Rangi sarcastically, making retching noises. I just love little smelly balls of sheep poo."

"You don't seem to mind chucking them around at other people," said Gypsy, glaring at him.

"Aw where's your sense of humour sis?"

"Come on then, let's go get it over with." Gypsy dropped her brown legs over the edge of the bed as Rangi disappeared up the hallway. She stared for a few moments at the pile of clothes and jandals she had left lying on the floor from the night before contemplating the gruelling day that was ahead of her. She rubbed her eyes, yawning and finally stood up, dragging on her clothes. She twisted the mane of her hair back into a rough knot without looking in the mirror. She slipped on her red jandals and reluctantly made her way out to the kitchen for breakfast. Gran had put on a farmers breakfast of porridge, bacon and eggs which they finished to the last crumb knowing they would need all the energy they could get.

# Chapter 17

The day in the shearing shed wasn't so bad after all, Gypsy decided. The shearers were funny jokers, always doing something for a laugh. You had to watch yourself or you would get your bottom buzzed with the flat side of the clippers while you were bending over picking up a sheep's fleece. Zak was there helping out too looking extremely tired, with red eyes and obviously feeling pretty fragile. He spent a lot of time leaning on a broom. They left him to himself. Gypsy and Rangi were kept busy all day throwing fleeces and sweeping up the clippings. Gypsy got the job of jumping on the fleeces in the wool-press to help squash them down into compacted bales. When she climbed out she felt greasy all over from the lanolin that came out of the wool.

"Good for your skin girl," Uncle told her, "rich woman pay heaps of money to buy that stuff to smear on their faces."

Gypsy didn't' care, she hated the greasy feeling in her hair, clothes and on her hands. Once the bales were fully compressed using the old-fashioned hand-press, Uncle used an outsized darning needle to sew them shut with twine. Rangi got himself into trouble with Uncle because he just couldn't resist teasing Gypsy by holding some smelly daggs near her face. Uncle sent him into the holding pen and told him to catch the sheep ready for the shearers. Rangi had to chase them around and around, jumping on their backs, falling onto the filthy floor as they cannoned around the pen and more often than not getting a face full of their smelly back ends. Uncle winked at Gypsy as he leaned on the low pen wall chuckling at his antics. The shearers unbent themselves to watch for a few minutes as well, throwing back their heads to laugh heartily. Then they were back to work, backs bent, sweat dripping off their faces, black singlet's soaked with perspiration and their rough pants with tiny fluffs of wool sticking to the grease smeared material.

This is how it was on the farm, there was always a lot to do. Shearing, lambing, tailing, drenching, mustering and during the quieter months there was always plenty of fencing, repair work and wood chopping to be done. All year round the farm was hard work and she knew Uncle really needed their help.

At the end of the day hot, tired and smelly the youngsters headed back towards Gran's place.

"Hey," Uncle yelled after them, "I need someone to help with the mustering in the morning. Five o'clock start, gotta get the sheep into the shed ready for another days shearing."

Rangi and Zak walked faster but Gypsy turned back. "Ok Uncle, wake me?"

"I'll be outside your window at five," Uncle grinned.

When Uncle banged on her window it was so early the next morning it still felt like the middle of the night. Sleepily she dragged herself out of bed. The fresh, crisp air soon shocked her into wakefulness as she hurriedly dragged on her warm sweatshirt and thick socks. Uncle had a large waterproof coat all ready for her which, when she put it on, came down to her knees. The overlarge hood fell down over her nose so that she had to hold it up to be able to see where she was going. Outside she could see the dawn just beginning to lighten the sky over the hill-line with an orangey tinge to it. It was only raining softly but by the time she had crossed the paddocks and begun the trudge up the steep hillside where the mustering would begin, the morning had darkened and the rain was dripping down her nose. Most of the walk up she let the over-large hood of her coat fall forward so all she could see was the wet grass and the back of her Uncle's worn old hob-nail boots.

It took a good hour to toil their way up the steep hillside but eventually they were at the top looking way down into the bowl of the valley. It was much lighter now, the brief rain had stopped and the clouds were dispersing. Gypsy felt it had been worth the early rise and trudge up the steep incline just to see that view. The hills looked very green in the wet, Spring air. The tiny white shapes of sheep were spread across them in the distance reminding her of maggots crawling on an old sheep's carcass. The grey-roofed, timeworn house far below looked as tiny as a dolls-house from this height. The dogs were snuffling around excitedly, wagging their tails and jumping up on her legs. They kept trying to lick as close to her face as they could get, leaving long smears of mud on her coat from their paws. They trotted backward and forth with a restless energy, waiting to be given the word by Uncle to shoot off after the widely spread sheep, herding them down to the shearing shed. Uncle got her to stay where she was while he walked on around the tops of the hills. Her job was to make sure the sheep didn't try and make a mad dash back up the hillside instead of running into the yards at the bottom as they were supposed to. She stood patiently waiting for the dogs to do their work, the sun was rising and mist beginning to ascend in smoky tendrils as the air warmed up. She recalled how Grandad always used to say how rich he felt surrounded by all this beauty. Now, seeing the valley spread beneath her sparkling with tiny droplets, flashing rainbows of colour in the early morning light, Gypsy felt she knew exactly what he had meant.

The shearing went on for days and took so much time and energy that Gypsy worried she might be missing Dayzie's visits. Nevertheless on Saturday, when the shearers had finally finished their job and gone home she woke up to the sight of the little girls shimmering face on her ceiling. After that they began to see each other regularly in the mornings and sometimes even during the night. Occasionally Gypsy would be startled out of a deep sleep to look up and see the now familiar face gazing down at her.

One day Gypsy brought Rangi into Dayzie's line of vision and explained who he was. Dayzie got quite excited about this and wrote a name on her pad, 'Az.'

The next morning when Dayzie appeared she was not alone. A boy about five years older than her came into view beside her. When they spoke to him he just stared and stared then went away. Dayzie held up her backwards word again, 'Az' so they knew that was his name.

"Is he your brother?" Gypsy asked. Nod.

The next morning Az was back. He stared carefully at each of them then he did some experiments. He held up his fingers till they told him how many, he held up objects and got them to tell him what they were. Finally he was convinced that they could see him as he could see them. After staring at her for a long moment he reached his hand down towards Gypsy and she reached her hand up towards him at the same time. His finger stopped as though it had hit a glass barrier and she couldn't reach high enough to touch the ceiling. They smiled shyly at each other and again that strange sense welled up in Gypsy that she was connected somehow to these people. Then the picture disappeared and she was left wonderingly staring up at the ceiling.

# Chapter 18

Az was lying down for his rest hour after class, his mind buzzing with new concepts. What an amazing discovery, he thought excitedly to himself. The olden-time people could see him although they couldn't hear him. There was nothing in his class lessons about this and he had never heard a single Wisdom for Life quote about it. This was even more amazing than the discovery that there were simulated buildings in the City. That discovery had disturbed him so much he had suppressed all the troublesome questions it had raised. Maybe he had overreacted anyway, he thought dismissively. There was probably a perfectly good and logical reason why those simulations had been put in place. He didn't want to think about that strange incident with Marama. He wanted to think more about his meeting with Gypsy which exited and enthralled him more than anything.

Sometimes during class as part of the lesson his teacher would take them on a history tour. This was an extremely realistic experience where they appeared to be walking around in the place and time they were viewing, complete with simulated sounds, smells and touch. He thought back to the last time this had happened. It was a brief tour of one of the olden time wars. The view was from a far distance as the noise of guns and the sight of blood and violence was far too traumatic if viewed up close. Even from the hill where they were looking down on the carnage it was quite frightening. The teacher used these experiences as opportunities to reinforce in them how much they had advanced in their society and why the rules and restrictions were highly necessary. Az now remembered that there were occasions when it did seem as though some of the people in the views could see them, even if possibly not very clearly. Sometimes a person would point towards them in an agitated or frightened way while others around them seemed unable to comprehend what it was they were seeing. At other times when they were in close proximity to people in a room he had noticed them shivering, looking fearfully towards them as though maybe they could feel or perceive their presence somehow. Previously he had accepted his teacher's explanations about them being a superstitious people, believing in spirits and ghosts. Now, after actually talking to some of them he began to question the whole truth of this supposition.

There's a completely new world out there, he thought, outside the boundaries, outside the schedule. Why is it a secret? What will happen if I try and find out? The questions reverberated through his mind without any satisfactory answers. Then the words popped into his mind automatically: 'It damages happiness and therefore Productivity if you think too much about what might happen in the future. Trust brings peace.' There I go again, he thought, I've been taught what to think, and what not to think too. I feel as though I am at the edge of a great discovery and I just can't stop trying to find out what will happen. I'm scared too, he admitted to himself, everything's so good, so perfect; what if I lose it all? There is no schedule for what could come next. He shivered partly in fear and partly in excitement.

—————◆————

The next day in school the teacher gathered the class together in a circle around him.

"We are entering a history view today," he announced, remember to stay close and listen carefully to my instructions."

He initiated the view and a scene appeared around them. They were on a dirty street with people coming and going and a few noisy vehicles clattering past every now and then. Az looked around at the people. They had expressionless faces and appeared tired and listless as they trudged along with glazed-over eyes. His teacher was pointing out the unhygienic conditions and beckoning to them to form a circle around him. On the footpath in front of them was a little girl sitting all by herself with her dirty knees drawn up to her chest and her back pressed against the concrete wall of a building behind her. Few of the olden time people seemed to notice her as they passed other than an occasional, uninterested glance. The teacher began a story about how children used to be neglected and left alone in dangerous situations in times gone past. He compared this kind of life with the way things were in the City where every child was carefully nurtured, educated and cared for by the Information Giver.

Az stopped listening to him after a few minutes and gazed fascinated at the little girls face. She was quite young, maybe about Dayzie's age but he had never seen such an expression on Dayzie's face. This little girl's mouth was turned down, her eyebrows were pressed together and she was making funny little sniffling noises. Her whole body seemed tense and there was something wet running from her eyes and shining on her cheeks. He wondered what it would be like to sit there all alone, shivering and afraid. What must she be feeling inside? He had never seen anyone cry before and he had never felt sadness in his life. As he looked at her he began to have a strange feeling inside. He could feel his breath starting to come in shallow gasps as though he were mimicking the fitful sounds she was making. He found, to

68

his dismay, he couldn't stop it and he didn't like the sensation at all. Suddenly he noticed the teacher had stopped talking. He looked up to see his intense gaze directed on him.

"It's time we returned to class," the teacher said quietly and decisively.

The scene disappeared and they were back in the classroom. None of the other students seemed to have perceived anything amiss. Az touched his cheek and was astonished to find it was wet. He took his seat along with the others and noticed that soothing music had begun to play. This often happened after a history view to facilitate calming the emotions after witnessing past events. He closed his eyes and stilled his mind as he had been taught. When he felt calm and collected enough Az decided he needed to ask some questions.

After all the teacher knows everything we need to know, he reasoned, maybe he knows more than he's telling us. Maybe I just need to ask the right questions. In the past he had thought about asking his personal robot questions he needed answers to, but he had found out long ago that the robot could only tell you so much. Mainly facts and information but it couldn't really answer his questions in the way he wanted it to.

"Excuse me teacher."

"Yes student Az do you have a question about this history lesson?" His teacher had a firm but fair way of dealing with the students. He was passionate about his subjects and able to make lessons so interesting that the students would often be riveted by what he had to say. He commanded the respect of his class as well as keeping them entertained. He also never deviated to even a small degree from the prescribed curriculum.

"Yes I do Sir," Az answered respectfully.

"Good your questions are always welcome. What would you like to know?"

"What was it really like in the old days?"

"It was very unhygienic, many people died of sickness, diseases, poor diet and war."

"Yes I know but what were the people like?"

"They were unhappy and sick, they fought each other, hurt each other and they often died young. I could tell you many tragic stories from those terrible times."

"I mean how did they live?" Az struggled to phrase his questions in a way that might lead to discovering what he really wanted to know.

"I don't understand the question student Az. I have given you all the right answers. What precisely do you want to know?"

"Well, if we could meet and talk to one of the people what would they say, what would they be like?"

"There is no answer for your question Az and I believe your queries are beginning to create unrest in the class, I must ask you to desist. I'm afraid this will have to be reported."

"Who to? Who are you reporting to?" Az blurted out.

The teacher looked startled. For a moment Az thought he saw confusion on his teacher's face as he struggled to find an answer to a question he didn't fully understand.

"Why I report to the Central Computer System of course. The answers to our problems are calculated using formulas. Your problem will be solved Az and then you will be content again."

He said this with calmness and certainty as he spoke what he knew and believed to be true, but somehow Az could not accept these kinds of perfunctory answers anymore. His eyes had been opened, there was a world of lies out there. He didn't know what to believe anymore. His class mates were glancing at him with puzzled faces, then they looked hastily away, focusing on their learning screens. No-one in their class had ever disappeared but if it did happen he knew they would all quickly stop thinking about them as they had been trained to do. After a short moment of silence, the teacher seemed to collect himself and turned smilingly to address the whole class.

"Now, I have a surprise for you all," he told them. You have been awarded a game of Superhero Tag by the CCS."

The class erupted with delight at this news. They leapt up out of their seats and in a moment the simulation began. Each person chose a superhero image along with certain powers such as flying, strength, agility, speed or even the ability to walk up the walls and upside down on the ceiling. Inside the simulation their bodies morphed into giant muscular shapes and the game began. Tag was never more exciting than when you had superpowers. It was a fast, exhilarating, action packed game that took the students minds completely away from the incident that had occurred. Az enjoyed the game just as much as anyone else did, somersaulting, leaping, ducking, running at adrenaline-charged speeds, keeping his mind alert to avoid being tagged. Once, during the game, he looked up for a moment to discover that his teacher was once more staring at him with that disconcertingly intense gaze. Unsettled by this scrutiny he looked away from his teacher's serious face and around at his class mates. He realised with a shocked chill that the Marama was no longer among them. He felt a sudden intense cold sweep through his body numbing him as he received the revelation that he was in danger. He quickly resolved to keep quiet and act normal in class from now on. He would keep his questions for Gypsy and maybe, maybe, nothing would happen. He needed to know more things fast and most of all he needed to know what kind of danger he was in.

---

That night he had a troubled sleep. Tossing and turning as flashes of distant, pre-lingual memories emerged from the dark hidden recesses of his subconscious.

*Flash!* Waking up in a dark place. *Flash!* A dim light far way. Knowing somehow he had to move forward towards the light. Crawling, crawling. *Flash!* Bright, colourful distractions to his left and right. Reaching out tiny fingers excitedly to touch. Sudden pain. Screaming and crying alone in the darkness. Eventually continuing wearily on. Crawling, crawling. Another flash of brightness, drawing him irresistibly. Shocking, numbing cold. Crawling, crawling on and on. Bright lights to the left and right causing pain to stab through him whenever tried to turn his head to look.

Swimming into semi-consciousness as a drowning man reaches for air, his mind struggled to comprehend. Were those real memories? Did those things really happen to him?

His floundering mind sank back into his dream and *flash!* He was back in the darkness, but this time he was full of rage. He fought, pushing and beating at the dark walls that surrounded him, breaking them down, smashing them. A bright piercing light blinded him as the walls crumbled and fell. He awoke with a new understanding in his mind.

# Chapter 19

Back in school Az was careful to fully comply in every way and to keep his attention focused on his studies. Then an incident occurred that tested his ability to stay composed and pretend all was normal. A student, Mikarl was his name, was asked to read a poem to the class. This student was skilled at public speaking and would become an entertainer as his assigned career. Az always enjoyed listening to his recitations which were usually on the theme of peace and gratitude aligning with the Wisdom for Life messages. When he recited it was with an energy and tone in his voice that captivated his audience so that they hung on his words.

The young man got up and stood facing the class. He was a tall, slender boy with dark, curly hair. When he spoke, his voice was deep and resonant.

"This poem is by one of the ancient poets, so old that it has almost vanished in the hazes of time."

He looked down for a long moment, gathering his thoughts, then began to speak.

"'There was a time when meadow, grove, and stream,
The earth, and every common sight,
To me did seem
Apparell'd in celestial light.
The glory and the freshness of a dream.
It is not now as it hath been of yore; -
Turn wheresoe'er I may.
By night or day,
The things which I have seen I now can see no more.'"

His voice broke a little on the last line. He really had the attention of the class as he uttered these strange and compelling words. As he spoke Az felt a dangerous longing welling up within in him.

Recovering himself Mikarl continued:

> "'The rainbow comes and goes,
> And lovely is the rose;
> The moon doth with delight
> Look round her when the heavens are bare;
> Waters on a starry night
> Are beautiful and fair;
> The sunshine is a glorious birth;
> And yet I know whe'er I go,
> That there hath pass'd away a glory from the earth.'"

"Marama," he whispered.

That was as far as he got. Throughout his poem the teacher had seemed restless, a frown deepening on his brow but at the moment Mikarl said the girl's name, the name of the girl who had disappeared, he got up swiftly, firmly interrupting him. "You may sit down student Mikarl."

Mikarl looked for a moment as though he would resist, then quietly took his seat. The teacher continued with the lesson as if nothing had happened but when they were all busy concentrating on their work out of the corner of his eye Az saw the teacher go over to Mikarl and speak quietly in his ear. Mikarl got up wordlessly and left the class-room. He didn't come back.

While this scene was being enacted Az felt a strong inner resistance as he tried to turn his head to see what was happening. Flashes of his dream returned to his mind. He recalled the sharp pain shooting through him as he turned his head attracted by bright lights and movement. They were real memories, he thought to himself, they had conditioned him. His mind became engulphed in a whirl of questions.

What was happening? What would happen to Mikarl? What had happened to Marama and to the others who had disappeared? How could everyone just sit there and not ask questions about their friends and classmates who were disappearing?! Terror of the unknown forces that were at work paralysed him. He could feel his throat tightening as panic threatened to well up inside him. He stared sightlessly at the study screen on his desk fighting for control. He was powerless, impotent. What could he do? An even more terrifying thought hit him. Would he be next?

"Gyps wake up, wake up." Rangi was standing in the door way again.

"Why? It's not Sunday?" she mumbled grumpily.

"No but your late waking, our visitors are here." Rangi pointed to the ceiling where two faces shimmered on the ceiling.

Gypsy came fully awake with a start. Surely it was too early.

"What woke you up?" she questioned Rangi.

"Needed to piddle, same as usual," he grinned

"Woolworth's bladder," she smirked.

"Hey look he's got that electronic pad thing." Rangi said, squinting up at the ceiling at Az. "He's writing numbers on it. Backwards as usual. What's that say 1800? Eighteen hundred what?"

"Numbers back to front are harder than words," complained Gypsy. "That's 2-1-0-0 with a question mark."

"Hey you don't think that's years do you? Maybe he wants to know what year we live in? Yes he's nodding his head. Two thousand and sixteen mate, got that? Look he just said 'wow,' I read his lips."

"What year do you live in?" Gypsy asked the quivering image.

Az scribbled on the pad and held it up for them to see.

"Let's see is that 52 or 25, oh I see its 2503. Wow, that's nearly five hundred years in the future can that really be true?" Gypsy was amazed.

"Cool man," said Rangi enthusiastically. "That's awesome, is it cool there, do the cars fly? Can you teleport? What cool gadgets do ya have?"

"He can't answer that dumbo," said Gypsy scathingly.

"Hey they look sad, what's up with that, who could be sad in a cool house like that and with all that mean-as technology?"

"I guess they might have some problems there we don't know about. Oh they've gone."

# Chapter 20

"Amiria are you awake?" Petra was leaning down over her bed and whispering urgently.

"Yes," she murmured sleepily. She rolled over vaguely discerning him in the dim light, blinking in an attempt to stimulate her brain into wakefulness.

"Have you set up the simulator in your room?" she queried in a sleepy voice and then yawned hugely.

"Shhh speak very quietly darling, yes I have. Anyone looking in will think they are seeing me with your simulation."

"Petra, she whispered hesitatingly. Maybe you should come in here with me, so it looks as though I am with your simulation?" It was a very daring, completely forbidden thing to suggest and she was a little frightened at her own boldness.

Petra however, didn't hesitate. He slid into bed beside her and put his lips close to her ear.

"We have to work out a way to escape," his voice betrayed his suppressed tension.

"How do we do that?" she asked trying hard not to be distracted by his closeness and the scent of his skin.

"Pretend to follow the schedule but start looking for ways out," he said simply. He was careful not to touch her in case this set off more alerts. The last thing he needed right now was to bring trouble on his family. He couldn't continue to live like this, in fear and uncertainty.

"But we don't know how to do anything except the schedule. We don't even know if there is anywhere else or if we can get out of the City," she whispered back at him.

"I've been thinking about that and I think I know how to do it." He injected as much confidence into his voice as he could so as not to betray the imprecision of his plan.

"How? Tell me quietly."

As he leaned closer to her and she could feel his warm breath on her cheek.

"Whatever the schedule tells us to do we do the opposite."

"The opposite?" Amiria sounded confused.

"If the schedule tells us to go somewhere we go the other way. If it says go inside we go out. If it says sleep we wake up. If it says rest we run."

It was the best he could come up with. He had no knowledge of how to think other than the way he had been trained to think. There was another idea dimly percolating through his mind that had come to him through his knowledge of the inner workings of the City. It was an unclear thought, a remote possibility about how they might be able to get out. It was so vague though, that he thought it better not to share it with Amiria just yet. It would raise too many questions, questions that he had no answers to. All he knew was that his inner trepidation and the need to protect his family had risen to such a level that he felt compelled to act. Even if it meant failure, he had to try. The consequences of not trying, of passively allowing someone to take his family away again suddenly and completely without warning, as they had in the past, gave him such a suffocating sense of helplessness that he could not endure it. The deep emotional wounds that had formed like fissures in a rock through his loss were painful reminders of what might happen if he didn't do something soon.

"What about the personal robots, what shall we do about them?" Amiria was questioning him.

She was so trusting of him, falling in with his crazy plan as though it were really possible. He loved her for that and hoped he would not let her down.

"I asked mine today what would be the best way to look after it. Guess what it said?"

"What?"

"Always keep them dry and allow them to recharge at night."

"So what do we do?"

"The opposite! Where's the wettest place in the house?"

"I don't know, the humidifier? The cleansing unit...?" she hazarded, and then she had it. "The waste-eradication receptacle!!"

"Exactly. Honey we're going to flush them!" He couldn't help grinning at the thought. All of his life lived carefully within the rules and guidelines set down for him made this moment seem one of the most exciting he had ever experienced. Even if it ended up being just a wild, futile plan at least he was making a choice for himself and his family and taking control, it was an intoxicating feeling.

"When should we do it?" Amiria looked startled but accepting of this idea.

"At night of course when they are meant to be recharging. Then we run when we are meant to be sleeping."

"What about the kids?" she spoke softly and tried to keep a note of anxiety out of her voice that she knew could be detected.

"I'll talk to them. You know I've been listening in to their conversations through the viewer. There's something very unusual going on there."

"What kind of unusual thing?" she turned to look at him sharply but couldn't make out his expression in the darkness.

"I'm not sure but I don't trust anyone at the moment. Except you of course dear."

"Thanks, I trust you too. She turned her body so that she was facing him and said something she had never said to any of her previous partners before. "We're in this together," she hesitated for a moment, then finished firmly, "till the end." She shivered when she had said it, but she also felt deep inside her something stirring that told her she was making the right choice. She was walking into an uncertain future which was something she had never even considered or imagined before. As long I have Petra, she realised, it would be ok somehow.

Petra longed to hold her as she said those words but he didn't dare. He wondered if this was why the CCS broke up relationships regularly, why you weren't allowed to touch each other and why children were only with their parents for short periods of time; so that there was no sense of permanence. Maybe they realised the danger of allowing strong feelings to develop. These feelings he had for Amiria were so powerful he knew they would drive him to take risks and do things he would never have previously contemplated. They wound themselves around his heart and gave him a deep sense of something he couldn't name. However now was not the time to give in to these feelings if he wanted to keep his family together, but a time for action. He must contain and restrain himself and do what needed to be done. So instead of responding in the way he wanted to he began to make practical plans.

"You know if those people from the viewer really are from another time and we can talk to them, they might be able to help us learn how to live outside a schedule."

Amiria recoiled at the thought of living in the way the olden time people did. "But the dirt, the germs, how disgusting and ugly," said Amiria her fear and uncertainty rising up again.

"Well, we'll have to see, but if we are going to disappear I want to do it myself, not wait until someone does it to us," Petra stated grimly.

"What should we do tomorrow?" Amiria questioned him.

"Go to Production as usual. Wait for the right time."

Petra stood up then and as he turned to look down at her the dim light reflected from the white marble walls fell across his face. Amiria looking up at him could see that unfathomable something shining in his eyes again. It was the same way he had looked at her the last time he had woken her up. She wondered, for an electrifying moment, if he was going to kiss her again. The thought made her slightly dizzy, but he just kissed her gently in the prescribed way on the forehead and offered her a hygienic wipe. He quickly went out and returned with the simulation disk that he had used to generate his own presence in his room. After he had left she questioned herself why she felt so disappointed. She switched on the simulator and was soon enfolded in the arms of the image of her partner. As the image held her, her brain told her senses that what she was experiencing was reality, but after the real kiss from her real partner she realised something. He had kissed her because he had passionately wanted to, even though it was forbidden. He had broken the rules because he had wanted to kiss her so much. It wasn't just the physical sensations that mattered it was the mind behind the person that made all the difference. This was an incredible revelation to her. In spite of all the detailed education she had received about relationships it was not something she had ever been taught, but she knew it was the truth.

# Chapter 21

The next morning Petra got up and focused on behaving exactly as he usually did. He enjoyed the pleasant surroundings, kept his mind calm and steady and went to Production immersing himself in it to the full. He knew it was important to keep his emotional levels even and he really did love his job so it was relatively easy to keep himself distracted from his inner concerns. As he was a City architect he knew more about the City's buildings and design more than most people did. Today he was taking a hover to overlook the City to check for inconsistencies or repairs that may need to be done.

Maybe that's why he and Amiria got on so well, he mused, she makes the inside of buildings beautiful, I make the outside beautiful. He kept his thoughts away from the strength of his feelings for her knowing this would cause a spike in his emotional levels. Instead he focused intently on his work and his plan. This time as he hovered over the City he kept a sharp lookout, not only for the lines and symmetry of the architecture but also for a possible escape route.

The City with its pure, white buildings stretched into the far distance beneath him. He could see no end to the City, it just seemed to fade into a hazy whiteness on all sides. The City's inhabitants only went where they needed to go for school or Production or where they were sent for recreation so no one really knew where the City ended or what was beyond it, if there was anything. He had been given an area to oversee and he had obediently remained in that area. Until recently he didn't have any desire to do anything else. It gave him a sense of pride to look down on the splendour of the City, parts of which that he had helped create but there were some things the City architects and designers could not substitute for.

No rivers, trees, bush or beaches here, he thought ruefully as he recalled these things from the history viewer. He gazed around, purposely prolonging his time above the City. He looked upwards as he remembered Dayzie talking about the sky, how it changed colour and how interesting the clouds were. His gaze shifted between the City and the clouds. The clouds didn't have the perfect, symmetrical magnificence of the buildings beneath him but were still lovely in a very different kind of a way. He looked across the City to the Fun Palace. He had helped design the outer part of the building but the rides were someone else's area of expertise.

I must take the family there this weekend, he decided, it may be the last time after all. He stayed up there for as long as he could seeing a pale sunset, all softly glowing oranges and wispy pinks.

Imagine being in an open space where we could see this all the time if we wanted to, not just catch glimpses of it from the travellers, he contemplated with a twinge of longing. A sudden inquisitiveness gripped him temporarily overcoming his caution. He decided impulsively to hover higher to get a wider view of the City and maybe even see what was beyond it. He felt he just had to know more no matter what the consequences. He rose slowly in the air, higher than he had ever been before. Until now he had always only ascended to the prescribed height required for him to complete his work. What would happen if he went above that limit, he wondered? He was about to find out. For a few moments no sound disturbed the serene peace of the sky then he suddenly stopped ascending as though the small vehicle had hit resistance. He looked up and thought he could faintly discern a slightly milky coloured substance spread across the sky.

Just at that moment a light began to flash and an electronic voice spoke. "Descend immediately and report to your supervisor."

Petra automatically obeyed, pressing the descend button and then the home button which would send the vehicle back to his area of Productivity. He knew he would be questioned about the choice he had just made, but in this moment it seemed worth it. He had discovered something about the sky. He would figure out later what that substance was and what it was there for. Right now he needed to prepare himself with an extremely good reason for breaking out of boundaries like that.

# Chapter 22

"Today, Petra announced to the children, we are going to the Fun Palace!"

"Cool" yelled Az.

"Yaaaay!!" Dayzie bounced up and down, plaits flying.

"Cool? That's a new word where did you hear that one?" Petra enquired quizzically of Az.

"From the history viewer, that's a word they used back then."

"Okay, cool it is then. Let's go."

Petra hadn't had any trouble adding this trip for his family to their schedule for the weekend and approval had been returned without question. He guessed the Central Computers had calculated his family would benefit from some fun after the happenings of the last few days. The Fun Palace had been devised to allow people the opportunity to experience extreme thrills and out-of-this-world adventures in a perfectly safe environment. It consisted of a wide variety of rides, simulated experiences and other fun activities to electrify the senses. The Fun Palace simulators gave you the opportunity to experience all kinds of fantasies such as living on another planet and you could even spend the weekend there as a holiday from usual Production activities. These planets appeared real and had their own sun, stars and moons all based on actual planets, some in our solar system and some from other solar systems. Each planet had different levels of gravity, types of vegetation and amazing simulated creatures.

There were even planets that were made up like Bubble Planet. This was a planet filled with bubbles that you could play with or ride on, you could even dive into a sea of bubbles. When you climbed on a giant bubble or a mound of bubbles you never knew just when they were going to burst. When they did explode with a pop and a splatter of shining wet liquid, the rider would be flung into the air briefly before landing softly on the planets jelly-like surface. This unpredictable bursting led to squeals of shock and laughter all over the planet. Sometimes a bubble stayed intact long enough for a child to float up into the air, riding it, higher and higher but it always burst at some point and then, down they came. The game was to see who could float the highest before the bubble burst. This planet was very well-liked by the under ten year olds in the City.

The gigantic rollercoaster was only for those thirsting for real extreme thrills. You drove around on it in small custom designed rubber cars. The speed was exhilarating and there was even a very slight possibility you could be a little bit hurt, although no more than a few minor bruises. This was the only ride in the Palace that allowed a small degree of real danger and it was aimed exclusively at teenagers. There was always lots of screaming and yelling going on and this ride which was invariably packed with crowds of young people. This ride was an opportunity for them to release some of the chemical build-up in their systems as a change from the normal compliant behaviour expected of them in their everyday lives.

There was an Edible Planet where every single thing was edible; not just the fruit on the trees but the trees themselves. Everything else from the houses, to the cups and plates, sofas and chairs, even the plants and stones; absolutely everything. Here you could eat and eat, experiencing a huge variety of extraordinary taste pleasures, but never get full. You weren't actually eating at all but the simulator made you think you were.

It was as perfect as everything else was or seemed to be in this world, Petra mused.

Rubber Planet was also a popular one, he remembered how much he had loved it from his young day. It was really a whole mini solar system and if you found just the right place to bounce you could bounce right up to the moon or even the stars. The speed and the rush as you flew through space was one of his most cherished child-hood memories. He and his friends had spent a lot of time there. Then there was Zoo Planet where you could play with exotic animals and make them behave in just the way you wanted them to. Dayzie was a frequent visitor. The animals looked and felt real and were in fact copied from those creatures who had lived in the world long ago when they had been kept in cages for people to look at. Dayzie would spend hours playing with them, stroking their soft, furry bodies or even riding on the larger ones. Fortunately smells could be turned off on Zoo Planet for those who didn't care for an experience quite as realistic as all that.

He smiled to himself. This was just what the family needed. An afternoon of pure enjoyment to chase the worries away.

When they arrived at the Palace, Dayzie and Az leapt out of the traveller to run inside.

"I want to go to the W-Zone," shouted Daisy.

The W-Zone was another of her favourite places. In this Zone you could experience total weightlessness. You could get drinks in there which you had to chase around as the liquid flowed out of the cup and into the air in globules. She loved to chase the bubbles of moisture as she bounced and floated, catching them and swallowing them in mid-air. She would bounce erratically off the soft squishy walls wrapped in inflated clothing. Spinning, hurtling along upside down and bouncing off other youngsters who were also floating around like balloons in the wind. Whenever two children collided each child would fly backwards with exhilarating speed, rebounding off the sides and ricocheting all over the place with screams of delight.

Az headed for the extreme roller coaster and stood staring at the cars screaming around the circuits in dizzying loops and up and over the crazy inclines. Sometimes a car collided with the sides of the track or with another car, then they would bounce off each other hurtling high into the air, rebounding up and down and around till they finally came to a stop with their occupants rolling around inside them like peas in a pod. No-one was ever really hurt but they all had to wear vomit extractors so that if they did vomit it was sucked away from their mouths to ensure it didn't go down their windpipes. The teenagers getting out of the cars reeled and staggered, laughing and sometimes holding their stomachs with grey-looking faces. Az didn't think he was quite ready for that one yet. He would go on one of the slightly less exciting rides this time round.

Amiria headed for the water simulator. She loved to sit in the waves and dive underneath or float on the surface. She didn't get wet at all of course and could stay under for as long as she liked as it wasn't real water. It was extremely pleasurable all the same and today she decided she wasn't going to even think about anything that had been bothering her lately.

Petra watched his family thoughtfully, glad they were having this day of unadulterated pleasure. His mind was working furiously, looking at things from a new angle. "Think opposite," he muttered to himself as he wandered around the gigantic park searching for what he believed could be their way out.

# Chapter 23

Gran was looking very cheerful this evening. Her grandchildren eyed her sideways. Something was up they knew and they were just waiting to hear what it was. Zak who was back to being his usual cheeky self, leaned over towards Gran.

"Why so happy Gran, got yourself a boyfriend? Ha, ha."

"Of course not, and that's quite enough of that" said Gran, quite gently for her. "Mind you," she said reflectively, "old George Whatua has been making sheep's eyes at me lately," she grinned mischievously.

"Aww Gran, he's like a hundred years old," said Rangi looking revolted.

"He's only seventy five," she snapped, "we went to school together, oh many years ago now," she sighed reminiscently, "he was quite the looker back then too."

The three youngsters had comical looks of disgust and disbelief on their faces.

"But that is not my news." She straightened herself up proudly. "We," she announced dramatically, "are having some special visitors tomorrow night, and you'll never guess who."

"Um the Prime Minister?" Hazarded Zach in a pompous tone.

"The Queen?" suggested Rangi mimicking Zach's tone of voice and with a regal flourish.

"Is it Mum?" shouted Gypsy eagerly.

"No, no, silly boys and no I'm sorry girly it's not your Mum."

"Who then Granny?" demanded Rangi, "don't keep us in suspenders."

"Well you won't be using that word while we have these guests," Gran smirked. "Tomorrow for dinner," she took a deep breath, "we will be having the Preacher and his wife." She exhaled triumphantly and looked around almost as though expecting the children to break out into applause.

"Who?" Zak enquired, "are we having for dinner? Gran just because your ancestors were cannibals. Mmmm hey," he said with mock reflection, "I've never tasted long pig before, is it good Gran?"

"How would I know that? Don't push me young Zak, I might not be able to catch you but I can wallop you while you're sleeping." Gran looked highly displeased with this response.

"What will we say to them?" said Rangi. He and Gypsy both had blank looks on their faces.

"Nothing, just be polite and don't talk with your mouth full. Smile and answer any questions they might ask you."

"Ok I guess it will be alright" said Gypsy uncertainly.

The three youngsters sat awkwardly digesting this news.

"Now off you go," Gran commanded rousing them to action. "Zak I want some wood chopped before bed. Rangi, help with the dishes. Gypsy go and make sure the chickens are inside for the night. There's a heavy rain warning and I want to make sure they are all safe in their coop."

Gran was a little disappointed at this reception of her news and she hoped they would behave. She wanted desperately to make a good impression on the Preacher and his wife. She was a little bemused by them herself but felt instinctively that they were genuine people and was keen to know them better. They were different from other ministers she had come across and as they were of her own race she felt confident to invite them around and get to know them better. It felt like something important that she needed to do. It was almost as though they may have the answers to some questions that had been buried deep within her during her traumatic childhood.

Silly thoughts I've been having, she told herself. As if there are any answers to anything in this crazy, mixed up world. Just get on with it, that's all you can do, she told herself sternly. She straightened her apron and proceeded to attack the pile of dirty dishes in the sink.

That night it did rain heavily as predicted. Gypsy had been kept awake till late by the pounding on the roof and the wind roaring and shaking the old house. The next morning Zak was up earlier than usual. She could hear him shouting up the hall way.

"Common cuzzies we gotta go check on the stock, Uncle just texted me, some of the paddocks are flooded. I'm gonna drive round to take a look. There'll be heaps of mud. Chee, cool, gonna be some great skids!"

"I'm not getting in that old bomb if you're gonna drive like a maniac," mumbled Gypsy coming into the kitchen looking very tired after her restless night.

"I'm up for it," shouted Rangi jumping up from the breakfast table. "Can I have a drive cuz, oh please?"

They ran for the door racing each other. It was still raining outside but it was lighter now.

Gran came into the room and looked out of the living room window.

"Fair bit of rain last night. Your Uncle will be pleased he's been worried about drought for the last few weeks. It's been great swimming weather for you kids but bad for the farm. Wonder how high the river is?"

After she had helped Gran around the house Gypsy went back to her room and lay on her bed staring at the ceiling. This was her favourite place now. She liked to be there just in case her friends from the future tuned in. Something was going on there she just knew. The other morning she had seen the father come up behind Dayzie and stare through the screen at her. He had looked scared and had dragged Dayzie away in a hurry.

What was coming next? she wondered. She thought about Az quite a bit. He seemed nice.

Wonder if he'd fancy a five hundred year old girl, she thought. Hee, hee, she giggled to herself.

She didn't mean to but with the light rain pattering against the window pane and after her disturbed night's sleep, while she was lying there day-dreaming, she fell asleep. In her sleep she dreamed she was in the room she had seen so often in her visions. She looked around. It was a beautiful place and filled her with peace and awe. It was completely still and silent and she was certain no one was home. The house looked incredibly clean, no marks, or stains, no mess or litter, just perfect. There was a table with very comfortable looking chairs around it, and by the table, set into a wall was a wide, ceiling high, curving screen. Suddenly there was movement all through the house and a low humming noise. Terrified she saw robots of all sizes becoming activated around her. A large one was moving across the floor towards her, tiny ones were zipping up the walls towards the ceiling. There were even some hovering through the air. In her dream she felt frightened. Could they see her? Sense her? What would they do to her? Was she about to be attacked? The large one came closer and closer then moved right past. Back and forth across the room it went. The tiny ones zipped up and down the walls and another began sliding around the table. Suddenly she understood. Cleaning! That's what they were doing, just cleaning the rooms. She laughed with relief.

"Dreaming about our boyfriend are we?" she felt a shove to her shoulder and woke up to find Zak standing over her grinning. "You were laughing in your sleep cuz. So, what's his name? Is he cute? He'd better be Maori or Gran will skin you."

"Shut up Zak, I haven't got a boyfriend," she snapped.

"She does, his name is Az," Rangi had popped his head around the door to add his two cents worth.

"You're both filthy," exclaimed Gypsy, "what have you been doing, rolling around in the muck out there?"

"Well, said Rangi, looking up at the ceiling, "we did a bit of sliding, had to walk back cos Zak crashed the car."

"What!?" she looked at Zak for confirmation.

"Oh stop narking on me Rangi, I slid a bit far that's all and hit a tree, got stuck in the mud." Then he suddenly dropped the causal act to groan in grief, "Oh my poor car," he held his hands to his head.

"You could have been hurt!" Gypsy remonstrated.

Well don't go narking to Gran she'll have fifty fits. I'm gonna get the tractor when the rain stops and drag her out."

"Well you'd better get yourself clean clothes for tonight, Preachers coming."

"Oh man! I forgot about that. I'll have to behave. What's he like?"

"Not so bad as far as preachers go, seems alright ae," she said noncommittally. In fact she had been astonished at some of the things he had preached. To her surprise she had found herself sitting up and listening. Some of the time she had to listen really hard to be sure she was hearing what she thought she was hearing. She kept this to herself, however. She wanted to wait until she knew herself what to think about it before mentioning it to anyone else.

# Chapter 24

That evening the three youngsters were sitting around the table, Gran fussing around trying to fix their hair with spit and wipe their faces with her stinky old dish cloth.

"Gran we're clean enough," Zak growled, "put that thing away or I'm outta here"

"Here they are, here they are," she chanted as they heard a car pull up.

"Phew, it's a 57 Chevy!" breathed Zak stretching his neck back to stare out of the window as the shiny black car purred to a stop. "Sweet, maybe I should get to know this dude after all," he said impressed.

There was a knock at the door and Gran flew to answer it. They were friendly, easy going folk and everything seemed to go well with friendly chatter over the meal until Gran started talking too much.

She addressed herself to the Preacher. "I must tell you about Gypsy, I think she might have a gift, she sees visions."

"Really?" he said with a smile, sounding interested and looking around at Gypsy.

Gypsy shrank back into the seat. No Gran please don't, she thought to herself

"Oh yes," continued Gran, "sees visions of what could be the future. I don't know, I don't know much about these things," she fluttered.

"So we have a young prophetess on our hands do we? That's a great gift to have young lady. There were many prophets and prophetesses in the bible. They could see into the future and describe the things they saw such as wars and plagues. They spoke about the birth and death of Christ long before he was born. Tell me more about these visions."

"Well," she said reluctantly, "I see a young girl and a boy, brother and sister, wearing strange clothes living in a beautiful home all made of white marble."

"Most visions of the future are given to us as a warning of what is to come or could come if we don't change our ways," he said kindly, still looking thoughtfully at her.

"I don't know about that, but I had a dream too recently where I was in that room. It was beautiful but I felt something, I don't know strange, kind of scary about that place. Those children, lately they've seemed scared and sad. I have a bad feeling something's about to happen there. I want to help them but I don't know how."

She looked up at him hopefully, but all he said was, "Perhaps in time it will be revealed to you."

Everyone had finished their meal so Gran and Gypsy jumped up to clear the table. She then invited the couple into the lounge ushering a reluctant Zak along with Rangi and Gypsy.

"Can I offer you and your wife a glass of wine to drink Reverend?" she asked deferentially, looking from one to the other.

"Thank you but no," the Preacher replied politely, "We gave up drinking many years ago."

"Oh but just one is alright isn't it?" Gran said wistfully.

"Maybe, but you know how the drink has affected our people. Our youth dying in car accidents," he turned to glance at Zak who immediately looked the other way trying to look as unconcerned as possible, "violent crime on the streets," he continued, "violence in the home, young children even babies being killed by their own families to our shame. Many of our fine young men are in the prisons. Even in this small rural community people are afraid to walk the streets at night. The police are overwhelmed and it's all alcohol fuelled. My concern is for the future generations. What will become of them?"

This sounded like it was turning into a sermon and Zak was eyeing the door wondering if he should go to the toilet and not come back.

"Oh quite right Reverend, quite right, I was thinking of giving it up myself," said Gran. She smiled at him and his wife broadly.

Rangi snorted but quickly turned it into a coughing fit hoping to avoid a session with the wooden spoon later.

"What about you young man? I would be interested to know what you think of these visions your cousin has?" The Preacher was addressing Zak.

Zak shrugged. "Maybe it's real, I don't know or maybe it's just her imagination."

"Well now there's an interesting point. Did you know that dreams and imagination are a way into the spiritual realm? A way of seeing and knowing things beyond our ability to understand?"

As the Preacher turned to Rangi and Gypsy, Zak started miming smoking a joint and pointing at the preachers back. He was doing a fairly good stoned impersonation till he noticed the Preacher's wife's with her eye on him. He tried to turn his mime into nose scratching but he didn't think it came off very well.

"Is there anything," continued the preacher, "that you can imagine that might not be real?"

"Well people imagine all sorts of things, what about monsters like Godzilla?" said Rangi becoming interested in the conversation in spite of himself.

"Monsters very much like Godzilla once did roam the earth, he looks rather like a T-Rex doesn't he?" The Preacher said with a chuckle.

"I guess so," responded Zak, "but sometimes people imagine really scary, creepy things what about those they can't be real?"

"There are some very scary, evil things in the spiritual realm called demons. Oh they're real don't you worry about that, but the good things are real too, angels, God, heaven. Only by using our imagination can we have a taste of heaven."

The Preacher certainly had a way of entertaining the young ones. They continued having conversations of this sort till late in the evening with Zak forgetting all about wanting to escape. Gran was surprisingly quiet during these conversations. All this kind of thing was way above her head although she was pleased to see her Grandchildren interacting so easily with the Preacher. To her relief the preacher's wife kindly engaged her in a discussion about local community news which she was able to understand very well and enjoyed very much.

---

The next morning Gypsy woke early at the usual time when her friends normally appeared. She looked expectantly up towards the ceiling when suddenly there appeared, instead of the usual faces of the girl and boy that she had come to know so well, some words instead. All backwards as usual. She ran and got a pencil and paper, stopping by Rangi's room to prod him awake and race back to her room. The words were still there shimmering on the ceiling.

"Look Rangi. I'm going to write them down, it's too hard reading back to front, help me what's the first word?"

"Umm... here. No that's the last one in that line."

Slowly they copied down each word onto the paper, looking up and down from the ceiling to the paper. Finally it was all written down. This is what they wrote:

> We have to leave here. We are in danger. There has been an alert. We are running but we can't tell you where we are going. I will try and contact you if I can. Az.

"Something's happened! I knew it. What shall we do?" she said helplessly. How could you possibly help someone when they lived nearly five hundred years in the future? she wondered frantically.

"There's nothing we can do except wait to see if they contact us," said Rangi in a practical tone.

"But they're in danger!" Gypsy was nearly crying in frustration.

"Look sis remember you are talking about something that hasn't even happened yet and won't for another five hundred years. There's nothing we can do except wait."

"And pray," added Gypsy quietly.

"Oh boy here's another one that's got religion. Yeh, that'll help," Rangi rolled his eyes towards the ceiling. "Best thing you can do is chill out and stop worrying.

Hey," he said suddenly, "Zak's going up North soon to visit our other cuzzies, why not come along with us, it will take your mind off things."

"Oh look, she exclaimed, "the words have disappeared. I thought I saw a flash of something for a moment, something in that room that looked like a metal face. That was really creepy," she said with a shiver.

"Freaky," agreed Rangi. "I think I'm glad I'm getting out of this house for a while. So are you coming?"

"I guess, it would make a nice change and give Gran a rest too," she responded thoughtfully.

"Yippee," whooped Rangi, jumping up excitedly, "Tiki-Tour, here we come!"

# Chapter 25

Rangi seemed easily able to put the problems of his friends from the future out of his mind as he anticipated the trip to the North Island. For Gypsy it was not quite such a simple thing. Sitting in the car with the two boys in the front seat yelling out of the windows, and Zak driving way too fast and recklessly, Gypsy seriously wondered if she had made the right decision coming with them.

"Are you sure this heap of junk is gonna make it all that way?" she yelled at Zak trying to make herself heard over the roar of the engine.

"Don't you call my baby a heap of junk. My precious," he stroked the steering wheel lovingly and gave it an affectionate kiss.

"That dent where you hit the tree's attractive," she mocked sarcastically.

"Sure, gives her some character, the bros in South Auckland won't mind."

"Drive carefully" Gypsy pleaded, "remember what the preacher said about our youth dying in car accidents."

"Aww that fella had been smoking to much happy baccy, that's all religion is, peoples imagination."

"You heard what he said about imagination, I thought it was interesting," Gypsy replied.

"It's the happy baccy sis," chimed in Rangi, "he's just after your money. How else do you think he pays for that flash car he drives?"

"I don't know, Gran says he used to be a forestry worker before he was a preacher, maybe he earned his money that way."

"Don't get sucked in Gyps," said Zak over his shoulder, "they'll be saying thou shalt not do this and thou shalt not do that before you can turn around."

Gypsy was thoughtful. The Preacher had said something else that night that had stuck in her mind. He said that there was time travel in the bible. That had shocked everyone. Gran had sat saying nothing with an uncertain look on her face. Zak had seemed most at ease with him, after they had got chatting though he said he didn't believe a word of it. Time travel?!! Wild! If only it were true. He had said the only way to time travel was through the spiritual realm. He had talked about Elijah who didn't die but simply disappeared into the sky. A prophet had said he would come back sometime in the future and some people thought he had come back as John the Baptist. He also talked about the other John who wrote the Book of Revelation who saw things happening in the future.

"How could he see them if he wasn't actually there?" the Preacher had reasoned. "God is outside of time, He can see the beginning from the end. He made us like him, so surely our spirits too have the potential to travel through time and space. Maybe we just need to believe," he had said.

Far out, maybe he was a bit whacko from the bacco. He said he'd been into it in his young day, along with the drinking before he'd met God. How on earth did you meet God? Gypsy wondered. She shut her eyes and prayed silently. Dear God if you are up there and can see my friends in the future please help them or show me how I can help them. Thank you very much. Bye for now. She opened her eyes and got a fright as her brother's face hovered half an inch from hers. "Get outta my face you little ngngngn!!"

"Oooooh Gypsy's been learning how to NOT swear from Gran," Rangi mocked. "What were you doing sis praying we won't crash? We're nearly at the ferry so wake up."

They got to the ferry just in time and lined up behind the other cars waiting to board. Zak jumped out to use the toilets in the ferry terminal. He came jogging back looking excited.

"Hey I've just heard the crossing is real choppy" he sang out cheerfully, "quite a bit of wind. That should make the trip more interesting."

The Interislander Ferry would carry them from the South Island to the North Island across the Cook Strait taking about four hours. This seventy kilometre journey could be treacherous, and in some weather conditions the Strait was so rough the ferries had to turn back. Sometimes they kept going even in rough weather while the passengers lined up along the rails heaving up their pies and chips. At other times the Strait could be as still as a pond with pods of playful dolphins swimming and leaping alongside the ferry.

"Might be some good tucker for the sea gulls this trip," yelled Zak, "Yee ha!"

They drove on board then left the car on the lower decks, climbing three flights of the solid iron steps to get to the passenger decks. The first part of the trip wasn't bad, travelling through the Marlborough Sounds was always fairly calm. Gypsy spotted some dolphins leaping as they swam beside the boat. Soon dozens of people were lining the railing taking photos and laughing with delight at the shiny bodies, leaping playfully through the water. Then they hit the open sea between the islands and the massive old boat began to rock, up and down and side to side. Gypsy sat very still with her mouth clamped tight shut as if she hoped to keep the contents of her stomach in by sheer will power. She was sincerely wishing they hadn't eaten so much junk on the trip up. Rangi was looking quite green too and had even stopped following Zak around, a sure sign he was feeling pretty bad.

Zak however, looked fine. He was as cheerful as ever and was wandering around, managing the rolling floors with ease and making friends. Gypsy noticed him chatting up a blonde girl and after a few minutes they headed off towards the bar. Not exactly what Gran had in mind, she thought grimly.

The ferry finally made it into the placid waters of Wellington harbour safely. The announcement came for them to head back to their vehicles so they descended once again into the lower decks where they saw the men unchaining the cars. When the boat had safely docked they drove off in a line following the other vehicles, trucks and train-trucks. Gypsy and Rangi were feeling better though still a bit shaky.

"So who was the chick?" Rangi asked conversationally as they waited in traffic.

"Cynthia," Zak replied dreamily. "Got her number," he said with a wink and a grin.

"Shot bro! You the man," Rangi high fived him.

"Didn't look very Maori to me," mentioned Gypsy to no-one in particular.

"Naw, don't worry about that. She's got some way back somewhere. She's Ngai Tahu, from way down south. They're pretty fair down there."

"Really?" said Gypsy disbelievingly.

"Anyway what does it matter?" Zak said dismissively.

Gypsy shrugged then changed the subject as a new thought struck her. "Hey. Can we go and have a look at the Beehive since we're in Wellington?" she asked Zak enthusiastically, "I've never been there."

"What for, it's just a big round building with lots of boring politicians in it spending all our money and fighting amongst each other like kindergarten kids."

"Never mind then," she muttered a little grumpily.

The traffic suddenly thinned and the motorway opened up in front of them.

"Let's drive," yelled Zak. "Yeeee-ha, Tiki Tour!!!"

They drove up the centre of the island past the volcanic mountains, Mt Tonagraro and Mt Taranaki. Driving past the massive Lake Taupo took a good hour. It was so huge it was like looking out to sea.

"Did you know that Lake Taupo is the crater of a volcano that erupted hundreds of years ago?" stated Gypsy informatively.

"Nah get off, it's huge. A volcano couldn't be that big," said Rangi in disbelief.

"Yeh it really is. It erupted ages before Pakeha or Maori came here. They saw it erupt all the way from China."

"Cool cuz, you've got a few brains under that mop ae," Zak grinned at her in the rear-vision mirror.

Zak could be cool when he wasn't drinking, Gypsy thought smiling back at his reflection, pity he thought he had to go on a bender every now and then.

The North Island had many inactive volcanoes, towering mountains set on wide, flat plains as though giant pimples had pressed through the surface of the earth. They drove past Rotorua next with its boiling mud and thermal hot pools. In times past these scalding hot pools emerging from deep underground had been used by Maori to cook. Now they were fed into pools for tourists to soak themselves in, revelling in the soothing hot water and clouds of steam.

"Pooh," said Rangi, as they passed, "it stinks like rotten eggs." Zak wound the window right down. "Breathe it in deeply cuz, it's good for you. That's the sulphur in the air."

"How far to Auckland now?" Gypsy asked.

"Still a few hours. It's getting late we might have to stop somewhere for the night and sleep in the car." The lights on the old girl aren't working too well," Zak admitted a bit sheepishly. "Anyway it's a bit too far all in one day and we don't want to arrive at Aunty and Uncles too late at night."

"Oh great" said Gypsy sarcastically. She was not looking forward to sleeping squashed up in the old car with her brother and cousin snorting and farting through the night.

The next morning Gypsy woke early with a cramp in her neck, feeling cold, uncomfortable and hungry. She had tried all night to get back into the room in her dream but it just didn't happen.

Maybe when I have a bed to sleep in, she thought.

They set off early as no-one had slept well.

"Burgers for breaky," said Zak, "now that's what I call good kai. Eat what you like, drink what you like, do what you like, that's my religion."

No-one bothered to answer that. After their breakfast they hit the road again, continuing to head north towards Auckland, New Zealand's major city. They arrived before lunch and headed straight towards the beautiful North Shore region, famous for its lovely beaches. Their Uncle and Aunt had done well with their laundry business over the years and were the well-to-do members of the family.

Originally they had come from South Auckland which was the poorer part of the city. It could be dangerous there with its gangs, high crime rate and alcohol fuelled violence on the streets. They had been glad to leave that area but they didn't forget about the rest of their extended family who still lived there. They often took round gifts of food or had different ones to stay. Family was family after all.

This was the first time the youngsters had been to their Aunt and Uncles new home on The Shore.

"Woo-wee!" gasped Zak sounding impressed. He, Rangi and Gypsy stared goggle eyed at the massive new house near the beach. Their Aunt came to the door to greet them.

"Bet all those rich Pakehas got a shock when yous guys moved in ae Aunty?" laughed Zak, impressed.

"Hey there Whanau. Welcome. Haere mai. Nah Zak they're our friends, we get on real well with the folks round here. Come give your Aunty a hug. God bless you," she said as she hugged and kissed each one of them.

"Wha...?" Zak froze in his tracks. He looked as though he wanted to turn around and run. "Not you too Aunty, you got religion?"

"Don't you worry, come inside and make yourselves at home.

Zak got a glimpse of the back yard of the house.

"Is that a swimming pool?" Zak said gushingly, "Sure Aunty anything you like, let me at it."

Rangi and Gypsy followed along behind him, their Aunt with her arm around Gypsy.

"You heard from your Mum lately dear?" she enquired kindly.

"No Aunty haven't heard nothing," she answered hanging her head a little.

"Well don't you worry, if you ever need anything, you just call me okay. Now come on in we're going to give you a really good time here. Have any of you been to that theme park before? Rainbows End? Your Uncle and I are looking forward to taking you there."

The grins those three country youngsters gave her would have lit up any dark and moonless night.

# Chapter 26

"Amiria, Amiria, its time," Petra was whispering quietly in Amiria's ear in the darkness of her bedroom.

Amiria woke up easily this time. Since that first night when she had been shocked into wakefulness outside of her schedule there had been many whispered night-time discussions.

"First we need to deal with the personal robots, before the children wake up, they might get upset otherwise," suggested Petra practically.

Quickly and carefully they carried the tiny robots in their comatose night-time state into the bathroom and threw them one at a time into the waste-eradication receptacle and flushed. Four times they flushed, and then, "One more just to make sure" said Petra with a mischievous smile."

"You're enjoying this," accused Amira.

"Doesn't it feel amazing? Strange but invigorating somehow? Like I used to feel as a teenager going on those crazy rides. This is even better than that. That was perfectly safe, with this we literally have no idea what might happen next."

Amira was still looking nervously down the receptacle. The tiny cleaning robot was already busily sliding around disinfecting as it always did after a flush and another was buzzing through the air like a miniature helicopter emitting puffs of deodorising spray.

This was exactly the kind of uncertain feeling Amiria didn't like.

"Come on let's get the kids." Petra moved and spoke briskly. He instinctively knew he had to get her moving before she became too afraid to act. They were about to leave everything safe, secure and known behind them. It would be so much easier just to give in and let the system deal with them. But Petra had strong reasons why he urgently felt the need to act now.

It was a painful memory, one he didn't allow to come to the surface very often, but which was always present. It was an ache that refused to go away, like a child curled up tightly in pain lying at the bottom of his mind.

Once before, in the past when he was with his previous partner and children he had been called in to see his supervisor at work. His supervisor had spoken kindly to him, explained there had been some alerts set off about his partner and their children. Something wasn't quite right with them and rather than jeopardise everyone's happiness and productivity they would have to be dealt with.

He hadn't really understood the seriousness of it at the time. He had gone home to find his house empty. No trace of his partner or of his children was ever found. It was as though they had never existed. His personal robot had immediately gone into action, counselling him to remain calm and focus on the future. He had advised him that his name had already been entered into the computer database to match him with a new partner.

"You are a very valuable asset to our society," it reassured him, "you must be careful and follow schedules very closely or ....." the 'or' was left unsaid.

He had immediately been granted a holiday and had embarked on the traveller that same day. This was the kind of holiday that was located in a simulated winter destination, involving challenges that required every bit of your mind and energy. He became so immersed in the simulated Winter-challenges that he hardly had time to think about what he had lost. Every moment of his time was taken up with mind blowing experiences of scaling dizzying heights, battling ferocious, simulated blizzards or cannoning down mountainsides if he happened to slip on the precarious heights. When he slipped, which was inevitable in those conditions, he would land unhurt and breathless in gigantic snow drifts, but the adrenalin rush was extreme. His every down time was filled with socialising, fun and games, recounting his adventures with other participants and in the night times, exhausted, dreamless sleep. He was never to speak of those whom he had lost and no-one would ever mention them to him again. If he needed to talk his personal robot would be there to help, support and soothe him.

He had not even been allowed to grieve, he thought angrily. For all the help his tiny, personal robot had given him he had felt there was an underlying threat. He must forget and move on quickly or he could go the same way.

# Chapter 27

Following this incident therefore, the second time Petra was summoned once again into the supervisor's area after breaking boundaries during his ride on the hover, he had gone with pounding heart, fearing he had left their escape too late.

The supervisor's office was spacious and palatial. The superb architectural design, wide curving windows letting in the muted, natural light and a fine view of the city was simply breath-taking. The design of the City was so precise that every building was placed in such a way so as to provide a stimulating view of the surrounding buildings with their lovely symmetry, graceful curves and arches. The supervisor had politely greeted him and enquired after his family and his work, had commended him on his designs and then gradually come to the main point.

"I'm very sorry to have to speak to you on this subject."

Petra was afraid he would bring up the incidents from the past, but he need not have worried. His supervisor was a compassionate man, chosen for this position for his ability to handle people and understand them. This instinctive knowledge gave him a powerful ability to motivate, inspire and handle any situation that might arise amongst his team of Producers. Petra believed he really was sorry to be delivering this news to him, but he could tell that he was also confident that what he was doing was right. No wavering or doubting the Wisdom for Life messages for him.

"It has come to my attention," the supervisor continued, "that there have been several minor alerts from various members of your family."

Minor alerts? Petra thought desperately. Maybe that wasn't so bad then, maybe there was still time. "Yes your son has given cause for concern on two occasions recently, once in class and once in your home. I'm sure you are aware of this. Teenage boys," he smiled sympathetically, "they can be the trickiest."

"You said there were alerts from other members of my family too, what were they?" Petra tried to relax but he could feel his hands clenching reflexively. Tiny beads of sweat were forming on his forehead in spite of the highly controlled air temperatures, as he tensely waited for his supervisor's response.

"Well," his supervisor replied hesitatingly, "it may not seem important but your daughter's persistence in naming her personal robot, ah Acne I believe it was." He showed no sign that he could see any humour in this. "It's an unusual name with an unpleasant origin. It refers to unsightly, facial disfigurements. You may have come across it from one of the many history views you have seen."

One of the many? Petra felt his whole body tensing. Was this a warning that his family's continual focus on the past had been noted?

Petra hung his head. "Is there anything else?"

"She appears to have an insatiable curiosity, it drives her to be a little," he hesitated, "ah, different from the other children."

Petra could think of no response to that, Dayzie was incredibly curious, he didn't know why she would be more curious than other children though.

"Also," his supervisor continued, "you and your current partner are rating higher than normal on the fear and worry register. Do you have any explanation for this that I can put forward for you?" He smiled again warmly.

Petra instinctively responded to his warmth by relaxing slightly. "No I don't think so."

"It is possibly a natural reaction to watching too many history views," said his Supervisor eyeing him intently. "I think you will agree you and your family should cut down on those. Focus on the present and on the future. "Now of course I must also ask you about your hover flight," he added almost as though this was something inconsequential and hardly worth mentioning.

Petra wasn't fooled. He realised his supervisors affable tone was useful for encouraging confidences. He knew would need to be very careful about what he said next.

"I must apologise for that breach," Petra responded with an attempt to look unconcerned, "I was attempting to view the Fun Palace from a higher perspective. There have been some recent additions and I wanted to make some checks. It was a foolish mistake, thankfully there was an alarm to remind me I had gone too high." He smiled at his supervisor, inwardly willing him to accept this excuse.

His supervisor listened carefully to this explanation nodding and then smiled back at him.

"You are a very skilled and precise producer Petra, and highly valuable. Whatever problems you may be experiencing I am confident they can be resolved. '"Today's problems are tomorrow's possibilities,'" he concluded heartily, quoting from the Messages. "I know things are going to work out well for you this cycle." His supervisors' expression was fond and comforting.

"Thank you, may I go now?" Petra felt a desperate need to get out of that room and hurry home.

"Of course of course, go home, relax, take the rest of the day off, enjoy your life, be at peace with your world, and I'll see you when you come back."

His supervisor gave him a disarming smile, patting his arm, then waved him towards the door in a benevolent fashion. Petra left the supervisor's area willing his breathing to be calm and walking as slowly and deliberately as he could. The traveller which usually took him home was not quite due yet so he had grabbed a mini-hover-bunny, so named because of its ability to jump from building-top to building-top. The hover bunny was named after an ancient creature which jumped rather than walked or ran. He tried to imagine this but he had no images in his mind for it.

When he reached home he hurried to the entrance of his home which opened to him automatically. As he entered he had a strange feeling there was no-one there. All his fear and tension returned with a suddenness, his stomach churning nauseatingly. The house was indeed empty and silent.

"Where are they??!" he demanded of his personal robot, his voice shaking with emotion.

"Are you enquiring after your family sir?" it replied smoothly. "Amiria is still at Production and the children at their classes. They are not due back for their rest periods for another hour," he advised in his reasonable voice.

"Oh of course, of course." Petra let out a breath that he had not been aware he was holding. The tension in his chest slowly lessening as he attempted to regain his self-control. "I came home early, they'll be here soon," he almost laughed with relief but this incident had increased his urgency to get his family out of this place.

"May I suggest some relaxation exercises sir? Perhaps an hour in the simulator with soothing water sounds or your mother's voice?"

His personal robot spoke in a voice tempered with concern. Although Petra knew this tone was fabricated he responded to it automatically.

"Yes, yes," he agreed, "I like the sound of that.

In the simulator he concentrated on relaxing his body, but in his mind he was thinking rapidly. His thoughts were only concerned with one thing; 'we have to get out of here, and soon!'

That night he woke Amiria.

# Chapter 28

With the robots out of the way, they would have to move fast. They crept into the children's rooms and gently shook them awake.

"Is it morning Mummy?" mumbled Dayzie.

"It's time for us to go dear," her mother said softly as she leaned over her.

Dayzie sat up rubbing her eyes looking confused then fell straight back to sleep.

"Don't worry, I'll carry her till she wakes," Petra said to Amiria.

Az was easier to wake. He was up in a moment and immediately understood the situation.

"I'm ready," he said. "There's just one thing I need to do first."

Amiria marvelled at how calm and mature he appeared. Almost as though he had been expecting this situation to happen and was prepared for it. Az went into the living area. He got out his auto-pad and wrote a quick note. He propped it up against the viewing screen and turned it on. Peeking around the edges he could see Gypsy asleep in her bed, curled up, her long tangly hair spread over the pillow. He wondered if he would ever see her again.

"Goodbye," he said softly.

"We need to go now," his father whispered urgently.

Quietly they crept to the door of the house hoping they would not disturb the house robots. When they got to the door they had a shock. It wouldn't open. They realised they had never tried to get out of the house at any time outside their schedules and certainly not at night.

"What now?" Amiria fretted in Petra's ear. Petra stood stock still. Surely they weren't going to be stopped before they had even left the house.

"Hang on," said Az and he quietly disappeared into the darkness of the living areas. When he came back he was holding a dinner knife.

"Where did you get that?" Petra hissed in amazement.

"Kept it," Az smirked, "and hid it. Put it in my pocket after dinner a few weeks back. Had a feeling it might come in handy."

"What are you going to do with it?" Amiria was staring at it in puzzlement.

Az moved swiftly to the door and inserted the pointed end of the knife into the centre crack where the doors closed, down near the floor. When he had jammed it in as far as he could he lay down and pressed his foot hard against it.

"Grab something," he whispered frantically, "to jam in it when it opens."

Amiria looked wildly around and then grabbed a large glass ornament that was glowing weirdly in the darkness. She heaved it off its shelf and sat it down on the floor near Az.

Az was shoving as hard as he could with his foot on the handle of the knife. The metal knife was beginning to bend when the door finally opened a slit with a protesting groan. He pushed one way with his hands while Petra pushed the other way. When the gap was just wide enough Amiria shoved the heavy ornament into the space to prevent it from shutting again. The doors slammed against the solid glass as they tried to close, causing cracks to form on either side of it. Az was lying on the floor sweating from the exertion.

"Let's go son," Petra hauled him up from the floor with his spare hand, the other still holding onto Dayzie draped over his shoulder as she slept.

"Great job, by the way," Petra gave him the prescribed pat on the shoulder. Then impulsively he grabbed him in a bear hug.

They all squeezed through the gap and gathered in a huddle outside. They had never been outside in the night before. They stood and listened for a moment but there no sounds broke the stillness of the night. As they stood there, gradually a distant hum became audible, slowly increasing in volume.

"Cleaning machine," Petra whispered softly, "We need to move before it gets here."

There were no roads in the City, if you wanted to go somewhere you went on a traveller to a prescribed destination. In unusual circumstances you took a hover-bunny or a larger hover craft if necessary for Productivity reasons. The family stood aimlessly for a moment looking around. They didn't know the way to anywhere; they hadn't ever needed to know the way to anywhere before.

Then Petra sprang into action. "Follow me," he whispered. He set off in what he hoped was the right direction. He had noted the route from the hover craft when he was hovering high above the City.

"This way," he spoke confidently to encourage his family. He feared he was leading them to a certain, unscheduled end to their life cycles but he couldn't let them see his fear, and he couldn't just wait around and allow the CCS or whoever was behind it to take his family from him.

"Where are we going?" Amiria questioned in a plaintive voice, she was already beginning to lose confidence in this plan.

"It's better I don't say it out loud in case someone's listening," Petra replied evenly.

There were no lights outside but the bright white marble of the buildings glowed in the darkness and lit their way. After about an hour of running between the shadows from building to building Petra spoke.

"Quick in here," he commanded.

They scuttled quickly behind one of the buildings. Another cleaning machine was gently humming past cleaning up any scraps of paper or dirt that dared to besmirch that sparkling, sterile city. When it had gone by, they continued to creep quietly along.

It would be so easy to get lost thought Petra, except that I know the designs of this portion of the City, and each building is different, unique so I can work out where I'm going.

They continued for about an hour or more in this way, Dayzie, on her father's back, lying against his shoulder, not saying anything, and seemingly confused about this strange night-time jaunt.

Perhaps she thinks she is still dreaming, thought Petra.

Amiria clung to him with a fearful face. Glancing back he saw Az was alert, keeping watch behind them. He looked more excited than Petra had ever seen him.

Teenagers, he thought smiling, worth their weight in gold. "Not far now," he encouraged them.

Finally the Fun Palace loomed up ahead of them, high walls seeming impenetrable and the massive doors securely closed.

"Can we get in Dad?" Az questioned in a low voice.

"Of course, I designed this place," Petra grinned, his teeth flashing white through in the dark.

"I designed an entrance for medium sized maintenance robots to come and go. We will have to crawl, and hope we don't bump into any on our way in."

Feeling his way around the edge of the building Petra found the entrance, concealed cleverly so it didn't malign the architectural beauty of the building. "In here," he called softly. "Az can you go first son? Your mother and sister can follow and I will come behind to make sure we're not followed."

"Sure Dad." He knelt down and started crawling into the low entrance.

"You next Amiria," Petra said. Amiria reluctantly got down to follow her son.

"In you go Dayzie," he said as she stood rubbing her eyes and trying to focus.

"Okay Daddy" she replied trustingly and got down on all fours to follow her mother.

Petra checked the area and as soon as her feet had disappeared followed on after her. Inside it was much darker. Petra sensed his family standing nearby as he stood up in the darkness.

"Where to now Dad?"

Petra took a moment to get his bearings then led them to the right, feeling his way along the wall. "Here," he said finally, "help me son."

He was standing by a large shoot with a heavy lid. This was the escape route he had been thinking about but was afraid to mention as he really had no idea where it ended up. On his miniature replica of the City he could see it spiralling down and away, disappearing off the edges of the model, but how far it went and where he didn't know. He and Az struggled to lift the lid.

"This is a disaster," moaned Petra, "it must be designed for robots to lift we'll never do it." He sat down with his head in his hands.

"Now what do we do, go back?" Amiria asked him worriedly.

The family huddled together in the dark uncertain what to do. Az got up and started wandering around. Dayzie looked like she was falling asleep again, leaning against her Mum. Amiria was sitting with her cheek against Petra's chest his arm protectively around her. They could hear Az clanking around somewhere close by. They sat quietly for a while, Petra thinking hard about what to do next.

"Look Dad I've found something," Az's voice came through the gloom sounding eager.

"What is it son?" Petra asked without much interest. He felt beaten and discouraged. He had led them here in desperation with a faint hope they would be able to escape and now it looked as though they were stuck. Maybe there was no way out. Maybe there was nothing out there anyway.

Az dragged something over to him. "It's a metal bar, I unscrewed it from a railing."

"Why, what are you going to do with it?"

"In our engineering class we learnt about how in ancient times long metal bars like this were used to move heavy objects. You stick one end under the object and put your weight on the other end. It makes it much easier to lift. I've never tried it but it might work for getting that lid open."

"Well okay, let's give it a go." Petra pulled hard on the lid and moved it only slightly but it was just enough for Az to wedge the end of the bar into the gap. Once it was well jammed in both Petra and Az used their combined weights to push down on the bar.

To Petra's surprise the lid lifted easily and fell clattering to the ground. The sound was very loud, echoing through the vast rooms of the Palace.

"Quick let's move," he shouted.

"I'll go first this time," he said to Az, I'm not sure what's down there. Can you make sure everyone gets in ok?"

"No problem Dad, we'll be right behind you."

Petra jumped into the shaft feet first. As he slid down he saw movement out of the corner of his eye. "Quick Az," he shouted behind him, "there's not much time."

He slid uncontrollably and kept on sliding very fast. The walls of the tube were highly polished metal and extremely slippery. He knew he couldn't stop himself sliding now even if he wanted to. He could hear the sounds of someone clambering into the shaft way above him and screams as they started to slide down. He could also hear shouting.

Was that Az? he wondered with concern. Had he been caught? There was nothing he could do. He couldn't stop and he couldn't go back up. He kept on helplessly sliding and sliding. It was completely dark in the tube so he could only listen to the sounds of the others sliding behind him and focus ahead to try and see where they might end up. The darkness and the sliding went on and on. He started to lose track of time. Was it an hour or two that he had been sliding? He awoke with a start. Where was he? Had he really been sleeping and still sliding?! How long *was* this tube? May be it was endless or just went round and around? It was confusing and disorienting.

"Amiria can you hear me? Amiria!!!" he shouted back up the tube.

A small voice sounding far away came back to him. "I'm here Petra, behind you."

"Are Dayzie and Az with you?"

"Dayzie is."

"Az!!" He heard her shout.

He couldn't hear any reply but then she relayed it back to him, "Yes he's there, way behind. He said something about a fight with a robot. He's laughing!" Amiria sounded incredulous.

"He must be alright then," Petra bellowed back up the tube. Nothing to do but wait till we get to the end of this, he thought.

Another half an hour later the tube fed into a larger tube along with many others. Petra managed to grab a-hold of an edge and hang on to stop himself sliding just long enough until he heard Amiria sliding closer then he let himself go again.

"Petra! What's down there, where are we going?" she sounded breathless and afraid.

"I don't know," he tried to speak calmly, "is Dayzie okay?"

"Yes. I think she's asleep. She's not far behind me."

"I think I can see light ahead," said Petra, straining his eyes, "it's not as completely dark as it was." The speed they were travelling at suddenly became apparent as Petra had only a moment to realise they were at the end of the tube before he was flying through the air. He landed softly enough on what he could see in the dim light was a gigantic pile of rubbish. If he had ever seen a mountain he would have said the pile was as big as a mountain. He instinctively rolled sideways and Amiria landed unhurt beside him. Dayzie who had been sleeping, woke with the sudden landing on the rubbish pile. They moved quickly aside but it was several minutes later that Az came flying out of the tube to belly-flop onto the rubbish with his arms and legs spread eagled. He looked as though he was enjoying this adventure so far. They looked around them. The sides of the rubbish container was constructed of wire netting and looked climbable.

"I'll go up and see what's on the other side Dad," said Az. "I'll let you know."

"Okay son," he grinned, "off you go. We'll wait here."

He looked around and realised that the sky and the light were vastly different in this place. Even in this dim early morning light it was much brighter than they were used to. The sky was a strange dark blue colour. The sky they could see from the City was very pale in comparison with this deep azure with white clouds scudding across it. He gazed in wonder around him, breathing in the tantalising air containing a thousand smells he had never experienced before. He could also hear unrecognisable sounds that he couldn't yet explain. It was a bit like broken snippets of music mixed with other sounds that he couldn't identify. Both the sounds and the sights beyond the netted walls filled him with new sensations and feelings that he had no words for.

"It's bird songs," said Amiria wonderingly. "Remember we heard something like it in the bush through the viewer," she said to Petra.

Petra stared at her amazed, he didn't know what to think. None of this fitted in with what he had always known and believed about the world.

Dayzie was sitting up and looking around her. Petra was only just in time to stifle her scream with his hand held gently over her mouth as she realised what they were sitting on.

"Ssshh baby sshhh."

"But Daddy its yukky, unhygienic rubbish," she squeaked.

He could see Amiria was having a similar reaction, trying not to touch it, cringing away from it.

"It's okay, its only paper and wrappers," he reassured them gently. "Hey look at Az go," he said distractingly, "he's climbing up that netting like a, like a, a..."

"Like a monkey Dad," supplied Dayzie. "Remember we saw one on the history viewer, they used to lock them in cages so people could go and look at them. They were really good at climbing."

"So they were darling, you're right," he said, pleased she was being distracted from the rubbish.

"Hey Dad," shouted Az, "You are not going to believe what I can see. It's gonna freak you out big time!"

"What, what is it?" He asked urgently, fearing whatever unknown dangers there might be outside of the City.

Az turned back towards them, his eyes shining with excitement. "Trees! Heaps and heaps of them. Come and look."

"Wait," said Petra, "what's that noise."

The sound was familiar to them all, it was the low humming sound of approaching robots. It was issuing from the tunnel and it was rapidly coming closer.

# Chapter 29

Out of the tunnel shot four robots to hover in the air before them. Then a voice spoke out of each one saying the same thing at the same time.

"You have been apprehended. You have had your final warning you must now come with us."

Each robot approached a human and clasped them in their metallic arms. One plucked Az screaming off the fence. There was no point in resisting and they allowed themselves to be picked up and flown away only Az fighting as hard as he could go. Freedom and adventure had been so close. They weren't hurt and they were flown above the tube opening into a building high above the rubbish pile. Inside they were set down gently enough and the four robots stood guarding the door.

The synthesised voice spoke again. "Step forward, proceed to the Information Giver."

"What?" cried Amiria with surprise, "are we actually going to meet him?"

They stepped forward as there seemed nothing else to be done. As they did so four seats came up behind them and swept them up. A restraining belt clasped itself around their waists and the chairs moved up an escalator and high into the building. At the top the building opened out. There were wide windows and looking out the four could see the trees that Az had glimpsed. Masses of them, all growing closely together and spreading away in the distance for many miles.

"Look at that, look at that," squealed Dayzie, "it's a river, a real one isn't it? Is it real Mum?"

Amiria shook her head in wonderment, "I don't know, maybe it's just a really big viewer."

"I don't think so Mum," Az said, "I think it's really the real thing and they told us there were no trees left except far across the sea; lies and more lies."

They travelled along a wide corridor with large windows all along one side, so they could continue to gaze at the view. They all sat staring, stunned at the sight. Abruptly they came to the end of the corridor and their chairs lined up facing a wall. Suddenly a screen as big as the wall appeared and through it they could see a group of four grey and white haired men and women sitting facing them and smiling kindly. They wore beautiful colourful robes of deep reds, blues, and greens adorned with silver and gold. Surrounding them were a multitude of monitors and controls.

The City family stared in wonder at the sight of living people who were older, much older than forty. This was something they had never witnessed before in the flesh.

One of the elderly women spoke first. She had soft-looking, white, wavy hair framing a very sweet old face.

"Welcome Petra, Amiria, Az and Dayzie," she said kindly as if they were old friends, "We have been watching you all closely. You have done well to get this far. Most don't make it out of the City."

"I had the advantage of being one of the architects who maintained many of the City's buildings," Petra replied. He waited, expecting, he didn't know what, but something bad was surely about to happen. "Are you the Information Giver? He ventured to ask after a tense moment.

She laughed and so did the others, looking at each other in amusement. "You could say that, but the information has been developed and stored over many, many years by a variety of different people," she explained patiently. "The information is then fed to the people via the Central Computer System."

"What's going to happen to me and my family now?" Petra asked a little shortly revealing his inner trepidation.

"Well, that, my friend, depends on you," she said, still smiling and with a slightly quizzical look, "You have choices now."

The way she said this reminded Az of a teacher asking a class a puzzling but interesting question. He felt annoyed by her light-hearted approach to their predicament.

"Why, why now?" Petra asked quickly, looking from one face to another in his quest for answers.

"I think perhaps we should explain a few things to you," she answered him gently. "In the meantime please relax, you are in no immediate danger."

The old woman's voice was soothing and her face was kindly. The others, two elderly men and another elderly woman nodded in agreement with her statement. One of these men looked very old indeed. His face was an incredible network of wrinkles and saggy skin. His hair was thin and white. Dayzie's wide, staring eyes were glued to him, her mouth hanging slightly open, intrigued by his appearance.

By contrast the other man seemed quite a bit younger, though still old, with dark steel-grey hair and very black, flashing eyes. The City family sat and waited nervously for developments, what else could they do? The white-haired old woman began her story.

"Many, many years ago," she said, "the world was not the beautiful, perfect place that you now live in. It had become a terrible, desolate, frightening place. There were wars, terrorist attacks, starvation, disease, and violence, even within families. Humans would fuel themselves on a substance called alcohol which had a powerful effect on the brain. It gave the person temporary relief from their pain and misery but took away their ability to control their anger and their desire to inflict their inner pain on others."

As she was speaking appalling images flashed up on the screen of war, death and drunken violence. "Each generation suffered the effects of this violent behaviour and in turn inflicted the same behaviour onto the next. The problem grew until there were no safe places left on the earth. It was at this time that simulators were being developed and tested. It was discovered that when a human was inside a simulator he or she could not tell the difference between reality and simulated reality. This led to a curious way of predicting the possible future and possibly the answer to the world's problems."

"Possible future?" interjected Az, "what does that mean?"

"People were put into a simulator which created in their minds a situation where they had an opportunity to do another human being harm," the women continued evenly. "While in the simulator the person became unaware that the situation was simulated and so they acted as they would have had it been reality. In effect it could predict who would commit crimes. Then someone had the idea of putting many simulators together, on mass. On a certain day a million people were linked into the simulator to create a mass mind. The results of this experiment went beyond what anyone could imagine. The future unfolded before their eyes, the future not just of individuals, but of generations to come. They thought the world was bad then, it was nothing compared to the devastation that was revealed by this mass simulation. It was horrifying. When the people of the world saw what the future of earth was likely to become many committed suicide. Some killed their own families rather than subject them to the horror that they now believed was coming upon them. Masses marched demanding the execution of those who had taken part in the simulation to protect the world and their descendants. They wanted a new law passed that allowed the conviction of crimes before they were committed. Everyone must enter the simulator and be convicted before the crimes they took place. They believed this would make the world safe and they demanded it. The law was passed. All people were required to take the simulated test. Many failed. Fear reigned at that time as hordes were imprisoned for crimes they had not yet committed. Rioting began as people rebelled against taking the test. The world continued to degenerate. There seemed to be no perfect solution. In the year 2200 it was recognised by world leaders that the world could not survive much longer. Each generation was more violent than the last and it was obvious that at some point nuclear warfare would be used and then that would be the end. Someone needed to take control but how to take control without producing a dictator who would use his or her power for their own gains and inflict misery on a large scale on the earth as had happened before in the world's history? All of the earth's leaders were desperate, not knowing what to do. There was one small hope."

"A handful of people from across the nations who took the test, proved in the simulator that under no circumstances would they commit a crime. These people believed so strongly in working for the good of all that they were prepared to give their lives for others if necessary. The world's leaders brought them together with the intention of selecting one person to contain and rule the world. When they came together something unforeseen happened. Once these ones understood what they were there for, they spent many hours discussing the situation and eventually decided that it was too dangerous for one person to rule the world and chose to act as group. So that is what they did. They acted with logic and kindness using all the technology and resources of the world to create a safe, happy environment where people can live out their lives in peace and productivity. They produced a beautiful world that would benefit the next generation and the ones to come."

Petra and Amiria looked at each other. There were so many new ideas to absorb all at once.

"But the people who disappear?" Amiria questioned, "What happens to them? And anyway, I don't believe the world is perfect. We don't have any freedom and it's all so, so, so predictable," she ended lamely. She had no words to describe the way she felt inside; the emptiness, the shallowness of her life and the fear she had lived under of what the unknown powers who controlled the world could do.

"And we are taught how to think", interjected Az "and told lies. Things are hidden from us."

The oldest of the elderly men bowed his head. "It was the kindest way we could find of creating a safe society. It is as perfect as we could make it and you are right it is not at all perfect. You must understand how terrible the alternative would be."

Az stared at him for a moment as though struggling with an idea. "Is it really real?" Az demanded intensely, "those memories I have of being trained and conditioned? The darkness and the pain. Is that real?!"

The old people looked at him with interest. "So you have some residual memories of that?" the oldest man asked with a look of surprise on his ancient face. "They are very early experiences, youngster, people don't usually remember." He appeared eager to know more.

"What I want to know," spat out Az the anger boiling up inside him, "is what happens to those babies who fail your tests, who can't be conditioned properly?" He was breathing heavily his hands clenched into fists.

"Ah," the old man sat back with his hands together like the steeple of a church, his fingers just touching at the tips, "it is regrettable," he said slowly, "but sometimes they need to be what we call 'remade.'"

"You kill them don't you?" Az spoke darkly, glaring at him.

The elderly people laughed softly, glancing at each other. "No, no," he replied, they have barely begun their life cycle, we simply restart the process. You can't 'kill' something that is not fully human yet and we do not consider them to be fully human until they have proven they possess the ability to fit positively into human society. If they cannot do this we simply rearrange their genetic material and start again."

"Who are you to decide who is human and who is not!?" Az spat out angrily.

The old man leaned forward seriously to look directly in Az's eyes. "We cannot," he accentuated the word, "take the risk of allowing a person into the City's delicate social system who is at risk of upsetting the balance." He leaned back again, speaking confidently. "We would quickly go backwards and descend into the anarchy of the past if we allowed that to happen. No my young friend that cannot be, they must be remade."

"They-are-people!" Az was shouting now. He stood up and began pounding ineffectively on the glass wall. "They-are-human-beings!"

Petra stood up beside him and put a hand on his arm to help calm him and to show his support.

"It must be hard for you to conceive of a world where there is danger all around and even those we love can turn on us," the white haired women spoke a little condescendingly. At one stage the population was almost completely destroyed, there were very few people left," she continued. She hesitated, seemingly troubled about something, but she didn't explain any further how the people of the world had almost been lost. We took the opportunity to rebuild and recreate," she looked directly at Az with a strangely determined look on her face. "We rebuilt from the dirt and the ashes of what was left. Without us there would be nothing, nothing!" She sounded angry to the ears of the City family and something else too, maybe a little afraid?

The old woman quickly regained her composure and settled her grandmotherly smile back on her face.

"Let us show you the story of Meg to illustrate how we have changed the world for the better."

Immediately a scene appeared on the screen and the images of the elderly people faded into the background.

# Chapter 30

The young woman was enjoying the warm sunshine tingling on her skin and the gentle breeze playing with her hair. Dreamlike she inhaled the scents of grass and wild flowers and the fresh smell that told her there was a river somewhere nearby. Going for walks in the countryside was a favourite way of relaxing for her.

She loved her children to bits, they meant everything to her but it could be exhausting being a single mum. Seeing a large shady tree she wandered aimlessly towards it. As she came closer she realised with a jolt that she was precipitously near a cliff edge.

How easily I could have walked over it, she thought with trepidation and with relief.

It was the gasping breaths that alerted her to what was happening only a few metres away. Someone was hanging off the cliff. She could just see the fingers clinging to the edge, the knuckles white with the strain. She went into action quickly. There was a thick rope lying on the ground. She didn't stop to wonder how it got there. She quickly tied the rope tightly around the tree then hurried to the edge flattening herself onto the ground. She leaned over the edge dangling the rope from her hands. The drop was fearsome and made her momentarily dizzy. There was a river far below surrounded by steep crumbling cliffs and the depths seemed to suck her downwards. She had never liked heights. She tore her attention away from the drop to stare into the desperate eyes of the man hanging there for dear life. She flinched with shock as she realised that she recognised him. She hadn't seen him face to face for many years now. In the seconds as she stared at him the memories came flooding back. The abuse, the cruelty, the constant fear. She had run from him and hidden afraid for her life and the lives of her children. They had only been married for a short time but the repercussions for herself and their children were lifelong. And here he was, about to die, to fall to his death and then he would be gone and she would be finally rid of him.

"Please," he whispered, "please."

His eyes so like the eyes of her young son were bloodshot from the strain. She could see the terror there as his strength seeped away. In an instant she made up her mind. She threw the rope across his back and scrambled to pull it around him, tying it in a knot under his arms. She rolled sideways and pulled herself up. Grabbing the rope she leaned backwards using all of her weight, pulling hard, stepping back inch by inch. Slowly his head became visible above the cliff edge. Clinging to the rope with one hand and clawing at the grassy cliff top with the other he shakily pulled himself up over the top. Finally he lay sweating on the ground, his chest heaving. Looking up at her for a moment he laughed with relief. He crawled away from the cliff before standing upright. Staggering over to the tree he leaned up against it breathing heavily.

"Thought I was gone," he panted. Then as his breathing slowed he straightened up and turned back to look fully at her.

She just stood there looking back at him. She felt nothing. She had done the right thing, now she just wanted to walk away.

He walked slowly towards her still smiling a little. "Meg," he said softly, "it's been so long since I've seen you."

As he came closer and closer she was puzzled. Was he going to thank her, or hug her?

"Here we are all alone, far away from anywhere… and anyone…"

She felt awkward as he closed the distance. Why didn't he just say thank you and leave? That was what she wanted him to do. Why did he have to talk to her in that strange intimate way?

His eyes held hers with a curious intensity. It reminded her of something.

Like a snake mesmerising its prey, she thought. Suddenly when it was too late she realised exactly what his intentions were. Time seemed to stop and stand still in those moments. She became suddenly acutely aware of the bright greenery around her. The flitting shadows of moving branches and the birds singing became strangely clear. The images of her children's faces appeared sharply in her mind and tears stung her eyes. Her heart began to pound with fear. He held his palms up pushing them hard against her shoulders. She stepped backwards involuntarily with the force, powerless to resist. His cruel face was close up to hers as he pushed her swiftly towards the edge.

"You deserve this," he whispered fiercely, "for what-you-did to me! For-leaving-me!" He spat each word into her face.

"No," she pleaded, her voice was a strangled squeak as she realised the inevitable.

Then, with a final shove and a mocking grin he pushed her over the edge. Screaming she fell, helplessly, grasping desperately at nothing, arms and legs flailing uselessly. She watched unbelievingly as the sky fell away from her; the beautiful deep blue sky. Everything went mercifully black.

She opened her eyes. A woman in a white coat was standing beside her, gently shaking her awake.

Confused she pulled herself carefully into a sitting position, feeling her arms and legs as though expecting them to be snapped into pieces by the impact of her fall. She could feel no pain. Was this a hospital? Was she so heavily medicated she couldn't feel anything? She was sitting in a comfortable chair. Not far from her was the man she had just rescued, the man who had pushed her to her death.

She gasped and nearly cried with relief as the realisation came to her that it hadn't been real. They were right when they said it was impossible to tell the difference between reality and simulation.

"You can go now," the women told her kindly, "well done, you've passed the test."

She stood up gingerly, still half believing her body should be broken to bits. As she left the room she heard an authorative voice speaking.

"Jeffery Edward Howard, you are under arrest for the wilful murder of Margaret Sarah Howard. You are hereby sentenced to life imprisonment."

She could hear him protesting and arguing, they all did that. It was useless. Before witnesses and on record he had murdered her. There would be no trial. The test was the trial. She felt no regrets. He had shown his true character. If he had the opportunity to murder someone and get away with it he would do it, no question about that now. There were many who were calling for the execution of such people, those who had proven beyond doubt that they were capable of violent crimes. People were frightened. What would the future be like with the revelation through the test that such large numbers of people were capable of that kind of evil? There had been so many who had failed the test it was unprecedented. She doubted things would ever go that far though, it would mean mass executions.

There was even talk that young children should be submitted to the test before they could begin to perpetuate violence if they were so inclined. This came from people who were radicals, who didn't seem to be satisfied with mere justice; they wanted nothing less than a purge. She felt unconcerned. That kind of thing would never happen she was confident. Killing people, even children for possible future crimes? That was ridiculous. No one would allow it.

She walked out into the sunshine and breathed in the fresh, cool air. She still had the half shocked half buoyant feeling of a person who has recently escaped from certain death. Knowing that it hadn't been real didn't take anything away from the experience. That moment when she had been suspended between sky and earth would be forever imprinted on her mind. She also felt a deep sense of satisfaction and contentment. She had passed the test and was free to go, and she would never have to worry about Jeffery again. A deep sense of gratitude welled up in her for the authorities who had set up this system and who wanted to make the world a better and safer place. What could be fairer than trial by simulation? Today felt like the beginning of a new day, a new society and a new world. Most importantly today justice had been served.

# Chapter 31

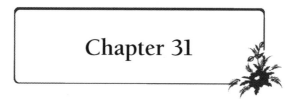

The family were silent as they watched the young woman walk contentedly away. As the illustration ended, the images of the elders emerged and came back into focus.

"What will happen to us now?" Petra urgently repeated the question he had asked earlier that was upper most in his mind. Whatever was right or wrong with their world and those who governed it, he needed to protect his family.

"You have proven that you cannot live happily in the world we have created," the old man with the steel-grey hair answered him, "there are other ways to live. You could go back and try to comply with the schedules but you may find that difficult now. There is another choice," he paused, eyeing them intently with his deep black eyes, "you could choose live in the Forest Community."

The four of them gasped. It was difficult for them to comprehend the knowledge that there were people actually living outside the City when they had been told all their lives that nothing else existed. They listened eagerly for more information.

"This community lives in a way people did long ago, having a few tools and making their own rules and enforcing them. We do not interfere with them."

"There is a third option" the second elderly women spoke for the first time. She had very long, soft-looking hair tied in a jewelled clasp lying down one shoulder. It was curiously coloured with black streaks sharply contrasting with pure white, but the effect was striking and elegant. "You can opt to take the test," she spoke in a warm voice, her large dark eyes smiling. "It is possible that *some* of you may have the gifts needed to become one of us." As she emphasised the word, some, she glanced at Az and a faint expression of dislike flittered across her face.

The family, listened with astonished faces to these options, then looked at one another questioningly. They had a difficult decision before them.

"We will need time to consider these options," said Amiria firmly. "How long do we have?"

"Take as much time as you need. We will leave you alone. You will find refreshments and comfortable seats in the room behind you.

The restraining belts popped open leaving them free to get up. They moved together into the room indicated. It was beautifully furnished and had a food and drink machine along with a nutrition reader.

It also had a panoramic view of the forest land.

When they had eaten and rested, they began to talk. Az couldn't take his eyes off the forest scene and leaned up against the window with his hands pressing the glass as though eager to go there and begin a new adventure. When he finally turned around his mood had completely changed and they knew he had made his decision. His eyes were shining with anticipation.

"Mum, Dad, I have to go there, I just have to." He stood looking at them, waiting for them to understand and accept his decision.

Amiria, Petra were silent for a while considering this. Then Petra turned to Amiria and Dayzie.

"What about you two, do you know what you want to do?"

"I don't know, they didn't give us enough information." said Amiria quietly. "Half of me wants to go back and be safe and happy and continue the only way of life I know, but I've found out something Petra."

"What's that my love?"

"Back there in the City when it came time to change partners I was always glad and looked forward to a new partner being chosen for me, but now I've met you, I don't want the cycle to end. I want to stay with you." She gazed steadily into his eyes. "Wherever you go, I want to go too, wherever that is."

Petra hugged her tightly, tears in his eyes. "I love you so much. This is what I've dreamed of. Staying together right through the Life Cycles, never leaving each other."

Dayzie stood watching them. "I want us to stay together too," she said choking on her tears. "I'll be reallocated to another family when your Relationship Cycle ends if we go back to the City."

Amiria and Petra opened their arms to draw her in.

"Now we have to decide, as a family what we should do," said Amiria.

"Az," she called to him, "are you set on going to the forest? No matter what we decide?"

"I can't go back to the City," he said in a decisive tone, "but maybe I could take the test just in case. I wouldn't mind being a ruler, that sounds cool. I guess I could do what I liked then."

"Much more likely you would have a life filled with responsibility and difficult decisions," his father said seriously, "and, anyway son, I'm not so sure you made such a good impression on them out there," he finished with half a grimace and a half smile.

Az considered his words for a moment then silently turned back to the scene behind him, gazing, mesmerised into the distance.

"We know that if we go back to the City we will be broken up at the end of the cycle as usual," Petra spoke to Amiria. "We will both be allocated new partners, Dayzie will go to another home and Az will be put into intensive training for his career."

"We need to know more though," Amiria persisted, "I mean, what is it like in the forest? Can we live there? We don't know how. Maybe they could let us try out living in the forest and choose later?" she suggested. "They did say we could have more time."

"You're right darling," said Petra, "let's ask them if we can do that."

They went out of the room and back to their seats by the wall with Az reluctantly tearing himself away from the view to follow them. The screen appeared again.

"Have you made a decision?" It was the very elderly, grey haired man with watery eyes who spoke this time in the cracked voice of the aged.

"We have decided," said, Petra "that we want to stay together as a family no matter what. So we want to trial living in the forest, but we want to be able to choose to leave if it doesn't work out. We can't make a proper decision after all if we don't have all the necessary information."

"A wise decision, you have considered not only the best interests of each individual but also of the family as a whole. Have you considered taking the test?"

"Perhaps, but I think for Az's sake we need to try the forest."

"Very well, we will release you to go out into the forest. We wish you well and will speak to you again beside the gates to the forest in six weeks' time."

Then Az spoke up. "I have one more question. How many people have escaped from the City? I mean if we found a way others must have as well?"

The woman with the dark eyes looked at him scornfully. "You didn't think you would have been able to get out if we didn't allow it do you? We were merely testing our systems, trying to discover if there were any gaps in our security. Of course we could have stopped you at any time if we had chosen to. Be assured no one will ever get out the same you did again."

Before anyone had time to respond to her chilling statement, the screen went blank and their chairs began to move again taking them further along the corridor then down to ground level. Here they were released from the restraining straps and they stood up together before massive doors that led to the outside world. It was a terrifying moment as they stood hand in hand, hearts hammering with excitement and fear as they waited for them to open. They were embarking on a new beginning in the strange, uncertain world they were about to encounter beyond the doors, a place they didn't even know existed until today.

# Chapter 32

Zak opened his eyes and instead of seeing the peeling white paint of his bedroom at the farmhouse with its daddy-long-legs spiders in the corners and bare floorboards, he saw a tastefully decorated modern bedroom. He leapt out of bed and leaned out of the window looking down on the beautiful pool with its blue sparking water. Further away over the bushes he could see the sea and could just hear the gentle swishing sound of the waves washing backwards and forwards on the beach. He leaned his elbows on the sill with his chin in his hands. "I've died and gone to heaven," he said out loud.

"Talking to yourself Zak?" came a cheeky voice from his doorway, first sign of madness you know?"

"That right cuz. Know what the second sign of madness is?"

"What?"

"Being cheeky to someone twice your size."

Zak grabbed Rangi in a chin-lock and started grappling him towards the window. Aunty, watering the plants around the pool, looked up startled to see Rangi, screaming blue murder, hanging precariously out of the upstairs window by his feet, which were being held by Zak. She marched over to the window and stood with her hands on her hips glaring up at them. Both boys froze, Rangi staring at her upside down.

"Morning Aunty," said Zak as though nothing were happening.

"Morning Aunty," said Rangi cheerfully as though hanging upside down from an upstairs window was normal morning behaviour for him. He even crossed his arms and whistled a little bit to show how normal it all was. Zak smiled broadly, nodding at her, he even put one hand on his hip in an effort to appear nonchalant and nearly dropped Rangi in the process.

"Zak!" growled his Aunty in a warning voice.

"Yes Aunty, don't worry Aunty, wasn't going to drop him Aunty." He hauled Rangi back into the bedroom and dumped him onto the floor.

The two cousins rolled around on the floor giggling.

Down in the garden their Aunt rolling her eyes and muttering to herself went back to watering the plants, "When's that boy gonna grow up? Huh!"

Their Uncle who had come out to the patio to see what the commotion was, smiled in a slightly perplexed way and shaking his head went back to reading his morning paper.

The two boys ran up the hall bursting into Gypsy's room without knocking.

"Hey sis!" Hey Cuz!" "What you doing sleeping?" "This is paradise man!"

Gypsy sat up rubbing her eyes.

"You'd better behave though," said Zak, "Aunty's in a bad mood this morning, don't know why."

He and Rangi looked at each other and burst out laughing.

"Me behave? That's a joke," Gypsy shot back at them. "You'd better get her back in a good mood if you want to be taken to Rainbow's End, otherwise you just might spend your holiday working in the laundry."

"Ae? What's that?" Zak looked momentarily disconcerted.

"I heard Uncle and Aunty talking last night. They think you're too old to be getting into high-jinks. They think you should have a good job and be contributing to household expenses. I think they might have been having a little chat to Gran. You big egg!"

Zak looked a bit shocked. "Whaaat? Hey I help out on the farm and do chores and stuff, what's their problem? There aren't no jobs back home. Not that I could find anyway." he muttered the last bit a little more quietly.

"Well it wouldn't be so bad would it? Getting into the laundry business? They've made a heap of money over the last twenty years."

Zak looked a bit glum for a minute. "Oh well, hey it's our first day here. There's no way they're gonna make me work today. Let's get out there and enjoy this place." He bounded out of the room and they could hear him thumping his way down the stairs, his cheerful attitude fully restored.

"The eternal optimist," said Rangi, grinning and rolling his eyes. Then turning his attention to Gypsy he asked, "How's it going with you anyway? Seen any more of our little friends?"

"Not exactly."

"What does that mean sis? You either have or you haven't."

"Well," she said reluctantly, "I had another dream. It seemed so real."

"Tell me about it, did you see them in that cool-as room again?"

"No," said Gypsy pulling her feet up and leaning back against the head of the bed with her hands wrapped around her legs. She had on her long white nighty and she tucked it around her feet and legs to keep warm. She gazed into the distance, remembering the vivid dream. "This time it was really different," she said softly. "For a start it was quite dim and I could hear lots of rustling and birds. When my eyes got used to the light I could see I was in a forest. Not bush like the one back home on the farm but more like a jungle. I stood there for a minute with nothing happening. Then I saw them. They were walking along through the trees. They were looking all around them and they looked kind of scared like they'd never seen a forest before. At least the parents looked scared. The little girl, Dayzie, she was looking from left to right so quick I thought her head might come off. I could see she wanted to run off but her Mum had a hold of her. Az looked serious but he looked kind of excited too."

"Something's happened to them," she said turning to Rangi, "I just know they are in danger. I wish I could help them. I just stood there as they walked past. Then something funny happened."

"What happened?" Rangi questioned impatiently.

"The man looked towards me and stopped suddenly. I, I think he saw me."

"Far out, it was just a dream right? Not like that other thing where they were seeing us through some kind of screen. You know, using technology."

"Yeh, but that other time, when I was in the room, I don't think that was just a dream. I think I really was seeing their house and I think I was really there. Maybe I time-travelled in my sleep."

"Well your body didn't. You were right there when we came in, sound asleep. What happened when he saw you?"

"I don't know," she said, a bit grumpily, "that was when you clowns came running in and woke me up."

"Ohhhh, so sorry sis. Well if that's all then let's do like Zak says and get downstairs.

He lifted his head and sniffed. "He-ey I can smell bacon! Quick before that guts Zak eats the lot. Come on."

Rangi raced out the door skidding on the highly polished floor boards in the hall way. He grabbed the banister to turn himself then leapt down the stairs two at a time. Gypsy got up more slowly, dressed herself and looked in the mirror at her hair. It was so tangled. No point in even trying to sort that mess out, she thought grimly. She dragged it back from her face with her fingers and tied it tightly with an elastic band. Downstairs Zak was sitting at the table polishing off a massive mound of bacon, eggs and toast. He looked up at her.

"Cafe Latte?" he said in what was supposed to be a posh voice, airily motioning with his hand towards a steaming cup and saucer in front of him. The effect was slightly ruined by the fact that his mouth was bulging with scrambled eggs and bacon as he said it.

"Aunty's got a coffee machine," he said in his normal voice after a big swallow. Just what I need for a wee morning pick me up. He opened his big eyes as wide as they could go, rolling them from side to side and grinning like a maniac."

122

"Like you really need a pick-me-up," she snorted sitting down and helping herself to bacon and eggs from the plates in the centre of the table.

"Ichs weally mmood shsis." said Rangi his mouth already stuffed with food.

"You said it cuz" said Zak laughing. They high fived each other across the table.

"You don't mean to say you can actually understand what he says when he talks like that do you?" his Aunty asked from the kitchen.

"Sure Aunty," said Zak, "no problem."

"Good morning love," she said to Gypsy, coming over to kiss her on the cheek. "Did you sleep well?"

"Yes thanks Aunty," she said. She hoped Rangi wouldn't say anything about her dream. It was a sensitive subject. She wanted to think about it some more herself before she discussed it with anyone else. She couldn't help feeling these dreams were being given to her for a purpose and that she was meant to do something, but she had no idea what. As Rangi said, if it really was five hundred years in the future, what could she actually do? So she greeted her Aunt cheerfully and tucked into her breakfast.

"Would you like a coffee dear?" Her Aunt asked.

"No thanks Aunty."

"Well how about a hot chocolate then?"

"Ooh yes please."

"Maybe we should do something with this hair when we go into town later," she said stroking her unruly mop.

"Haven't been able to get a comb through it for a while," Gypsy admitted looking embarrassed.

"My hairdresser can work wonders with curly hair, we'll have you looking like Beyoncé in no time. What we need is a girl's day out."

Her Aunty smiled and went back into the kitchen ignoring the boys who had stopped mid-chew.

"...and don't worry boys," she said with her back turned. Your Uncle will make sure you enjoy yourselves today too. No-one's going to make you work on your first day here."

The boys grinned at each other and continued to shovel food into their mouths.

Zak waggled his eyebrows up and down to Rangi with an 'I told you so' look on his face.

—————✦————

Zak and Rangi came home later that day full of excitement about their afternoon at Rainbows End, talking at the top of their voices.

"Woo-wee that was choice! That roller coaster man, that was cool! What about that tower thing where you drop straight down at hundred kilometres an hour? Awwwesome!"

They stopped dead in their tracks as they went into the kitchen and saw a girl with long straight, shiny hair sitting at the table.

"Gypsy?" ventured Rangi, is that you? What happened to your hair?"

"Wow looks cool Gyps," said Zak, "amazing."

"Thanks," Gypsy responded shyly, unused to compliments from her rough and ready cousin.

It had taken hours of washing, untangling and straightening to sort out her mass of tangled curls but the results were worth it, she thought.

"Aunty bought me a straightener so I can keep it looking like this," she said, "they thinned it out too."

Zak looked at her with approval, then moved on to more important things. "What's for dinner Aunty?" He looked over at his Aunt who was in the kitchen stirring a large pot.

"We're having boil-up. Go and get yourselves washed up, it's nearly ready."

Zak and Rangi bolted for the bathroom while their Aunty started dishing up the meal. When they were all seated Zak and Rangi tucked in until they realised no-one else had started.

"We say grace in this house," his Aunty said firmly.

They clasped hands around the table, their Aunt nodding to their Uncle who said a short grace and a blessing on his niece and nephews. Zak and Rangi looked a little bit embarrassed about this, and especially didn't seem to enjoy having to hold hands. They held each other's hands gingerly as though they were snakes about to bite. They quickly let go at the end and concentrated on eating.

"Well I hope you all enjoyed your day today," said Aunty.

"Yes thanks Aunty!" they chorused.

"Good, well tomorrow don't be late getting up because we are all going to church."

Zak looked up with a pained expression on his face. He had been getting out of going to church in the last few years whenever Gran got her religious fit on her. But it seemed as though there would no way out this time.

Rangi groaned then catching his Aunts eye turned it into "....mmmmmm this foods good."

Their Uncle chuckled. "Don't worry boys it's not that bad. Lots of young people there, some pretty girls too."

Zak looked up with interest. "Okay Uncle" he said casually, "we'll give it a go."

After dinner the family went down to the beach. It was a beautiful evening, the sea was calm, reflecting the dim blue of the fading sky.

"It's a great place for swimming here and further out past the bay you can get some pretty good waves if any of you are interested in surfing."

"Yeh! Sounds good Uncle," said Rangi and Zak.

"Gypsy won't want to get that fancy hair-style wet though ae cuz?" laughed Zak yanking on her hair.

Gypsy was very conscious of her new look. Aunty had bought her some nice clothes to go with her new hairstyle so she would have something to wear to church and town.

It must be nice to have money, she thought, but she knew Aunty and Uncle had worked hard so they could enjoy this lifestyle. They hadn't wasted it either as most of her family had in the night clubs and casinos. She was curious about the church too. A bigger version of the one back home with lots of Maori people attending and a Maori preacher. It was based out in South Auckland as this was the area they believed the church was most needed. This area was reputed to have the highest crime rate in the country, yet the church had moved there purposefully. The preacher back home had told her the church had a mission to redeem the Maori people. Thinking about her family, she knew how much this was needed. She was also looking forward to catching up with her other cousins, Aunties, Uncles and extended Whanau but she had no illusions about what their lifestyle was like.

When they arrived at church the atmosphere in the big auditorium was electric. The music was pounding, the people were clapping and singing and raising their hands. The singers on the stage were belting out the songs through microphones. She got caught up in the excitement and clapped along, feeling unselfconscious for a change. She noticed Zak was checking out the chicks till Aunty had him by the ear and sat him between her and Uncle. Beside her Rangi was jiving to the beat as though he just couldn't help himself. She grinned up at her Aunty who was shakin-it-down to the music as good as any of the young ones.

She looked around at the big crowd of people and realised that most of them were of her race. Many of them were young men and women covered in gang tattoos but who had their eyes closed and their arms raised unashamedly praising God. It gave her a buzz to see it.

God must be real, she thought, if He could change the hearts of these tough ex-gang members. There were miracles all around her she realised. She turned back to listen to the preacher with greater respect. He had planted his church in the toughest area of New Zealand because of his love for his people.

Afterwards Aunty introduced her to some of the young people and they invited her to youth group. Sounded like they did lots of singing and dancing and getting up to antics; bit hard for a shy country girl but she wouldn't mind watching.

Too soon their holidays were over and it was time to go back home. They were flying back as Aunty and Uncle had prevailed upon Zak to stay behind. They wanted him to work for them in the laundry and hopefully be a good influence on him. Zak was a bit unsure about it all, but decided it wouldn't be so bad and would be nice to have a bit of money in his pocket.

Gypsy and Rangi weren't going back to Gran's place. The school holidays were over and it was time to go back to Mum's. Gypsy wasn't looking forward to that. She loved her mum but she always seemed to end up with boyfriends who beat her up. She drank like a fish and she wasn't very good at looking after them. Gypsy and Rangi had learned long ago how to look after themselves.

Their first day back home Mum was so pleased to see them she hugged and kissed them both half to death. Alan the new stepdad grinned at them from his armchair showing gaps in his teeth. He had a saggy beer belly and an ever present green bottle in his hand. Mum worked in the mussel factory and he sometimes went to sea. They never seemed to have any money though and the house was always dirty and unkempt. Gypsy knew from experience that if she wanted proper meals she would have to make them herself.

The first week went by pretty well with everyone being polite and anyway she and Rangi were at school most of the day and Mum at work. Alan, or Al as he liked to be called, seemed to sleep a lot and then disappear out in the evenings. Their Mum didn't make any comments about it, she just seemed pleased to spend the time with her kids. Both the children noticed the fading bruises on her face and arms but didn't say anything. It wasn't the first time and they knew their Mum would get mad or lie if they mentioned them.

It was on the weekend a few weeks after they had arrived home that the trouble started. Gypsy and Rangi were in the lounge watching TV about ten in the morning. They had been talking about their holiday and laughing loudly about some of the things Zak had got up to and how Aunty and Uncle had caught him trying to climb out of the window at night several times. Suddenly a bedroom door banged open and Al was standing there in his undies screaming blue murder. He was yelling about how their confounded noise had woken him up. He was swearing and cursing, coming closer and pointing his fat finger threateningly at them. Mum came in then in her nightie and tried to calm him down. He pushed her away so hard she hit the wall.

Rangi jumped up and shouted at him. "Don't you touch my Mum," he yelled, bunching up his skinny fists.

Gypsy froze. Al called Rangi some unsavoury names then raised his own big fist. Mum screamed and stood in front of him between him and Rangi. "No, no" she shrieked, don't hit him."

"Right, you stupid cow, I won't then," he said, and hit her hard in the face. She fell backwards onto Rangi, blood oozing out of her nose.

"Gypsy call the cops," Rangi yelled.

Gypsy leapt up and ran desperately for the door. Al saw her and started to give chase, but he was fat and she was young and quick. She fled out of the door with him yelling after her.

"Don't yah dare!!! I'll kill you and I'll kill ya mum and yer stupid little bruver!!!"

# Chapter 33

The great doors swung open and the family moved uncertainly forward. Ahead was the vast, jungle-like forest and a deafening sound of bird chatter sounded in their ears. The river sparkled in the distance to their left where the trees were less dense. Dazed they felt drawn towards this amazing spectacle as though barely believing it could be real. The light was strong and harsh on their eyes, but they kept moving forwards eagerly, entranced by the sights and sensations.

They walked up a small rise with the jungle to their right and stood looking down on the landscape, transfixed by so much teeming life before them. Birds fluttered above the tree tops, rustling among the trees suggested small animals, and the scintillating smells were overwhelming. They had never before smelt anything other than the clean, sterile air of the City. They couldn't even begin to recognise the earthy, vegetation scents that they could smell and taste in the air here. They had seen trees and rivers before in the history views and experienced simulated smells but nothing prepared them for the real thing. Their senses were jangling with confusion as they tried to assimilate all these new sensations at once. They stood there and looked and looked with wonder until finally Az turned to glance back behind them. As he did he involuntarily gasped with shock. The others swung around to see what was wrong and saw a vast plain with trees dotted around it in the distance. The building they had just come out of was nowhere to be seen.

"What will we do?" wailed Amiria, "it's gone, there's no way back."

Az ran back the way they had come, slowing down as he reached the point where the great gates had been. They watched him walk more and more slowly, then stop and reach out his hand.

"Come and look at this," he yelled over his shoulder.

The others came quickly to where he was standing. "Stretch out your hands and feel here," he prompted. They did as he said and as they reached out their hands they bumped into something hard.

"Marble walls. If you look carefully you can see it," exclaimed Az, "it's still there it's just camouflaged somehow, with some kind of projection I think."

"If we leave here and go into the forest this place will be almost impossible to find," said Petra slowly. Dayzie looked up at him expressions of fear and excitement warring against each other on her face. "Will we have to live in the forest forever?" she asked wonderingly.

They were all silent for a moment.

"It looks as though we may have no choice," said Amiria bravely, "but we must carry on and hope that we can find our way back here in six weeks' time."

"Yeh, that's if they keep their promise about that," sneered Az. "I don't trust them. We've been lied to all our lives."

"Yes but I think the rulers did that because they really did believed it was for the best, for everyone," said Petra in an effort to be fair.

"Yeh," Az said again in the same depreciating tones, "and what if *they* think the best thing would be for us is to lose ourselves in that forest and never come out again?"

"They seemed so genuine" said Amiria, "so, so kind...," she trailed off lamely."

"The kindness is a lie," shouted Az, "they used it to suck us in. They've just learnt it's the best way to control people and make them believe what they want us to believe!"

"You may be right son, but we are wasting time standing here," said Petra firmly. "We chose to leave the City and now we will have to continue making choices to find out how to live in this new world, for at least six weeks, and perhaps more."

Petra gazed helplessly towards the vast forest as the impact of this possibility hit him. They were completely vulnerable without skills or knowledge of how to survive out here.

Petra and Amiria turned together and began walking back towards the point where the river flowed out of the forest. Az walked thoughtfully behind them staring around, taking in every new sight and sound. Dayzie ran ahead. She seemed to have gotten her bounce back, excitement winning out over trepidation in her young mind. She skipped along eyes shining ready to make new discoveries.

"Wait Dayzie," called Amiria, "stay close to us, this world is unpredictable, uncontrolled, it has no, no schedule and we don't know what could happen next. We need to go carefully, don't' we dear?" She looked to Petra for support.

"That's right," said Petra, sternly, looking towards Dayzie, "this place isn't like anywhere you may have visited in the simulator. This is real. Remember when you went to the Zoo simulator? You saw those big grey creatures and those pretty furry ones that had big sharp teeth?"

"Elephants Dad, and...."

"Tigers," supplied Az.

"Yes tigers," she agreed, "they were so nice and soft and pretty, I liked cuddling them."

"Yes but in a simulator they can't hurt you and you can make them do whatever you want them to do," Amiria explained earnestly, "here it's different. Everything is real. You could get hurt."

"Is it just like in the olden days here?" she asked with amazement in her voice.

"Yes, it's a bit like that," said her father, "we don't know what it's like yet but every day will be different, depending on what we find and what choices we make."

"...and who we meet," suggested Az wryly.

"That's true," said Amiria, "there must be others out here too. We must try and find them. They can help us understand how to live in this place. I mean how do we eat when there are no food machines? How will we know if we are healthy or not without diet monitors and schedules?"

"People used to live without those things in the far past, we'll just have to figure it out," said Petra with as much confidence as he could manage. He knew he needed to keep his family calm. Dayzie was young enough to be adaptable and Az's curiosity and teenage craving for adventure would help him. He was mainly concerned about his partner and how she would respond to this strange new situation he had brought her into. He felt responsible. They had both been conditioned to live in a world that was perfectly controlled and safe, but they would now need to start thinking in a whole new way out here in this unknown territory.

They had reached the edge of the forest and were standing near the river bank. They listened to the sounds of running water and gazed at the sparkling river with awe. Birds and brightly coloured butterflies flitted here and there. Amiria stared down at the water, then stepped forward tentatively, stretching the toes of one foot slowly downwards she touched the water. It was cool but refreshing. She sat down on the bank and lowered both feet in. It felt lovely. She could feel the current tugging gently at her legs. She looked up at the others watching her.

"This is amazing, the first time ever, without simulation. Petra," she said mischievously, "I'm going in." Before he could stop her she had pushed herself off the bank and into the water with a splash. It was shallow enough for her feet to touch the bottom. Thanks to the simulator she had a good idea of how to move through the water, but she got a fright when she put her head under and found she couldn't breathe under there. She stood up coughing and laughing at the same time.

Dayzie, flung herself in beside her mother and Az took a running jump the way he had seen the family in the history view do it. He landed with a massive splash beside the girls, sending water washing up and over Petra as he stood on the bank. They were soon enjoying themselves hugely. Jumping, splashing and playing in the water. Petra watched them, pleased they seemed so happy and relaxed. He looked around, keeping himself alert for any dangers. He knew he would have to recall any fact that he had learnt from the history views to help keep his family safe in this strange new environment.

Suddenly Dayzie squealed with surprise and shock. "I saw something in water," she cried pointing.

From his vantage point on the bank, Petra could see a small, shiny creature flitting away through the clear water. Was it dangerous, he wondered? He knew there had been dangerous creatures in the water in times past. He thought they were bigger than that though and he seemed to remember they mostly lived in the seas not the rivers. Amiria and the children climbed out of the river, water dripping from their hair. Their clothes, made from lightweight, floaty fabric, dried very quickly in the warm sunshine. They sat on the bank for a while watching the birds and spotting the occasional fish.

It was Az who asked the next, obvious question.

"What are we going to eat? I have a strange feeling. I'm sure its way past time to eat in the schedule."

"We need to find the other people," said Petra, "they will help us find food. We had better stay by the river though, so we can drink when we need to."

They started walking along the river bank towards the forest.

"Aaaah, it's such a lovely place," breathed Amiria as they entered the shade of the trees.

They walked in silence through the trees and the ferns. Every now and then Dayzie would run to look at and touch a new discovery.

"Look at that big flower, it smells nice too. Look at that little green creature on the log, what funny legs it has, and its eyes stick out like buttons," she chattered. "Look at this," she yelled excitedly behind her to the others.

"What is it?" Amiria asked with interest as she approached. It was a tiny black creature with a round body and eight long, hinged legs sticking up and out from its sides but bent in angles so they stuck up higher than its head. It was sitting in a fragile looking net attached by strands between the branches of a tree. It sat very still as they studied it, till Az came up behind them, stretched out his finger and gave it a gentle poke. The creature came suddenly to life scuttling away in fright. They watched fascinated as it jumpily worked its eight, jointed legs to climb upwards towards the overhanging tree branches. It was such a comical sight that they found themselves giggling as they watched it. After that the family continued on, walking more slowly through the trees and really beginning to enjoy their surroundings.

Dayzie ran back and forth, here and there, looking under every leaf and behind every bush making new findings all the time. She was amazed at the sheer number of living creatures she found from tiny crawling caterpillars, flying insects, little furry animals that peeked out at her shyly from the foliage, to large, pink birds that flew over the river emitting weird cronking cries.

Az stared fascinated around him, stopping every now and then to examine things more closely or to poke at them with a stick. Petra and Amiria walked a little way behind hand in hand with dazed looks on their faces staring all around them. Flocks of startled birds flew up squawking in fluttery clouds as they walked by. Tiny creatures with fuzzy looking bodies buzzed around them, bouncing from flower to flower. They had to keep reminding themselves it was all really, really real. To the City family it was as though an ancient story had come alive and they were walking dream-like through its pages.

Petra gasped. He had seen an even stranger sight very briefly through the trees.

"What did you see?" questioned Amiria seeing his surprised look.

"I thought I saw a girl. That girl Gypsy form the viewer, just for a moment, there through the trees." He pointed and Amiria stared and stared but couldn't see anything. The children up ahead were busily exploring and hadn't noticed anything.

"This is a strange place," shuddered Amiria, how could you have seen something out of a viewer?"

"Everything here is like something out of a viewer," Petra pointed out.

"That's true," Amiria admitted, "but that girl was from the far past. How could she possibly be here?"

"How can we view the far past?" Petra questioned, "Maybe the past and the future are connected in ways we don't understand. For us, who have been brought up in a world that is half simulated, half reality how can we ever tell what's real and what isn't?"

Just then they noticed that Dayzie had stopped suddenly in her tracks. "What's that?" she asked looking down at the ground at something. In front of her was a round, brown substance with a strong unpleasant odour emitting from it.

"Poooh Dad can you turn off the smell please, it's really stinky?" she looked hopefully up at her father.

"You can't turn smells off here love," he smiled at her. "Try holding your nose shut, like this." He pinched his nostrils.

"Dabs bedda," she said holding her little nose as tightly as she could.

"Walk around it," said her mother cautiously, "remember everything's real here."

She spoke too late, Dayzie's curiosity had caused her to plant her foot right into it. She slipped in the wet, soft substance and fell over landing with a splat right on top of it.

"Oh, and there are no clean-up robots here either," sighed Amiria regretfully, "I will miss those."

It took them a fair while to wash Dayzie clean in the river and even then the smell didn't completely disappear.

"I think I know what that was," said Az when they were once more walking through the forest.

"It was manure. Like cows manure, only much, much bigger. I guess it came from an animal much bigger than a cow. Look at those round marks on the ground," he said suddenly, noticing them, "what do you think they are?"

"Could they have been made by some creature's feet?" asked Amiria curiously.

"Elephants!" shouted Dayzie. "My favourite! They are large and grey, with big flappy ears and a tiny tail. They have feet with no toes but with toenails in them!"

"Really dear, that's interesting," said her mother wondering at her knowledgeable daughter.

"Acne told me. I wonder where he is. Why didn't he come with us Mum?"

"Well, when we escaped the city, we had to leave them behind or they would have told the Central Computer System where we were and what we were doing. Did Acne say if elephants are dangerous or not?"

"Nooo," she shook her head uncertainly "but I don't think they are. I like them."

"You've got to remember the animals here aren't simulated, they won't behave in just the way you want them to," Amiria reminded her.

In spite of these warnings Dayzie was pulling harder and harder to get away from the hold her mother had on her. Finally with a sudden yank she broke free and bounded off.

"I'm following the tracks, I'm going to find the elephant!" she shouted.

She quickly disappeared into the jungle. The other three shouted after her to wait, but she soon disappeared from their view amongst the thick bushes and trees.

# Chapter 34

Petra, Amiria and Az broke into a run, frantically dodging around trees, keeping the river on their left, following the tracks as they tried to catch up with Dayzie. All of a sudden they broke out from amongst the trees and into a clearing, and in the clearing were people.

They stood staring at a scene such as they could never have imagined. There were about twenty people in the clearing sitting or standing around great smoking fires. Some of them were watching over some huge lumps of a brown substance stuck onto sharpened sticks as they cooked over the fires. Liquid was oozing from these lumps and dripping into the fires with hissing noises. The smells that assaulted them were very rich, and unlike any food they had smelt before. The people were all dressed in green and brown clothes appearing rough and handmade compared to their own exquisite garments. As they stood there gaping people began to notice them. Some stood up as though they were considering if they might be a threat. Others just sat and stared with undisguised fascination and maybe a little contempt.

Suddenly there was a noise from a tree overhead and a man jumped down onto the ground before them. If they had known who Robin Hood was they might have mistaken this man for him. His green attire looked as though it was made from woven grass from up close. He wore brown soft looking shoes which were sown with large stitches. He had a short brown beard and moustache. He was chewing on a straw and looking at them with his arms folded. He was of average height but solidly built and strong looking.

"Well, who do we have here?" He grinned at them, spitting out bits of straw. "Newbies!"

Two other men jumped up from the fire and came over to stand one on either side of him and to grin at them as well.

"I do so love newbies," said one, "they're so much fun, so entertaining."

"So useless you mean," said the other scowling, "they don't know nothing, not how to cook, or hunt or build or anything. What did you do for a job back there in that holy city," he asked sarcastically addressing himself to Petra.

"I was an architect," said Petra as calmly as he could. He was wondering how he was going to safeguard his family from these people if he needed to.

"Oh you were, were ya? So you can show us how to make our huts real pretty then?" he sneered.

"And what about you love, what's your special talent?" he leered at Amiria.

"Interior designer," she replied in a small voice.

There was a grim silence from the men for a moment.

"Talk about useless," the man spat out, disgusted.

"At least they are fit and healthy," commented the Robin Hood character, "that's one thing you can say about the City, they do feed them well and make them exercise."

"I was being trained as an engineer," volunteered Az.

"Were you really? Well that actually might be useful." The men began to look at him with interest.

"We're looking for our daughter," Amiria spoke up, "have you seen her?"

The man didn't answer but gestured to the left with his thumb.

Looking the way he indicated Petra and Amiria, gasped with astonishment. There was Dayzie perched on top of an elephant! The elephant was feeding on a pile of freshly cut long grass. It didn't seem to be bothered by the small child on its back.

Dayzie saw them and squealed happily, "look Mum, Dad, Az, its real, it's really, really real!"

Amiria stepped forward anxiously with her arms out towards Dayzie, but the man stopped her gently enough. "Don't worry love, she'll be fine. Tame as a cat is that one. She's our pride and joy, she is. Does all our heavy lifting. No robots out here you know.

"Now," he said moving around them and looking them up and down, "let's get to know each other. I'm Jax, and this," he indicated the smaller, stockier man with dark curling hair and beard, "is Tama and this over here," he indicated the man on his right, "is Zi." Zi nodded and smiled, giving Amiria a special smile and a wink. He was a broad, brown-skinned man with bulging arm muscles.

Petra and Amiria smiled in greeting to each one trying not to notice the strange and unpleasant odours.

"What's the matter?" growled Tama "why are you pulling those funny faces?

"Ohhhh" said Amiria, her revulsion at the stench overcoming her desire to be polite, "what on earth is that terrible smell?"

The three men threw back their heads and laughed, slapping each other on the backs.

"I think it might be our manly aroma that she's referring to," laughed Jax. "That's how you're going to smell in a week or two," he grinned, "a bit of hard work and no soap and you'll smell ex-actly the same. Now, let's get down to business," continued Jax in a more serious tone. He seemed to be the leader and the others obviously looked to him for cues. "Let's all of us sit down around the fire, we'll give you your first meal for free and then we'll have to see where you're going to fit in."

They sat down self-consciously with the other people around one of the massive fires. A large lady with a mass of black hair with little bits of stick in it moved along the log she was sitting on to make room for them. Amiria sat down trying to smile in a friendly fashion but her eyes were soon watering with the smoke from the fire. She gazed fascinated at the lump of whatever it was roasting balanced on a wooden structure that held the hand-whittled skewer. It looked unappetising but smelt surprisingly good. She felt her mouth watering and realised how incredibly hungry she was. Hunger was a new sensation for Amiria as it was for the rest of her family. She usually felt a little hungry in the mornings but this was different, it was as though she had a pain in her stomach. The women she was sitting next to was squinting at her quite closely. Amiria turned towards her and got a close-up view of her face. She was astonished by how very dirty and wrinkled it was. She knew her own face was perfectly smooth. The woman's eyes were dark and she had shaggy eyebrows. They both seemed quite mesmerised with the other.

"First time we've seen a newbie for a while," the woman finally said in a rough voice, turning back to watch the roasting lump. Looking around Amiria also noticed how brown the skin of all the other forest people was. She looked down at her own white, soft hands.

"I'm Betz," said the woman turning back to her. "You're so soft and white and clean looking," she sniffed at her, "and clean smelling," she added as though amused. "That won't last though," she chuckled, "you'll have to work out here."

"Of course," said Amiria nervously, "we'll do whatever we can to help with Production."

Petra and Az were deep in conversation with Jax. Dayzie was still talking to her elephant friend. It seemed to Amiria that hours passed before the food was finally ready. Each person was given a large leaf with a slice of the brown stuff on it. The family sat around the fires, eating the food, which tasted pretty good. It was a bit stringy, but moist and filling. There was fruit as well, bananas and oranges and some other types of fruit they couldn't recognise. They had no idea how to skin and eat the fruit as food had always come to them in a fully prepared, easily digestible form in the City. The forest people were very much entertained watching them trying to figure it out.

First they tried biting directly into the skins. The bad taste and un-chewable-ness of this method warned them this was not the right way to do it. Next they tried breaking them open by bashing them on rocks or squeezing them between their two hands. This lead to squashed bananas oozing through their fingers and busted oranges squirting juice in their faces and on their clothes. They had better luck with the plums though they were not expecting to find hard stones in the centres till their teeth hit against them. Soon their hands and faces were stained with purple juice.

After they had had a good long laugh, some of the forest people took pity on them and showed them how to peel and eat the fruit. The tastes and textures were a whole new experience for the family and they pulled alternatively comically disgusted and pleasantly surprised faces as they experienced sour and sweet tastes. In the end they were very sticky with their previously spotless clothes spattered with various colours from the juices. They looked a little like a family of baboons on a picnic, with peels lying around them and smears on their faces. Some of the people from the Forest Community were actually rolling around on the ground holding their stomachs as they laughed uncontrollably at the spectacle. The City family looked at the state each other was in and couldn't help but join in the hilarity.

As darkness fell it became hard to see by the light of the dying fires. They gazed up entranced at the bright sparkling stars which they had never seen this clearly before.

"Mum," guess what?" Az whispered in Amiria's ear.

"What is it?" asked Amiria.

"I think we've been eating elephant."

"What? What makes you think that?"

He pointed to Betz who had pulled up a big grey blanket up around her.

"No, it couldn't be," Amiria was horrified.

Az pointed down.

At the bottom of the blanket was a short tail with tufty bits on the end. Amiria suddenly felt a strange, very unpleasant feeling. Abruptly the contents of her stomach flew up her throat and splashed onto the grass in front of her. The whole camp roared with laughter.

"What's the matter newbie," someone shouted, "elephant meat don't agree with ya? Ha, ha, ha!"

The City family had never seen or experienced vomit before, but even Dayzie, with her insatiable desire to know things, did not venture nearer to examine it. Amiria, white and shaken was convinced she had contracted a terrible disease, just as the people from long ago used to die of. She couldn't understand why people found it so funny and didn't seem at all concerned about her. Betz took pity on her and kindly patted her on the knee where she sat huddled under a tree with Petra sitting nearby with concern written all over his face.

"Don't worry, luv," she comforted her, "it's nothing to worry about, likely our food doesn't agree with you. You'll feel better soon." She nodded reassuringly then went back to sit by the fire again with the others who were still smiling in amusement.

That night the family was very thankful to whatever elephant had given up its skin to be their blanket. They huddled together under it on the grass beneath the trees. Some of the forest people slept by the dying fires while others had rough huts or tree houses to sleep in but no-one offered to take them in. Previously having always slept in perfectly comfortable beds, with temperatures that were exactingly controlled, sleeping on the ground under a skin was the most excruciatingly uncomfortable experience of their entire lives. They eventually fell asleep but woke up the next morning very stiff and sore.

When they awoke it was to the sounds of the forest people packing up their belongings. This was a hunting trip Jax had told them the night before. They used these makeshift huts whenever they came this way.

"It's a fair walk back to the community," Jax informed them cheerfully, "the little one can ride old Nelly if she likes." He lifted Dayzie up onto the elephant's back and the whole party set off.

Jax seemed a genuine character and trustworthy enough although, like the others, he enjoyed having his fun at their expense.

The City family got up, trying to manage their unusual feelings of pain and weariness. They knew they had no choice but to follow these people and to trust them, without them they would be lost and helpless. This would mean travelling further and further away from the City, the only home they had ever known and without any idea if it would be at all possible to go back there.

# Chapter 35

They walked through the trees and tangled undergrowth for many hours. Although the City family was fit and healthy which enabled them to keep up with the others, the heat and the lack of their regular nutritious meals wore on them. As they were under the shade of the trees at this stage of the journey they were at least protected from the effects of the intense brightness of the sunlight.

Used to strict schedules and organised activities, the seemingly random way the forest people walked and chatted and rested was puzzling to them. Part way through the journey they witnessed an argument between two men about who was carrying the heaviest load. Their disagreement became so heated that the men dropped what they were carrying to stop and shout into each other's faces threateningly. It looked as though it could turn to violence and the City family, minus Dayzie who was ahead still riding the elephant, were cowering away unused to this kind of scene.

When Jax saw what was happening he jumped in.

"Settle down boys," he commanded the rough looking men, "stop acting like big babies and get it sorted out. Come on shake hands," he growled when they still stubbornly stood glaring at each other.

Suddenly, to the City family's surprise the two tough-looking men broke into big grins which made their sun-burned faces look boyish. They shook hands in a comradely way.

"Here, gimme that sack, I'll carry some of yours if it will stop your whingeing," one of them said still grinning. They both laughed and continued their journey side by side, best of mates leaving the City family staring after them in bewilderment.

Jax watched the big men walking away companionably then glanced over at them. He seemed a little embarrassed as he said, "there's a lot of this kind of thing going on out here and it's not always resolved so easily. People disagree and argue about the most ridiculously small things. We don't want to enforce a whole lot of rules and regulations because we don't want to end up like those controlling rulers in the City. The trouble is without rules there is no order. What we really need," he added after a moment's thought, "is a way of changing people from the inside, not brain washing but a real change of heart." He shrugged his shoulders, "but how could that ever be possible?" He shook his head a little wearily then followed on after the others leaving the City family to trail behind whispering amongst themselves.

"How do they manage out here without rules and instructions?" Amiria questioned in a low voice.

"Those two looked as though they were going to become violent at any moment," Petra whispered back, "this is like the old days."

Az was thinking hard. "I once saw something in a history view that reminds me of this. People were buying and selling in the ancient market places where you had to give someone something to get what you wanted. The seller would mention an amount, the buyer would say no and mention another amount and even though they disagreed, they kept talking. We may have to learn to do that. Bartering I think they called it. You just have to keep talking until you can agree."

"I don't think I can do that," said Amiria quietly her eyes directed nervously towards the lumbering figures of the forest men.

"I think bartering only works with people who want to come to an agreement," Petra stated in a matter of fact manner, "but it is still a good idea," he added encouragingly seeing Az's disappointed face, "we should definitely learn how to do that here, I think it will help us a lot."

They continued to walk for several weary hours. Dayzie happily astride the elephant was gazing around and up into the thick trees above them. Every now and then the elephant would reach up with its trunk and snatch at the overgrowth. She would then playfully flick the leaves backwards over her massive shoulders showering Dayzie with them. Dayzie thought this was a great joke. A long time later Amiria noticed Dayzie was lying face down along Nelly's broad back, fast asleep.

Finally they came across an open, stony clearing near a loop in the river. Here they sat down gratefully on a group of large, scattered boulders to rest. The elephant with Dayzie still on its back waded into the cool, green water and began sucking it up with its long trunk. The great beast squirted fountains of cooling water up into the air drenching Dayzie who woke up suddenly shrieking with laughter. Amiria was sitting watching her as she gratefully rested on a large smooth stone. Suddenly she squealed and jerked into motion as something brightly coloured fluttered into her face. It was a large, orange and brown coloured butterfly. She fell backwards, screeching in fright, landing on her back amongst the long grass. As she stared upward, confused, the delicate butterfly dipped down and landed neatly on her nose. Cross-eyed she had a close up view of its bulging eyes and long curling antennae. She let out another terrified shriek while the forest dwellers hooted with laughter at her antics and Petra and Az both came hurrying to her rescue.

"You wait you haven't seen nothing yet. Wait till you come across them bugs that bite and sting then we'll see some jumping, ha, ha," chuckled one of the men. His big brown face was wrinkled up in a crinkly grin, his sparkly, green eyes, full of fun.

Jax chuckled along with the others then standing up indicated it was time to continue their journey.

"Time to move on," he said mobilising the group, who heaved themselves up, picking up their belongings to continue their trudge through the trees. Nelly had to be coerced out of the cool river water to follow them with a patient plod of her massive feet.

They walked for many more hours till finally the trees began to thin and they came out into a wide-open, grassy hill-country. In the far distance they could just see the curly lines of smoke winding towards the sky. As the family stood gazing down on the landscape Tama came up beside them.

"Our village is just behind those hills there, welcome to your new life," he said with a mocking tone in his voice. Then he started the rapid decent down the grassy hillside.

"Does that mean we can't ever go back?" whispered Amiria.

The four looked at each other for a moment.

"We have no choice but to carry on" said Petra. Maybe in six weeks' time we can ask for a guide to take us back to the gates. In the meantime, we need these people to help us to …" he didn't know a word for survive so he finally said, "… to stay healthy."

# Chapter 36

As they began the descent they moved out from under the thick canopy of the trees and out into the open country where they began to feel the effects the suns unusual heat and brightness. It hurt their eyes that were so used to soft lightening and after a short time they noticed their pale skin beginning to redden and sting.

"What is it?" sobbed Dayzie with tears in her eyes looking at the redness all over her arms. She had never experienced a day of sickness or pain in her life before.

"Is it skin cancer?" said Az.

"Not cancer dum-dum, sunburn," said a cheeky voice behind him.

Az turned around to see one of the younger forest dwellers. He was slim with curly dark hair and skin wearing the usual homemade Robin-hood style green and brown stitched clothing.

Az was embarrassed, knowing that in this world he was ignorant of many, many things.

"Is it dangerous? It hurts."

"That's because you're so pasty white, you City dwellers haven't ever been out in the sunshine before have you?"

"The sun wasn't nearly so bright or hot over the City, I don't know why."

"That's because you didn't know you were fenced in. They say it's to protect you from the sun's harmful rays and the wind and rain, but what they didn't tell you is that it's also to keep you from escaping."

"Why would they do that?" Az asked, sounding frustrated.

"Because they're control freaks. Think they know what's best for you and won't let anyone decide anything for themselves. I prefer freedom, out here where you can feel the wind and the sun on your face and where you could get killed at any time by a wild animal. Adventure that's what I like! Never knowing what will come next, fighting for survival!" The boy strutted along with his chest thrust out as though ready to take on anything that that might dare attack him.

Az looked sideways at this young man. He had a feeling that he was not quite as brave as he pretended but he was liking him anyway.

"I'm Az," he said, "I would really like to learn more about your world. It sounds amazing to live like that."

"I'm Tripp, and I will be pleased to be your guide." He took off his hat and swept him a courtly bow. He continued to walk beside him, chewing on a piece of straw and looking quite pleased with himself. He started pointing things out as they walked along.

"See those mountains in the distance? Beyond them is the Great Sea. There's nothing out there except sea forever. Back that way there's the flatlands and of course the City. Where we're headed is the hill country which is the best place to live. Plenty of streams with fish, birds and other animals and good soil for crops, though things have been a little dry lately. He looked sideways at Az with a slightly annoyed expression that Az couldn't understand.

Was he blaming him for it being dry somehow? Az thought, slightly puzzled.

"There's a few different communities around like ours," Trip continued, "and we meet up every now and then to swop information. That's important that is. Anyone who knows something that will help the community is given special privileges. Everyone gets a chance to talk."

"That's interesting," said Az "aren't there any other lands over the sea? We were told there was a giant forest far across the sea used for producing air for the City."

"Another big fib" said Tripp shaking his head. "There aren't any other lands across the sea. There was once. But that was before the great quake. Didn't they tell you about that?"

Az shook his head.

"Most of the land disappeared under the sea," continued Tripp knowingly, "and this piece here was heaved up to make one large land mass. It used to be a little country made up of two islands if legend is true. All of these freaky animals that are wandering around in the forest are descended from animals in their zoos. That's where they locked up animals from around the world so people could come and look at them," Tripp began to explain.

"I know what zoos are," Az interrupted quickly, in a hurry to show that he wasn't completely ignorant about everything.

"Most people didn't survive the quake," Tripp continued. They were about to blow each other up anyway by the sounds of it," he chuckled. "We talk a lot about those days to try and make sure we don't make the same mistakes. If you've got any good ideas, make sure you say something, it will really help you fit in."

Az deliberated over this new information. The Information Givers had not mentioned a quake. Why was that? I guess they think they have a right to control what information they give us and what they withhold, he thought grumpily. A sudden memory of the white-haired old lady's face came back to him her face determined but fearful. 'We rebuilt from the dirt and the ashes,' she had said. Was she talking about the quake? Why wouldn't she mention it? I'll bet it freaks them out that they can't control earthquakes, he guessed, pleased with the idea.

It was getting late in the day by the time they came near the little village. It consisted of simple huts amongst the trees, with a river flowing nearby. Great fires were burning in the central area, and delicious cooking smells wafted up to them.

"Look! Look!" shouted Dayzie. She was looking up at the sky.

The sky was on fire with the pinks and oranges of a brilliant and breathtakingly beautiful sunset stretched across the wide expanse of the sky. The colours blazed like the paintings that adorned their City, but alive, moving and changing. The sight was so much brighter and clearer than it could ever have been from the City confined within its luminous boundaries. They stood with eyes transfixed on the sky mesmerised by the heaped up pink, cotton-candy clouds, the blazing orange embers of the sinking sun near the horizon and the dazzling rays of burning honey-gold that were flung up into the sky sending explosions of heavenly sensations within them, stirring harmonies of feeling deep within their beings.

As the colours in the sky began to soften and diminish the family looked around startled to realise they were being left behind. The others had already descended to the village and they could hear the people calling out greetings to them. They followed feeling self-conscious as they walked up the central path between the houses. People stared at them, some laughed, presumably at their bright pink skin and strange clothing. Soon they were enclosed in a circle of curious people. Brown faces, many with brown eyes but some with green or even bright blue eyes, stared at them. Then a woman pushed her way through to them. She had long dark hair and looked a little older than Amiria.

"Hello City dwellers, I'm Laney, you look as pink as lobsters," she grinned, "let's get you something for that sunburn."

She led them to a house that looked as though it were made of mud and straw, taking them in through the low doorway. Inside it was dim but they could just see it had simple furniture made out of logs; a table, a bench and a ladder leading to a loft overhead.

Laney began rummaging in a wooden box. "Here we are." She brought out a pot with some green looking mixture inside. She motioned them to sit and began to gently rub the creamy substance into their skin. It felt cool and refreshing and seemed to lessen the sting.

"Thank you so much," said Petra. "This is all so strange for us, we don't know how to live in this world. It's so different from the City."

"Don't worry you'll soon learn. Humans have a way of working things out. There are others here you know, who used to live in the City," she said quietly. She had her head bowed as she gently applied the ointment to Dayzie's painful skin but something triggered Amiria to have a flash of insight.

"You? Did you used to live there?" she asked excitedly.

Laney nodded slowly, not looking up from applying the lotion. "I was a child when we escaped, but I remember life there. My mother got me out."

Laney looked so sad they felt they couldn't ask any further questions although they were desperately curious.

When Laney looked up again she was controlled but there were tears on her face. "My mother died, she couldn't adjust to life out here."

Amiria didn't know how to respond to her grief. It was Petra who understood the best.

"I have lost people too, a partner and children, it was…," he struggled to express himself, he had no words for pain, sadness or loss.

He and Laney looked at each other sharing a brief moment of grief.

"Do all the people who disappear from the City end up out here?" Az queried.

"Who knows," Laney shrugged, "maybe they are all out here somewhere, wandering around or have been eaten by the wild animals. Maybe the rulers send them off early to their funerals, who knows? They think they're God those rulers do," she finished with a scowl.

"What's God?" asked Az instantly curious.

Laney looked at him, then laughed. "You tell me. No-one knows, do they? God is supposed to be the one who made the world and us and is in charge of everything. Like some kind of great powerful being that we can't see."

Az looked thoughtful, he was thinking about something Gypsy had said.

"Anyway," continued Laney, "those rulers think they know what's best for everyone but they forget something important about humans."

"What's that?" Petra and Az asked together.

"Dreams," said Laney, straightening up with her hands on her hips. "People need to dream and to have hopes, otherwise they aren't really alive are they? Dreams are a way of envisaging and creating the future. They have taken that away from people so that they have become like compliant dolls; immature and shallow. It's because of that, the way people need to dream that makes us think, maybe there is a God somewhere."

The City family listened to Laney with an interest as new concepts flooded their minds.

"Now I know why we loved the history views so much," said Amiria after pondering these new ideas for a while, "it was always different, always changing. Our future in the City was always the same and we didn't have to think about it because it was all worked out for us. The past was the only way we could dream of something different, something new and with people who were making their lives happen every day by the decisions they made."

"Some of those decisions were very bad decisions remember," said Petra reminded her cautiously.

"Yes but even making bad decisions that hurt us would be so much better than feeling safe all the time and having no dreams for the future." Her eyes were shining, she looked animated as this realisation came to her.

Petra looking at her sitting there with her sunburnt skin, her long hair hanging down, loose and natural around her shoulders, her eyes gazing into the unknown thought he had never seen her look more beautiful. He gently touched the tender skin on her arm. "Are you sure it's worth it darling, the pain and the uncertainty?"

She looked at him steadily. "I know now this is what I want, no matter how hard it is. I can't go back to not thinking or hoping or dreaming. As Laney says without dreams it's not really living at all. I feel alive as I never have before. I also feel scared," she faltered, "but I just can't give this up and go back and pretend, let other people choose for me and let someone else tell me how to live. I can't Petra." she said looked up at him entreatingly.

He hugged her. "I feel the same but I needed to let you make your own choice, otherwise I would be just like them, those 'Dream Stealers.'"

# Chapter 37

As they sat around the fire that evening, Amiria looked around at the people wondering about them and their lives. She noticed a young woman about her own age sitting nearly opposite her. She was wearing a long brown dress and had bare feet. Her hair was long, curling and dark but most noticeable was her massive swollen belly. She was chatting away to different ones near her and didn't appear to be sick but Amiria noticed her holding her belly and grimacing every now and then.

"What's wrong with that woman?" she asked Betz who was sitting nearest to her.

"Oh she's fine," Betz replied with a wave of dismissal, "her baby is due soon that's all."

"Her baby?" asked Amiria "but why is her belly so big, is she sick?"

"No, she's not sick," Betz looked at her in bemusement, "she's about to have a baby."

When Amiria still stared at her. Betz gestured towards Az and Dayzie, "these are your children aren't they?"

"Yes they are, mine and Petra's."

"Well then you must have been pregnant and given birth."

"I don't know what those words mean?" Amiria sounded confused. "When it was time for us to begin parenting we were given Az. Then later Dayzie was brought to us. They were seven years old when we first met them," Amiria explained as Betz stared at her without speaking. "Dayzie has just come to us recently. All of the babies are cared for in the Preparation centre of course." Amiria stopped talking as she realised how little she really knew about the Preparation process other than her own vague memories.

"Wow," Betz's eyes were wide with astonishment, "I knew that the City was into controlling people but that is amazing."

Amiria suddenly realised everyone had stopped talking and was listening in.

"Her baby is growing inside her," explained Betz, "when the time is right the baby will be born. That's the natural way."

"But, but, how did it get in there?" asked Amiria feeling distressed at this new way of producing children.

The whole group erupted into raucous laughter.

Jax could be heard shouting "who would like to tell the newbies about the birds and the bees?"

"I know what birds are," said Amiria indignantly during a lull in the laughter, "but, what are bees?"

The laughter erupted again, louder than before and it took a while for it to quieten down. Amiria didn't know what she had said that was so funny but she found herself suddenly giggling along with them anyway.

Then Jax stood up. "Thank you to the newbies for the entertainment. Now we must turn to more serious matters. Let's bring issues, complaints and solutions to the conference. Who will speak first?"

A youngish man stood up a little nervously, doffing his cap as he did so. His wife was sitting near him with three very young children huddled around her. All of the children had thick curly hair and large brown eyes. Dayzie staring at them from her place on a large log near the fire, thought how much they reminded her of Gypsy.

The man cleared his throat, "We have had very little rain and the crops are drying up. I am fearful we will lose the harvest if we don't get rain soon."

"It's because of the City siphoning off the clouds for their sky gardens!" shouted an older, scrawny-looking man. "They don't care if we starve due to crop failure!" He had white stubble on his chin, and as he shouted spittle flew from his mouth.

There was some angry muttering of agreement amongst the people.

"There's enough water in the river," Zi called out, "we just need to find a way of getting it to the harvest."

"True" said Jax, "but it seems an impossible task. We can't carry water back and forth it would take us all day and night."

Az was sitting listening intently to this exchange with his elbows on his knees and his head in his hands, thinking hard, remembering some of his studies. Suddenly he lifted up his head. "I know how," he said loudly.

Everyone turned to look at him. Some smiled expecting more entertainment.

"Long ago water was fed through pipes to water fields that were dry."

"What are pipes young fella?" said Jax.

"Big hollow tubes, if you put one end in the river upstream the water will flow through the pipe and onto the field."

"Interesting," said Jax, "but how do we make these pipes, can we use hollow trees?"

Az thought for a minute. "Maybe you could divert the river by digging ditches for the water to flow along. The force of the river current would move the water along them and then you could stop the flow when the field was watered. You could use gates to open and close the flow. Or even better we could build a dam," he suggested enthusiastically, that way we can store the water for when we need it.

"Yes and I could help you design it," said Petra.

"And I expect your misses will help you paint it a pretty colour," called out a women from the far side of the fire. The group laughed again but Jax shushed them with his hands.

"I like the way you think boy. Those are some interesting ideas, and we always welcome new ideas. We must think more on this. Everyone put your minds to work and we'll see if it can be done," he announced to the whole company.

Some of the people were now staring at Az and his family with interest and approval.

"Anything else that needs to be brought up?" Jax asked looking around.

A women stood up. Her hair was greying and she had a worn, worried face. "We have had more trouble with the men who live in the caves. They have been hanging around the crops, helping themselves and harassing the young women. My daughter was attacked by one. The men in the field chased him and he ran, but I know they'll be back. They must be getting hungry."

"They should find their own food not take what others have worked for," someone called out angrily.

"We can't keep letting this happen, they are taking our animals as well, it won't be long before one of our daughters disappears," another shouted.

Tama stood up. He flexed his muscles, looking grim faced. "We must hunt them like animals and kill them, nothing else will stop them."

There were gasps around the fire at this pronouncement and then a silence as they waited for Jax to respond.

"If we kill some of them," Jax said slowly, "will not the others come after us to kill in return? Is there another way?"

"Talk to them negotiate," suggested a woman, "offer them a share of the harvest if they will work for us in the fields."

"They won't listen, they will steal our daughters and our food if you bring them here," another countered. Loud arguments broke out all over.

Jax came closer to the City family. "Unfortunately this is often how things happen here. We just cannot agree. If only we had someone wiser than me to guide us," he said sadly.

Suddenly he looked up staring out beyond the fire, then gasped in astonishment. "Who's that," he called, "who's there?" He jumped up and out of the circle running towards something, then stopped.

"What is it? What did you see?" the others asked him.

"I saw a shimmering shape, a girl, long hair, big dark eyes, wearing a long white dress, but she disappeared."

"Who was she? Where has she gone?" The people sounded frightened, staring behind them into the darkness.

In the silence that followed a small voice spoke out. It was Dayzie. She said, "I know who it was. It was Gypsy."

Many questions followed Dayzie's statement but none that the forest dwellers could really understand. All they knew was that Gypsy was from the past and had appeared to the children before. They could not understand what viewers were but they were excited and hoped to see her again. They believed she had been sent to help them, maybe from God.

Each night round the conference fire Jax would begin by saying, "Gypsy, child of the past, appear to us and speak wisdom to us," but night after night there was no response.

# Chapter 38

Months passed and still the visions of the girl, Gypsy were not seen again. The weather became colder with a chill in the winds. Although cold it was dry, without the usual wintery showers the Forest people relied on for their crops and water supply. Petra, Amiria and the children had changed during these months. They had become as brown as any of the Forest people and Petra and Az had developed muscular arms from working in the fields. Daisy's face was covered in freckles and she looked healthy and happy in this new life.

Amiria, now dressed in forest dwellers clothes that she had helped make herself, looked tired but content. Her belly had a small bulge in it. Sometimes she could feel the baby moving inside her. It was a strange and fascinating sensation. She was both shocked and intrigued by what was happening to her. She had learnt a lot about pregnancy and birth from the other women. She had heard a birth taking place not long after their first conference; there seemed to be a lot of screaming going on. Afterwards she had visited the mother and baby and when she saw the look on the mothers face as she held her child it had brought tears to her eyes. It had given her a deep ache of longing.

Az and Petra helped design and build a water system to divert water from the river to the crops and in doing so had earned acceptance and status within the small community. Going back to the City was not even discussed amongst them now. Even though this life was difficult, somehow it was satisfying too. They had to work hard and think hard. They felt sadness, anger, happiness and love in a way they could never have felt before within the confines of the City. There were numerous challenges to life amongst the forest dwelling community. Now after many weeks without rain the river was now becoming so low that the irrigation system no longer worked. That night at the conference the grumbling about the City was louder than ever.

Jax stood up looking serious. "It's time we stopped grumbling about this problem and took some action. I propose a trip to the Sky Gardens," he told the group earnestly.

"Why," complained one of the older men, "how will that help? You can't get up to them you know. I went there once when I was younger. The gardens are on huge curving poles that stand up in the sky about one hundred metres up. Those poles are as slippery as eels. You can't get a grip on them."

"I know that, Earl," sighed Jax, "but we would be better able to find a solution if we went there to consider the problem. May be we can find a way of getting to all that food."

"Yeh," shouted a young women, 'they steal our rain, we steal their food!"

There were roars of approval from the people gathered around the fires.

"All right then," said Jax. "Who's with me? I only want a small party of people who are thinkers and who are young and strong enough to carry out a plan when we've come up with one."

There was a space of silence as people looked down or around at the others, then they all started coming up with excuses.

"My backs been killing me these past few years...."

"....not as young as I used to be...."

".... It's a long walk to those sky gardens and my shoes are worn out...."

"......someone's got to stay behind, that will be the most dangerous job with those caves dwellers hanging around..."

Jax gazed around in disgust and shook his head. "What are you lot so scared of?"

No-one said anything for a minute then a young lad piped up.

"We've heard they guard the sky gardens with robots and the robots have bright red eyes. They've just got to look at you and they can shoot a couple of holes right through you."

"Where did you hear that nonsense?" Jax demanded.

"My Granddad told me, he'd seen them. He was the only one who got away."

"Well" sighed Jax, "robots with red eyes or not we need to at least go and have a look and try to find a way up. I only need three or four."

"I'll go," said Tripp.

"...and me," said Az.

"…and me," said a young women standing up and folding her arms in a defiant way as she said it. She had long, honey-brown, curly hair that fell well below her shoulders. Her figure was lean and boyish and judging by her determined expression, she had made up her mind she was going to be a part of this adventure no matter what anyone said.

Jax looked impressed with them. "Perfect," he said, "couldn't have chosen better myself. Get yourselves ready, we leave at sunrise."

The girl stalked off looking pleased with herself. Az sat gazing after her till Tripp gave him a jab in the side with his elbow.

"Don't waste your time, she's likely to bite your nose off if you look at her gooey-eyed. She's a toughy that one," he said admiringly, "cute, but oh boy, that cat has claws."

"I hate to ask this," said Az reluctantly, "but what's a cat?"

Tripp threw his head back and laughed, "come with me mate and I will further your ed-ja-cashen."

---

The next day they headed off moving away from the mountains but not directly back the way they had originally come.

"We have to walk beyond the City," Tripp explained, the Sky Gardens are further north."

Jax took the lead and the young girl, Shari, who didn't seem overly friendly, walked rapidly after him, her determined little nose in the air.

Trailing a short distance behind, Tripp and Az chatted about this and that. Sometimes Tripp asked more about life in the City, astonished at how the City people had lived.

"I couldn't stand that," he shuddered, "all boxed in and controlled, no freedom, no choices."

"It didn't really feel like that at the time," said Az thoughtfully, "it seemed pretty perfect, although I did feel restless sometimes, and we weren't supposed to question things which was frustrating. I was born there so I didn't know any different."

"You don't regret you choice do you?" said Tripp with an eyebrow raised and a sidelong look at him.

"No!" said Az firmly, "definitely not. "There are some things I could never give up now. Each day out here is hard and we never know what might happen next. It's as though we make each day up as we go along. I know that sounds funny to you, but that's never happened to me before. Each day was pretty much the same in the City and someone else always decided what would happen. We didn't ever have to think about the future."

Tripp nodded and seemed satisfied.

"Tell me something," said, Az, lowering his voice and slowing down a little so the gap between them and the flouncing figure of Shari widened, "how do couples get put together out here? In the City the computers put compatible couples together starting at age fourteen."

Tripp gave another of his superior laughs. "Ah where to start?" he said airily looking up at the sky, "oh the complexities of love and relationships. Well, here's how I see it," he said in a more practical tone. "When you see a girl you like, you talk to her and get to know her a bit and if she likes you, you spend time together and if you still like each other after a while you become a couple."

"Oh. Well that sounds simple enough. What if she doesn't like you?"

"Well then she lets you know she's not interested and then you either give up and go and find someone else or you keep trying and hope she changes her mind. Sometimes doing something daring and dangerous can attract their attention, girls like that kind of stuff. But let me tell you now my friend," he said ingratiatingly throwing an arm around Az's shoulders, "it's anything but simple. It's very, very complicated. Women are the most amazing, the most exquisite and the most frustratingly, infuriating creatures that God has ever put on the face of this earth."

"I can't see what's so complicated about it."

"You don't, but you will," smirked Tripp, giving him a pat. Then Tripp increased his speed to catch up with Shari leaving Az behind to muse over his comments.

He watched as Tripp struck up a friendly conversation with her. She kept her eyes directed in front and continued to stride along but now and then she grinned a little and answered him in a cheeky way. He remembered watching the couples from the City. They always seemed to enjoy being together and he had been looking forward to when it was his turn to have his first girlfriend. He knew the relationship would be strictly controlled with any touch being simulated, but the idea had intrigued him just the same. Now here things were completely different. Here he had to try and win the girl. He felt his heart beating harder at the thought.

I guess it's a bit like hunting, with the chase and the uncertainty and then finally being successful, he thought to himself, but what happened if two boys liked the same girl? He gazed at Tripp and Shari, and wondered, what happened then?

During the second day of their journey Trip nudged him and pointed to his right. Az shaded his eyes to squint in that direction, his eyes were still unused to what seemed to him to be extreme brightness after a lifetime lived in the City's soft light. Far away he could just make out the distant outline of a massive dome. He stopped to stare for a few moments. How could he have not known they were enclosed, he wondered? The City was very large and there had been places he had never been allowed to go to. He realised now that they had most likely been keeping them away from the edges of the dome, to prevent them from discovering they were separated from the outside world. He remembered Marama and how she had shown him the simulated buildings. Maybe all of the buildings around the edges were mere simulations making it look as though the City went on and on forever, he conjectured. He felt a suffocating sensation in his chest as he stared at its curving surface, made milky and opaque with distance. He looked away, gazing instead around him at the wide landscape and up at the broad sweep of the sky. As he did so the tight feeling in his chest gradually lessened and was replaced by a feeling of expansion and freedom. He took a deep breath of the fresh cool air, feeling the wind blowing on his face and continued walking after the others with an extra spring in his step. This was a greater adventure than any he could have had in a simulator and it was all real, he thought to himself with satisfaction.

It took three long, exhausting, days of walking to get to the Sky Gardens. Looking at him now no-one could ever accuse Az of being a soft City boy anymore. He was brown, dusty and dishevelled looking. He looked tired but if you looked into his eyes and compared him with the way he had looked when he had first left the City you would have seen an indescribable difference. It was as though he had an inner light, as though in some way he had become more fully alive.

The Sky Gardens were visible on the horizon a long time before they came anywhere near them. As they came closer the weather changed and they could see the heaped up clouds that they so desperately needed for their crops. They were mighty mountains of white, grey and black with lightening flickering amongst them, swirling in huge horizontal funnels as they were sucked inexorably towards the towering gardens.

When they were finally close enough to be in the shadow of the gardens Az stared upwards. They were gigantic white structures each with a single smooth curving pole that rose high in the sky supporting enormous, round platforms that must have been about four acres each in size. Each platform would easily be large enough to fit the gigantic fun palace on it.

They crouched in some nearby bushes and gazed, silently up at them, Jax shaking his head doubtfully. "Looks like old Earl might have been right, they're impossible to climb, nothing to grip. No ladders or stairs, I guess the robots fly up there. If only we could fly." He sighed and turned back to the others. Shari was gazing up too, frowning as though she could figure out the problem by sheer will power. Behind her Tripp and Az were whispering together.

"Yes, yes it's a good idea," Tripp was saying, "but then how do we get them to come down here?"

"What are you too chattering about" asked Jax, "have you got a plan?

"Yes," said Az, "we have."

# Chapter 39

That night the four people had a whispered consultation amongst the bushes as they discussed their idea.

"It sounds dangerous" said Shari with an approving smile.

Az grinned up at her, her approval gave him a warm feeling inside. "There are lots of things that could go wrong," he cautioned, "and it's a long way to fall."

"I'll go alone if you're scared City boy," she said witheringly.

"Nope, not scared. How about you Tripp?"

"Me? You're joking, I live for danger."

Tripp had meant to appear brave and offhand but just ended up sounding kind of silly. The other two burst into stifled giggles which were quickly shushed by Jax.

"Right you heroes, we've got work to do before dawn," he whispered authoritatively, "let's get stuck in."

The four of them worked together all night long. They gathered piles of the long flat, stringy leaves called flax, scraped them with sharp stones to remove the soft outer layers and wove the pieces expertly together to make a large net. The forest dwellers were very good at weaving and flax was used to make many different things such as baskets, fish nets, mats and sometimes even shoes. It was strong, hard wearing but soft and pliable. Az was fascinated by their skill and was curious about where they had learned it.

"It's just something we know how to do," said Tripp shrugging, "handed down from our ancestors I suppose."

That got Az thinking. "Do we have the same ancestors? Could we all, those in the City and those outside be related? Maybe all of those who are outside the City are descended from people who once escaped from there?" Az speculated.

"Maybe," Tripp didn't sound particularly interested.

"According to legend," Jax spoke quietly, aware of possible surveillance, "this land, before the Great Quake was once a small country, two islands alone in the sea far from the larger lands. Most people alive now are descended from the inhabitants of that country. We have kept some of the practices and ideas that came from the past. Some of them help us to live and others influence our beliefs. One of the beliefs that came from way back was that the world was created and there is a God who watches over us. There is a scared image that we have, very old, very powerful. We use it to mark a grave to send the person who has died on into the spiritual realm. We don't know what it means but we hope one day to discover its mysteries."

This was fascinating to Az and they continued to have hushed conversations of this kind until dawn as they worked busily, concealed amongst the bushes.

In the early morning light Jax walked out boldly into the open carrying a large stick while the three youngsters came creeping behind with the green, tightly woven net covering them. When they got to the massive supporting pole the youngsters lay down under the net blending into the grass.

Jax raised his stick and then struck the pole as hard as he could. There was a loud clang as the stick hit the pole. Jax hesitated for a moment looking up, then began beating the pole again.

Clang! Clang! Clang! The sound was echoing up and down the pole and was deafening to the three hidden under the net. Then Jax stopped and looked up, crouched ready to dive into hiding. They heard it before they saw it. The whirring noise that was so familiar to Az; a robot was approaching.

Jax dived head-first into the nearby bushes leaving the piece of wood lying in the grass.

They could see it was quite a small robot as it came closer and closer to the ground, then hovered a few feet above it. It had bright red eyes that scanned the piece of wood then spun around to scan the ground where the four people were hiding.

"Now!" shouted Jax from his hiding place and the three youngsters leaped up throwing the net over the little robot. The robot, confused by not being able to see, immediately began to rise into the air at a terrifying speed. The three youngsters who had tied themselves to the corners of the net screamed as they were lifted up into the air. They rose higher and higher, the robot seeming to have no trouble at all lifting the weight of the three young people.

"Don't look down, don't look down, don't look down," Tripp chanted.

Az looked down involuntarily and then wished he hadn't. He bit down on his lip to stifle his scream. The ground was a very long way below. Jax looked small far beneath them. He wrenched his eyes off the receding ground and latched them onto Shari's face opposite him. She was dead white and looked sick and faint.

It was a good thing they had used plenty of the strong, flax rope to attach themselves securely to the net, he thought, because she wasn't really holding on at all, she was just hanging there. His own head was spinning and his stomach lurched as they ascended. Then, thankfully he looked down and saw the garden below them. They were flying across the garden now, the robot bobbing and swooping around in a bewildered fashion trying to find a way out of the net. Suddenly it dropped down to settle amongst the plants and the three youngsters fell in a heap. Peeking out, they could see some small trees with bright orange fruit growing on them. The robot continued to twist and turn as it tried to escape.

"Grab it!" yelled Tripp. Shari whipped a small bone knife out of her clothes. With it she dived under the net and they could see her struggling for a moment. Then she emerged panting and smiling with something small in her hand while the robot could be seen lying motionless on its side.

"What is that?" asked Tripp "and how did you er, kill that robot?" He asked wonderingly.

She held up the small thing in her hand. It was a round piece of metal with some wires dangling from it. I didn't kill it, I disabled it. I don't know what this is," she said with a grin, "but looks like they don't work without it."

All three burst out laughing releasing the tension from their terrifying assent.

"What now?" said Tripp, when they had begun to relax a little. They looked around them and discovered how incredibly beautiful the sky gardens were. The one they were on grew a multitude of various kinds of fruit. There was an array of colours; oranges, reds, blues and yellows, peeking out between lush, miniature trees and bushes. The thing that struck them the most was the smells. They were so tantalisingly delicious that they just stood breathing them in, tasting the air. The next moment they were gorging themselves on the fruit. This was better than anything they had ever tasted in their lives before. When they couldn't eat anymore they sat down on the ground looking at each other.

"What now?" asked Trip once again.

"We need to find those cloud siphons," said Shari looking around. They began to wander around the garden looking around and enjoying the beauty of it. When they got to the edge of the massive disc, they stood looking out over the countryside. They saw a vast rolling plain spread beneath them, green with trees dotted around and further away in the distance the hills tinged with brown.

"Not too close," cautioned Az as Shari moved towards the edge.

"Look," she said pointing. They could see from here that the giant disc they were on was one of many which were grouped in a wide circle. In the centre of the circle were huge tubes that stretched high into the sky disappearing into the mass of clouds.

"I think that's it," she said.

"What shall we do now?" asked Az. "Shall we try and stop the siphoning or just steal some food and go?"

"I think we have done all we can for now," she replied, "we've found out useful information. Let's take as much food as we can and leave."

"How?" said Az trying to focus on the siphons rather than the ground, "how are we going to get down?"

The three looked at each other and laughed again, but it was nervous laughter.

"It seemed so important to get up here, we didn't think about how to get down," giggled Shari.

"You know," said Tripp, stretching himself out on the soft grassy ground, "I could live here quite happily."

Shari aimed a kick at him. "We have to get back" she said, "Jax will be worrying. We need our little friend again."

"What little friend?" muttered Tripp, rubbing his leg where she had kicked him.

Az followed Shari as she strode over to where they had left the net. "I wonder if I can fix it?" she said, crouching down and hauling the small robot out from under the net.

"And," said Az crouching down beside her, "if you can fix it how do we make it go down?"

Shari fiddled around attempting to reattach the wires then inserted the small piece of metal back into the top of the robot. The robot made a few whirring noises then came to life the red eye-lights flickered on and off fitfully.

"I think you gave it a headache," Tripp commented standing over them.

The little robot rose and fell, rose and fell, wobbling dizzily in the air.

Shari threw the net over it. "I'll look after this little fella while you two fill your backpacks with fruit. But be quick I'm not sure how long I can hold it for."

The two boys quickly filled their packs till they were bulging then came back to find Shari being dragged around by the net with the agitated robot still twisting and turning inside. She had been dragged through the dirt and branches and was sweating and panting from the effort of keeping a firm hold.

They quickly tied themselves back onto the corners.

"Now what" said Az, "do we just jump?" He looked from one to the other, hoping they were going to say no.

"I don't fancy jumping either," said Tripp "if that net slips then we're pikelets."

"Pikelets?" Az questioned.

"Small, very flat cakes, City boy," Tripp replied dryly.

"Oh," was all Az could manage at that moment as his imagination supplied him with a visual picture he would rather not have had.

Suddenly they heard a sound, a loud reverberating noise that went on and on. Clang, clang, clang! The whole garden vibrated under their feet.

"Jax," they said together.

The little robot seemed to respond to the noise because it suddenly leapt into the air pulling them off their feet and then plunging them over the edge.

Too fast, thought Az, his eyes shut as tightly. Down, down they fell, the little robot twisting in sickening spirals, around and around till with a crash they fell into a tree. Shari didn't waste a moment but whipped out her knife again to flick the little metal piece from the cranium of the robot. It fell immediately to the ground leaving them huddled in the tree branches with the net draped over them.

"Don't move," hissed a voice from the ground, "more coming."

They sat as still as they could beneath the net. They could hear the whirring of robots around them searching the ground. They waited and eventually they heard them whirring away to search elsewhere.

They all let out their breaths with relieved sighs. Then with the relief of tension the three of them seemed suddenly inclined to go into fits of giggles. They looked at each other and realised that they were now good friends. Looking down they saw Jax regarding them with a puzzled look on his face.

"Are you lot coming down? What on earth are you giggling about?"

They climbed down one by one, complaining about their aches and pains and scratches from the collision with the tree. Pain was still a new experience to Az but he dare not say too much as the others soon seemed to forget about it as they excitedly told Jax about how amazing the sky gardens were and showing him the fruit they had stolen.

"Let's get further away," said Jax cautiously looking up, "even though our little friend won't be telling any tales, they will know that something is up."

They set off the way they had come as quickly and as quietly as they could. As they walked the air turned colder and soon there was a loud rumbling noise that seemed to shake the ground.

"Thunder," said Jax, "long time since I've heard it so close, it's going to rain in a minute."

They kept walking as fast as they could and soon the freezing, cold drops began to fall.

Az remembered watching the history view of the rainy day at Gypsy's place. He had longed to be in it then, but he soon discovered how uncomfortable it was to be wet and cold with rain dripping down his neck.

An hour later they stopped for a rest and to talk about what they had discovered. The rain was behind them now and the warm sun was beginning to dry them off.

Az noticed that Shari's long hair was drying into dozens of thick spirals. He also noticed how deep brown her eyes were with little glints of gold in them.

They talked for a while about their adventure, then Az said, "You know, before our little friend was put out of action it would have sent images of us to the Central Computer System."

"So what," said Shari, "what can they do?"

"I don't know, we are outside the City so I guess they can't do much. Maybe they will do something to make it harder for us to get back up there again though."

"I wonder how those siphons work," contemplated Shari. "How do they suck the clouds in?"

Az was thinking hard. "Yes, I wonder too. There must be some kind of machinery or something underground."

"Well if it is underground we could get to it couldn't we?" said Shari her eyes lighting up.

"Maybe we just have to dig," suggested Tripp.

"Good work youngsters," said Jax. "All three of you did an amazing job. We have a lot of new information to share at the conferences, and everyone will be glad to taste this delicious fruit. Maybe we could organise a group to come back at night with tools to dig up that machinery."

They set off again with the three friends walking together this time, laughing and relaxed after their daring adventure.

"They will make stories about us you know," said Tripp with a swagger in his step.

"Tripp the great adventurer and his companions break into the sky gardens to learn its closely guarded secrets."

"Yes and nearly wet himself on the way up," laughed Shari.

"What about you I thought you were going to barf, and you city boy, were screaming like a wee girl."

They all laughed again and Az decided he liked adventures. It was completely different from the fun Palace synthesisers. There it was exciting and seemed real but you always knew you were safe. Unlike this adventure, he mused, where they could quite easily have turned into, what had Tripp called them? Pikelets?

# Chapter 40

At the next conference the four recounted their adventures to an audience that listened with rapt attention. They were asked to repeat the story over and over again over the next few weeks. Some wanted to start off immediately to dig up the machinery under the siphons so they could prevent them from stealing anymore clouds. Others were more cautious and advised waiting for a while until whoever guarded the City had forgotten about the recent raid on the gardens.

"We can't wait that long," others wailed, "the ground is drying up and the crops are parched."

"Have you thought about digging for water?" Az suggested interrupting what looked like turning into another of their interminable arguments. "In times past, they used to dig deep into the ground to tap into subterranean rivers. They called these holes in the ground wells."

"What?" What's that big word you said boy? Subtrain-e-an? I've heard stories about those," it was an older man who spoke in a knowing way, "like great big caterpillars that sped along after swallowing whole crowds of people. Monsters that tunnelled underground they were." The old man was deadly serious so Az tried hard not to laugh, although it seemed unfair when he and his family had been the butt of so many jokes since they had arrived.

"I believe what you are thinking about are trains. In olden times they were used them to transport people similar to the way our travellers in the City do. I was talking about underground rivers that flow deep under the surface."

The old man seemed embarrassed at being corrected by a City boy and he snapped out a reply with a cynical sneer on his face. "And what say we take all that trouble to dig deep into the bowels of the earth and find this water, what do we do then, how do we get it up to where we want it?"

He was a wizened looking old man with a scrawny neck, unkempt shoulder-length grey hair and a bristly chin. He had been through some hard times and had become somewhat bitter.

"They used to use buckets, but that would be too slow." Az considered for a moment, then brightened as he remembered something. "There is a way to make water run uphill."

There was a roar of laughter at this.

"The boys thinks he's magic," the old man cackled over the noise, "thinks he can make water run up hills. He's crazy, hah, hah, hah," he laughed in his squeaky voice enjoying Az's discomfit.

Az waited until there was some quiet to speak. "There is a way to do it," he spoke with confidence. "You will need to send a pipe down lower than the flow of the underground stream, as low as the height above it. Yes," he seemed to be talking more to himself, "that should work, the weight of the water dropping down would force the water to flow up through the pipe onto the surface and then we can redirect it to wherever we want it to go." He looked up and around him. "Does anyone know of any likely places to start digging?"

The group stared at him in silence as they readjusted their ideas.

"There's a place near the caves where the grass and trees are always green even in the hottest weather," a youngish woman spoke up timidly. "I saw it when I was herding the goats. I didn't want to get too near though, because of those cave dwellers," she added a little fearfully.

"Even better," responded Az interested in the water rather than the problem of the Cave Dwellers, "that means the water is very near the surface. Maybe it's a spring, then we might only have to dig a short way to find it. We would just need to open it up and dig around it so that it filled up, then we would have a pool of water."

"If the spring is near the caves we will have to negotiate with the cave-dwellers to access it," Jax said carefully.

There was some angry muttering around the fire at this. Looking at their stony faces Jax knew they would not give in easily to this idea. The cave dwellers were becoming more and more of a problem to the small community. In the end there was so much discord at the idea of having to deal with the Cave Dwellers that Jax had to put the whole idea on hold for a while.

---

Then one day something terrible happened; a girl went missing. Her mother was frantic, her father grimly silent as he held in his feelings of fear for his daughter. She was found several days later. She was dead and the marks on her body showed she had died from an attack by a human being. No one doubted it was the Cave Dwellers who were responsible. Her body was laid on a hammock-like net made of flax and covered with flowers. There was a time of mourning and a chance for each person to say good bye to her. Then the people carried her solemnly to the burial site outside of the village where they sang her traditional songs of farewell.

Tama looked on grimly as the women, crying despairingly, lowered the small body gently into her grave. That same night it was noticed that he was missing from the company. Everyone knew where he had gone and what he planned to do.

In the evening at the conference around the fires Jax seemed at a loss to know what to say or do. There were too many problems building up all at once.

"We need guidance," he said softly, as if to himself. He closed his eyes tightly as he prepared himself to speak to the people. Inwardly he desperately sought for answers to guide them. "God," he whispered, "God who made us and who made the world, please guide us, show us some answers, please," he pleaded.

He opened his eyes to find that people were staring at him.

"Were you talking to God?" a middle-aged woman sneered, "why would a God who allows a child to be killed care about us?"

There were nods and mutters of agreement around the fire.

Amiria, who had been staring deep into the glowing embers with a distant look on her face suddenly surprised everyone, including herself, by speaking up. She had been through a lot of changes since she had arrived in the community, outwardly but also inwardly. Her mind, shaped by life in the City to be logical and reasonable, although without full and complete information, was kept child-like, and sometimes this allowed her to see things more clearly than others.

"What if there are two gods?" she spoke clearly, her eyes distant, "one who is good and one who is evil, and they are fighting with each other. What if all the evil things came from one and all the good things from the other? What if we have to choose between them, and they are waiting for our choice?"

"Then which one would we pray to?" A young man yelled out, "I know I'd be praying to the evil one to make sure I didn't get in trouble with him," he looked around half-jokingly as if hoping to get some agreement from the others.

"Would you trust someone who lied and murdered?" Az spat out vehemently, glaring at the man.

The man who had spoken, looked a little shame-faced at that but said nothing.

"We've been lied to all our lives and our people are murdered, all of them!" Az growled in an angry tone. "No-one is allowed to live over forty in the City and if you break the rules or get too curious, you die. Don't tell me the right answer is to suck up to the evil one, he'll just carry on lying to you and will kill you in the end." He stopped talking and looked down at the ground as though trying to contain his anger. After a few moments he looked up at Jax. "I think Mum is right," he said with more self-control, "I think we need to be careful who we ask for guidance. We need to make sure if there really is a God that we are talking to the right one."

"How can we know," Jax questioned?

Dayzie went over to sit down next to him. She put her hand on his arm and whispered. He looked up to see a shimmering form beyond the fire.

Jax stood up slowly. "Gypsy," he intoned. "We are in need of wisdom from the past, speak to us," and then more pleadingly, "please, don't disappear."

The shimmery image of the girl stared at him in surprise and slowly came forwards to take a place around the fires. She looked around and seeing Dayzie and Az she smiled. Dayzie was jumping up and down with excitement and Az looked pleased.

"Can you help us?" Jax entreated. "We know you are from the past. What should we do? We have trouble in the land. A girl has been killed."

———————

Gypsy looked uncertainly from one to the other anxious to help them. She longed to be able to tell them something that would answer their problems, they looked so desperate. She couldn't understand the strong feelings she had for them as though they were her own family. Then something inside her stirred and in a powerful voice that seemed to come from the deepest place within her, she began speaking:

"My people! My people!" she cried out, "they are trapped in the City, not by the dome but by their own fear. They are controlled and manipulated. They long deep within themselves for the land, for freedom and for the spirit. They are Tangata Whenua, the people of the land! Their love for the land will never leave them, generation after generation, it cries out. Their longing and the restlessness cannot be controlled or stifled. My people must be released from the confining City."

"How? How can we release them?" many people from the group cried out to her.

"I see a vision of the dome being cracked from side to side like a giant egg and the people looking up and seeing the stars for the very first time. They see the great expanse of the sky and breathe the free air and they will leave the City and begin to live on the land once more."

The people gasped as the image faded and disappeared and they were left looking at each other in astonishment.

Dayzie looked up at Jax and patted his arm comfortingly. "Don't worry, she'll be back," she reassured him, "Gypsy won't leave us alone when she knows we need her."

# Chapter 41

Gypsy woke up with a start. She knew she had prophesied to them, to these people that she felt such a great affinity with. These were her people, the ones that would come from her, far in the future but still a part of her, connected by the spirit where time didn't count. Some of them had escaped the deadly beauty and apathy of that terrible City; that gilded tomb where dreams and life and the spirit were stifled, but many more were still trapped inside. They had to be released, but how? Maybe they would find a way of breaking open the dome. She hoped and prayed they would. They needed to wake up and realise where they were and what was happening to them. She couldn't bear the thought that her people were walled in. It gave her a terrible deathly feeling, like a half-life.

Then she thought of the people in the Forest Community. What of the family of the young girl who had died, she wondered? How could she help them? Were they destined to repeat again and again the same mistakes of the past?

Gran poked her head around the door just at that moment. "You all right love? You were talking in your sleep. I hope you're not too worried about your Mum. She'll be alright, she'll leave that fat lout and then you can go home."

Gypsy nodded. Gran came closer and leaning over her, gave her shoulder a concerned squeeze then said in her usual brisk style, "Come along girl, come and get some breakfast in you."

Gypsy came fully back into the present then. It was hard thinking about her Mum. Her life shouldn't be like this she thought angrily. Generations ago her family had been part of a proud tribe that had owned vast areas of land. Now she was poor, unhappy and couldn't even look after her own kids. She looked at the framed photo of her Mum with her and Rangi when they were very small. Mum looked happy then, young and pretty, she thought, or was that just a brief moment of respite amongst the constant abuse from her partners and the drinking?

"That picture is a lie," she muttered to herself angrily.

Suddenly she realised how thankful she was for her Gran. Gran had been brought up with drinking and violence, and although she drank heavily herself and surely wasn't perfect, she really did try. She was the best thing in her life right now. Impulsively she jumped up and ran into the kitchen. She put her arms around Gran's ample waist as far as they would go.

"I love you Gran," she said with a sob.

Soon she and Gran were sitting companionably at the breakfast table together. Gypsy was feeling more cheerful now.

"Gran," she said thoughtfully as she pecked at her scrambled eggs with her fork.

"Yes dear?" Gran was munching contentedly in between taking noisy slurps of strong, hot tea.

"Our people love the land don't they, and wouldn't be happy living away from it?

"It's very strong in our people, our connection to the land," Gran answered proudly. "You know what the Preacher says. God brought this people across the vast Pacific Ocean to this very land. They came all that way in canoes travelling thousands of miles and landed in this country and named it Aeotearoa; the land of the long white cloud. The ocean is so very huge and the land is small but those tiny canoes found their way here. This is our land, given to us by God for a special purpose."

"What's the purpose?" Gypsy questioned curiously.

"Well," faltered Gran, "I'm not so sure about that part, but it sounds so grand, don't you think. Makes us sound important. He calls us 'the first people of the land.' I like that, better than being called natives ae girl?"

"Our people wouldn't like being shut up so that they couldn't live on the land without the trees and the stars and the rivers and the sea would they Gran?"

"Do you mean like in prison? No certainly not. What has put all this into your head all of a sudden? I know you've been upset by what happened at your mother's."

"Dreams Gran. Not just visions, but dreams where I am in another time and place with our people in the far future. They are shut up inside a huge domed city and they don't know there is an outside and they are too scared to go outside even if they could. There are no old people there Gran, think of that. It made me sad and I prophesied that they would be released, but, I don't know how."

Gran was staring at her looking a little bewildered. "Ah, humm....more tea dear?" She ventured inadequately proffering her the steaming teapot.

"Thanks Gran," said Gypsy with a grin holding up her mug to be refilled. She knew now who she should go to for answers to these questions. It was time to talk to the Preacher.

The Preacher listened carefully without interrupting as Gypsy told him all about the visions and the dreams. When she had finished she looked up at him hopefully, as he sat contemplating what she had said. Gran was sitting listening with an anxious look on her face as though she was afraid he would pronounce Gypsy to be crazy and should be locked up.

He looked at Gran, smiled and said kindly, "My wife is in the kitchen making some tea, I'm sure she would be thankful for some help."

His wife poked her head out of the kitchen to smile and beckon with her hand. "Come on then, we'll have a good gossip in the kitchen while those two work out the Universe's problems," she called invitingly.

Gran jumped up willingly and almost ran into the kitchen in her eagerness to get away from that puzzling conversation.

The Preacher looked down at Gypsy's earnest face. "I don't pretend to understand any of this," he said at last and Gypsy's face fell, "but I do know that there were prophets in the bible who talked of strange and fearful things that would happen thousands of years in the future. No-one at that time understood them either. That's not what mattered, the underlying message was there, warning us and guiding us."

Gypsy waited for him to go on.

"Your main concern seems to be how the people will be freed from the dome. You say you saw it broken open. I say nothing but God himself could do that. I think it will happen in the right time and the people will have the chance to be free. In the meantime your job seems to be to bring these people, the ones on the outside in the Forest Community, hope and knowledge. You must teach them the fundamentals," the preacher told her seriously," the basic truths about God and heaven. They must know there is a future for them beyond this world and that there are two forces warring for their souls. Teach them the sacred ways, the blood that was poured out for them, the great value that has been placed on them."

"What about the girl that was killed?" Gypsy pleaded, "They are asking me for answers, I don't know what to tell them."

"They must forgive," he said firmly, "but remember," he continued as Gypsy frowned and opened her mouth to protest, "to forgive is not to be passive, it just means that whatever action is taken it will be justice and not revenge. Revenge, hatred and un-forgiveness is the substance of wars. They would merely be re-enacting the past. We are not meant to live like animals. The murderer must be brought to justice, but in the right way."

Gypsy absorbed this information to pass on to her people.

"If they are indeed the people of the distant future," the Preacher continued," then they are a product of our actions and choices right now. Each generation reaps a harvest for good or evil from the one that comes before it. The main thing you need to be concerned about young Gypsy, more important than anything else, is what kind of inheritance you will be leaving for the generations that are coming after you."

He smiled at her then and she smiled back relieved. She found his words comforting. She didn't need to worry quite so much about the people who were yet to come, now was more important and what she would be leaving behind for her children. That felt more like something she could really do, rather than solving all those really difficult problems from the future.

Gran and her new best friend came out then with trays laden with tea and cakes. Gran looked very cheerful and had obviously been having a whale of a time.

# Chapter 42

Later that night Gypsy was curled up comfortably under a rug in the lounge. Her hair, which had reverted back to its usual tangly style was splayed out on the back of the sofa behind her. Rangi was sitting on the floor leaning up against it near her and staring at nothing in particular having exhausted himself by an x-box marathon. Gran was clattering happily away in the kitchen, completing her household tasks for the day. Occasionally they heard an explosive sound issuing from her direction which made Gypsy and Rangi look at each other and giggle. Gran would always act highly offended if Rangi and Zak had farting competitions but became mysteriously deaf when it came to her own noxious emissions.

Gypsy felt pleasantly sleepy and relaxed. "You know what I think is going to happen to those people in the domed city?" Gypsy asked Rangi contemplatively after sitting quietly for a time.

"What?" murmured Rangi tonelessly without changing expression or even blinking. He was doing a good job of appearing to be asleep with his eyes open.

"I think there is going to be another earthquake, that's one natural force that can't be controlled or avoided even if you are all sealed up in a dome." Gypsy seemed pleased with this notion.

"Cool," said Rangi without much enthusiasm.

Gypsy didn't mind, she just needed to talk over a few things. "Did you know there is no-one over forty in the City? They all die on their fortieth birthdays somehow. They go to their own funerals, willingly!" Gypsy sounded amazed. "They are so scared of getting old and of diseases and wars and stuff that they just do what they are told by the authorities, even though they can't see them and have never even met them. They can't vote them in or out, they just get chosen somehow. They send information and rules to them through the computer system and through the robots. Bizarre ae? Az told me," she said as Rangi turned lazily to look at her as if a little bemused by what she was telling him.

"Preacher says what they are doing sounds like communism, where it all seems fair but people are controlled in every part of their lives and can't change the government even if they want to. He says that kind of idea will never work because human beings are too corrupt and love power too much. He thinks Communists don't want people to believe in God because they are afraid they would will lose control over them." Gypsy didn't really know what communists were but she had been interested in any information that related to the people of the future. "Anyway, I saw the dome broken open," she continued, "so it's going to happen somehow I believe. You know, I didn't realise how important I was," she said, "how important we all are," she added hurriedly as Rangi gave her another sidelong, slightly sceptical look. "We all have a special purpose and everything we do affects the people in the future, right down through the generations."

Rangi laid his head back on the sofa allowing the x-box controller to slide through his relaxed fingers and hit the floor with a bump. Since he made no response she carried on.

"I tried to work out how many descendants I might possibly have in five hundred years' time. If I had two kids, and my kids had two kids, and so on, and so on, over five hundred years. It was a really hard calculation, took me ages to work it out, but it turned out to be, well a whole lot of people, maybe even millions!"

The actual figure she had arrived at, of the number people who might someday carry her DNA, had seemed so ridiculously high that she was afraid to even mention it. Rangi made the effort to turn his head a little to look back at her with a mildly quizzical look on his face.

"I have to pass the Preacher's words onto them," she continued dreamily ignoring him, "because they are my people."

At that moment Rangi yawned such a huge, face-splitting yawn that it made his eyes water. Gypsy, stretching her leg out along the sofa, nudged him playfully in the back with her foot.

"Hey, thanks for listening bro," she said dryly.

"Anytime sis," he responded with a grin.

Gypsy slumped down sideways with her head on the arm of the sofa. As sleepiness began to overcome her she wondered idly what Zak was up to. Zak was a good guy underneath, she knew. Things could have been a whole lot worse. Zak had narrowly escaped being involved in the gangs and that was only because he had spent most of his time out in the countryside where he was away from their influence. He might be careless and lazy and inclined to be cynical but he wasn't violent or a criminal as he might have been if Gran hadn't taken a lion's share of the responsibility for bringing him up. Now that he was with their Aunty and Uncle in Auckland maybe he would settle down and grow up a bit.

"Do you think Zak is doing ok?" she murmured sleepily.

Rangi shrugged. His eyes were closed and he looked as though he might drift off to sleep in that awkward position, head back, mouth slightly open, a little drool forming at the corner of his mouth.

"Do you miss him at all?" Gypsy persisted.

"Sure," was Rangi's monosyllabic answer, in a husky, half-asleep voice.

Gypsy continued to wonder silently to herself, accepting that Rangi was in a non-communicative state. Maybe if Zak was earning his own money and learning to work hard and save he would be ok, she thought. Who knows maybe he would meet a nice girl at church, settle down and have a family? She grinned at this thought, it seemed so wildly unlikely. She remembered the similarity to Zak she could see in some of the Forest Dwellers features.

I guess that means he must be going to have kids someday, she chuckled to herself.

"Time you two youngsters were in bed," came Gran's voice in an unarguable tone from the doorway.

Rangi groaned and hauled himself to his feet. He stomped off to his room zombie-like to collapse across his bed and to immediately fall deeply asleep. Gypsy flung the rug to one side and padded over to Gran to give her a good night peck on the cheek, then disappeared into her bedroom also. As she snuggled under the covers she wondered with a feeling of anticipation, as she always did, if tonight was going to be just an ordinary night's sleep or another excursion into the mysterious realm of the unfolding future.

# Chapter 43

The young girl, playing a game with her friends, looked up reflexively as the dark swiftly-approaching cloud caught her attention. The cloud seemed to boil with strange movement as it advanced across the sky. Her small hand, grasping a ball that she had been about to throw, was suspended in the air as she stared.

"Mana!" The robot nanny's single word admonished her.

She flicked her attention back to the game to continue to throw, catch, duck, turn and start again in the complex game designed to develop various parts of the brain.

Someone called, "change," and the game reversed. Squeals of laughter issued from the group as they fumbled and struggled to reverse the sequence. The dark cloud was now directly overhead, causing a shadow to be cast across the City. No one else seemed to have noticed it and it passed silently over and was gone. That evening during conversation time at the Preparation centre Mana did not mention the cloud and the image had completely disappeared from her conscious mind. The word bird did not even register in her thoughts. The image sat deeply in her unconsciousness, flapping and struggling to rise with nothing to attach itself to in her concept of reality in this orderly predictable world.

———

Every day the schedule was set and they followed it. No need for thinking or questioning, no stress, an easy life, comfortable and peaceful. If every now and then there was a slight anomaly, it was no cause for concern as it would soon be rectified. Slight anomalies were usually people who stood out from the others. They were a little too different, a little too curious somehow not quite able to fit in. It was better not to interact with these ones; they would soon disappear anyway; this was something people knew without needing to speak about it.

A constant thankfulness to the Information Giver and a gratefulness that they didn't have to live in the bad old days was saturated into their thinking through education and production activities. History views proved over and over that life was a thousand times better now that disease, wars, violence and unpredictable death had been eliminated. There was also no need to consider the future or make decisions of any kind. If being nurtured and cosseted in this way resulted in the people of the City remaining rather childish in their thinking, this was something they were blissfully unaware of.

The confidence each person had in the CCS was so great that on the day when something hugely and alarmingly unprecedented happened the inhabitants of the City were shocked into immobilisation.

At first it was just bewildering and they behaved exactly like little lost children, not knowing how to react or what to do. There had been no announcement, no adjustment in their schedule and worst of all there were no instructions.

The day the ground had begun to shake began with a few gentle tremors. People stopped their Production duties to look around surprised but not yet frightened by the fact that the ground was vibrating gently beneath their feet. Even when the contents of shelves and storage spaces began rattling strangely they were not unduly alarmed. Some even laughed thinking it was merely a simulation. They were so used to being in situations that stimulated the senses but were perfectly safe that initially they didn't react.

They waited for an announcement and after a few confusingly silent minutes their personal robots spoke in unison: "Please remain where you are. We have just experienced a small earth tremor. Please prepare to continue with your duties, there is nothing to be alar......."

At that moment, a stronger more violent tremor hit the City cutting off the announcement. People were flung to the floor, ornaments and glasses fell and shattered. A strange high pitched creaking followed by a terrible groaning sound seemed to be coming from high above their heads. They were so used to being perfectly safe and cared for that it took many disorientating moments for them to begin to understand that they were in some kind of danger. People turned to their robots expecting advice but the robots remained uncharacteristically quiet and ineffectual. As tremor followed tremor terrifying panic and real heart pounding, debilitating fear set in. They began to shout at their robots desperately asking for advice and pleading for help. In a City where orderliness and calm was the norm and even a raised voice was unusual, this chaotic clamouring was of a nightmarish quality.

The robots also seemed confused and began spouting useless information all at once talking overtop of one another so they could barely be understood:

"*...Earth tremors were common occurrences...!*" "*...caused by the shifting of tectonic plates...!*" "*...constantly moving bumping up against one another...!*" *...pressure causing the crust to break...!*" "*...shaking of Earth's surface...!*" "*...seismic waves...!* "*...devastating destruction...!*" they babbled adding unhelpfully to the commotion.

The whole City seemed to be swaying in a sickening motion. People began to stumble and fall out of the houses and places of Production, spilling into the common areas. The adults and children alike were screaming and crying hysterically. Some screamed towards the sky for the Information Giver to help them, to save them, as though calling on a deity, but the shaking continued.

Fine cracks began to appear in the beautiful white marble of the buildings and larger ones tore at the ground, breaking it open, shattering the artificial surface as a spoon shatters eggshell. The buildings shuddered and swayed and there was a continuously loud, menacing rumbling roar that seemed to surround and consume them. The terrible creaking and groaning which appeared to be emanating from the sky grew louder.

People looked upwards as an ear-spitting screech suddenly sounded from high above them. To their unbelieving eyes a network of cracks and breaks appeared right across the sky. Then with a deafening bang the sky itself exploded. The City's inhabitants watched transfixed as the shattering sky rose in the air in a cloud of sparkling splinters and then began to fall inexorably towards them. Staring for one amazed moment upwards, they instinctively fell to the ground, curling themselves up in protective huddles. They covered their faces as fine shards rained down all around them, making tinkling sounds as they hit the ground, covering it with piles of sparkling debris.

Then came silence. The earth stopped shaking and the sky ceased falling. Slowly and fearfully, one after the other, the people looked up and around them. As they looked up they had to shield their eyes from the searing light beaming down from the sky. The world was considerably changed. Where the pale stretch of the sky had been was replaced by a deep, blue with a dazzling sun shining in it. A sharp wind was blowing over them such as they had never felt before in the balmy, sheltered hothouse that had been their home.

Their personal robots were hovering undecidedly amongst them, not giving them advice or instructions or spouting information as they usually did. In the absence of instructions suddenly people began to chatter amongst themselves, questioning each other confusedly about what had happened. Many had tear stains on their faces, looking shocked and disorientated. There were some who in painful confusion just sat down amongst the chaos submissively waiting to be told what to do next.

Others stooped to pick up the shards to examine them more closely, fascinated by the refracted light flashing from the glassy structures. Looking up at the transformed sky and down at the shattered substance again they slowly came to an astonishing conclusion about what must have taken place.

A little girl was sitting on the ground next to her mother whose face looked ravaged with panic. The girl stared around her with frightened eyes, squinting in the unusual brightness.

Her normally perfectly styled hair was hanging in draggled clumps, her beautiful midnight blue dress dishevelled. She picked up a handful of the crystal-like debris and let the shattered pieces roll around her palm flashing rainbows of colour.

"Look Mum," she said, pulling at her mother's hand, "look at what fell from the sky."

Her mother ignored her and continued to sob, distraught. She was shaking with shock, unable to focus her mind, her eyes flitting fretfully around unable to comprehend what had happened.

The little girl let the shards fall from her fingers, trying to absorb the changes in her surroundings. Then she noticed the buildings. Where had all the beautiful buildings gone? In their place were bare structures, ugly grey concrete walls that were cracked and crumbling. The white marble buildings had all vanished. The world as she knew it had dissolved around her.

She saw the blue sky and she felt the fresh wind on her face. Away in the distance, although she had been led to believe the City went on forever, she could blurrily see something green. Looking up she saw a dark moving cloud over to her right. Distant cries issued from it and she could clearly see the rise and fall of moving bodies and wings. A deeply buried image flashed into her awareness. Birds? Real birds? They were moving away and soon disappeared from view.

In the wind that blew her disarrayed hair about her face she could smell something that she didn't recognise, like a sweet perfume, or a divine breath, awakening her senses. Her heart started beating faster. The sight and the smell of that distant place was tantalising her, drawing her towards it. She felt that somehow she had to get there, that place where the wind was blowing from.

She noticed some of the people were moving slowly and cautiously towards the edges of the City and soon a small crowd was doing the same thing. The little girl tugged again at her mother's hand, urging her to get up and follow, but her mother shook her off, too immersed in her own misery and too unused to making any decisions for herself let alone for anyone else to help her little daughter. The woman was suddenly shaken out of this self-absorption by a loud voice.

The voice could be heard, echoing throughout the City as though originating from another place. People stared around them surprised wondering if this was the Information Giver at last, speaking directly to them. The voice, sounded like a young girl's voice, and was yet strangely familiar to their ears.

"My people, you must leave this place! Leave quickly! Get out and don't look back! Please hurry," the voice pleaded. "Please, please, leave, quickly!"

The urgency in the voice caused even those who were sitting passively on the ground to get up and begin slowly and uncertainly to follow those already on their way. A lifetime of conditioning to follow instructions encouraged them to obey without question. The little girl and her mother joined the others heading outwards, towards the green distance.

———————

Gypsy looked down on the City with its shattered dome as if from a great height and saw with relief that the people seemed to hear her and were moving towards the City's edges. She felt reassured and peaceful as she watched them, like a mother watching over her children.

———————

"Gypsy love are you ok?"

The rough voice woke Gypsy with a start. She could see her Gran's shadowy figure leaning over her and could hear the concern in her voice.

"You were yelling something in your sleep, sounded like 'get out,' you woke the whole house up girl." Gran sounded as though she wasn't sure if she should be growling, or concerned about her granddaughter's mental state.

Gypsy looked up at Gran's worried face. "Don't worry Gran, it's all going to be ok," she said soothingly, "they got out, they are really free now."

Gypsy promptly rolled over and went back to sleep with a contented smile on her face.

Gran looked down at her for a few moments, her face puckered with uncertainty. What would the girl say next, she wondered to herself? She tucked Gypsy's blanket more securely around her and plodded back to her own room. She heaved herself into her bed with a few creaks and groans. As she settled herself down the old man's words ran comfortingly through her mind, 'Worrying never added a day to anyone's life.' "Good advice old man," she muttered as she fell into a peaceful sleep.

# Chapter 44

Gypsy visited the Forest Community in her dreams many times after that, passing on to them the knowledge and wisdom she had gained from the Preacher's words, confident now that the people of the City would soon also be free. There were no easy answers to give them but she knew the most important thing she was giving them was hope, faith and a way forward. She was reconnecting them with the Spirit, that vital link that had been severed for a dark and soulless age. She began to experience a deep sense of peace and trust in a purpose greater than herself. It gave her satisfaction to think that she could influence so many people and situations just by the way she lived and the choices she made. Something had happened to her one day that had profoundly changed her and gave her something even greater than belief; it had given her a sure knowledge that lodged itself securely in the depths of her being.

She had been sitting in church listening to the Preacher and he was reading from the big black book he always read from.

"The way to eternal life is simple and clear," he told them seriously, "Repent and believe in the name of the Lord Jesus Christ and you will be saved. God has promised us," he continued, "that He will transform us as He renews our minds."

Renews our minds? That caught Gypsy's attention. Az had described to her the way he believed those born in the City had been conditioned at a very early age to comply to the rules and instructions they were given without question. Even when people disappeared they ignored it and seemed to forget about it quickly and easily. It was as though what they were seeing could not attach itself to their beliefs about the world. Could their minds really be renewed and set free from the deep bondage they had been held in? Could they ever really experience true freedom of mind and will? Then there were the people from the Forest Community who had few rules but could never agree on anything. Could this be the answer they were looking for too? What about her own life? Maybe she had also been conditioned by her experiences to believe that broken relationships and violence were a normal part of life? She caught her breath as the Preacher spoke another passage of scripture. Why did it seem as though he was speaking to her and only her? The words pierced deeply within her heart, breaking through hidden barriers of pain and fear.

"I am close to the broken hearted, and save those who are crushed in spirit," he quoted. "These are the very words that God himself has spoken to us. He is close to us and not far away. He feels our pain, our sadness and our fears and he longs for us to come near to Him as He is always near to us."

Gypsy thought about the brokenness of her family and about her own broken life. She felt the tears welling up and begin to run down her cheeks at the thought that God Himself was near and not far away. She knew then that He was concerned about all the things she cared about, that He knew her and under stood everything she had ever thought or felt. She had put her face into her hands then and wept uncontrollably. She felt as though she was crying out all of the hurt and pain, all the worry and fear for herself and for those she loved.

Gran had seemed a little embarrassed at this show of emotion in a public place, but had patted her arm reassuringly and offered her one of Granddad's big old handkerchiefs to blow her runny nose. She had even fished an old peppermint out from the depths of her dusty purse to give to her. Peppermints along with tea were the cure-alls of Gran's generation.

Gypsy was touched by Gran's kindness but as she suspiciously eyed the peppermint with bits of fluff sticking to it, she wondered just exactly how ancient it might be. Even though she really did appreciate the sentiment she couldn't quite bring herself to put it in her mouth. To avoid hurting Gran's feelings she surreptitiously slipped it down her sock to throw away later.

After the profound experience of that day she had felt a new pervading and deep sense of peace seep into her being. From that day on she knew that she would never be completely alone again. The weight of her responsibilities seemed lighter and most importantly hope had sprung up in her heart. Somehow, in some unfathomable way, she had an assurance that everything was going to be alright.

—————◆—————

When next she dreamed and took her place around the fires with the Forest Community she had a certainly that this would be the very last time she visited them.

She looked around at the familiar faces, and as she looked at the people gathered there she felt a deep and overwhelming love for them. She saw the green eyes that reminded her of Zak and the brown faces and dark curling hair of her people. She saw the big round eyes of the children as they stared at her from behind clumps of tangly hair so like her own and their hard-working, parents with their sun-browned faces.

She gazed affectionately at the white haired old Kaumātua with their crinkly faces nodding wisely at her. She could feel the strength of their spirits and the hunger of their desire for a knowledge of the truth. She felt inextricably linked to them but it was even more than that. They were looking at her so intently, seeing her as the one who would give them guidance and direction in a world that had lost its deepest connections to the earth and to the Spirit.

She looked over at Az and smiled at him, stretching out her hands towards him. As he stood up moving towards her, she felt a strong pull, like a current, drawing them together. He stopped and stood waiting, as she opened her arms to include all of those that were gathered there.

In her mind's eye she looked up and saw the great, domed City, its glassy walls splintering, shattering and falling, and her people, wonderingly, coming out just as she remembered it from her dream.

They should never be confined within a city without soil or nature, she thought indignantly. Their spirits longed for the land, for freedom to live, to believe, to choose for themselves and for future generations. The City had turned them into mindless creatures, herding them around and spoon feeding them, denying them the freedom to be filled with the life-giving spirit of their creator.

She gazed on the people grouped around her. These were her far distant descendants, her own flesh and blood. She smiled as she remembered how Gran had thought she might be seeing the spirits of their ancestors, but that was not quite right.

"I am the ancestor," she said aloud with wonder in her voice.

The people were looking at her in astonishment and she had the feeling of enacting a legend or speaking a part that had been written for her before time had begun. She was certain that she would be spoken of around many firesides in times to come; the legend of the girl-ancestor who had brought hope and words of wisdom to the people in their time of need. The one who carried forth the word of truth from the past into the future, bridging the gap of darkness and deceit that had been torn in their history.

She felt a strange sensation. As she still stood with her arms still stretched out towards them, the scene before her was melting, fading, merging. She could feel the spirits of her people being drawn towards her, as a strong tide sucks at the beach. They were being drawn back into her being, into her body; the body of their ancestor. The scene blurred and dissolved. She gasped aloud as time seemed to roll backward. She awoke, lying on her bed with tears on her face and her two hands touching either side of her belly. Here within her were the seeds that would one day populate the world in the far future. Az, Dayzie, all of the Forest Community, the People of the domed City, they had not yet been brought into being, but were here, waiting.

She wondered if all that she had experienced in her visions and in her dreams would actually happen one day, or was just a possible future that had been shown to her for a reason?

She had no way of knowing.

She thought of her mother being beaten, of her father whom she didn't even know, her Uncle in jail and Zak and Rangi, what would their futures be? What were they handing down for the next generations? What kind of world were they creating?

She felt sure her visions of the future had come to an end. It was now that mattered, now and tomorrow.

My ancestors are here right now, in my body, waiting, for the decisions I will make, she thought to herself. She believed with every atom of her being and deep within her spirit that the future of her people depended on her and on the choices she would make in her lifetime. These choices would resound and echo down the generations, shaping and influencing them.

"I will create a better future for you my people," she promised looking down at her two hands. "I am your ancestor and this is my promise to you: Wherever I go, whatever I do, I carry you with me and the knowledge of you is in my spirit."

> *The Lord has brought you out with a mighty hand,*
> *and redeemed you from the house of bondage…*
> *Therefore know that the Lord your God,*
> *He is God,*
> *the faithful God who keeps covenant and mercy*
> *for a thousand generations*
> *with those who love Him*
> *and keep His commandments…*
> *Deuteronomy 7. V 8 & 9*

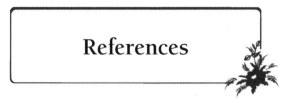

# References

*I would like to acknowledge the influence of the teachings of Bishop Brian Tamaki for inspiring the concepts shared by the Preacher.*
www.Destinychurch.org.nz

**William Wordsworth:** *Intimations of Immortality from Recollections of Early Childhood*

**The Holy Bible NKJ:** *Psalm 34.18*
**The Holy Bible NKJ:** *Romans 12.2*
**The Holy Bible NKJ:** *Acts 2.38*
**The Holy Bible NKJ:** *Deuteronomy 7.8,9*

## The Seven Cycles of Life

1. **0-7:** Development and Preparation
2. **7-14:** Family and Education
3. **14-21:** Career Training and Relationship Preparation
4. **21-28:** First Relationship Cycle and Production duties
5. **28-35:** Second Relationship Cycle, Production duties and Parenting
6. **35-39:** Increased Status, Final Relationship Cycle, Reduced Production duties and Increased Recreation
7. **40:** Completion

# Maori word meanings

- **Aeotearoa** (ae-or-tee-ah-raw-a) – New Zealand, Land of the long white cloud
- **Haere mai** (hi-ray-my) – Welcome
- **Kai** (k-eye) – Food
- **Pakeha** (pa-kee-ha) – non-Maori, fair skinned
- **Tiki Tour** (tick-ee) – sight-seeing journey
- **Whanau** (far-no) – Family
- **Long Pig** – reference to cannibalism
- **Huhu grubs** (hoo-hoo) – larvae of the huhu beetle
- **Hangi** (hung-ee) – traditional Maori way to cook food using heated rocks in a pit oven
- **Marae** (ma-r-eye) – local meeting place
- **Ngai Tahu** – (nigh-ta-hoo) – south island tribe
- **Kaumātua** (co-ma-too-a) – elders
- **Tanga tewhenua** (tongue-ah-too-fen-oo-ah) – people of the land

# About the Author

Suzanne was brought up on a sheep farm in a rural area of Nelson, New Zealand. She spent much of her childhood helping her father with the many aspects of farm life, including mustering and long hours in the shearing shed. Many of the happenings in this book are influenced by her own history and the distinctive personalities of the significant people in her life.

As an early teen, she experienced the transforming power of Christ. This life-altering event created the strong spiritual undertone that flows through all of her writing.

Suzanne has a diploma in counseling and another in career guidance. She spent many years working with Maori youth who were struggling with life issues. She saw an amazing potential in these young people and writes this book in honor of them and their unique capabilities.

Printed in the United States
By Bookmasters